# The Queen's Sorrow

# The Queen's Sorrow

SUZANNAH DUNN

Harper
Press

Harper*Press*
An imprint of HarperCollins*Publishers*
77–85 Fulham Palace Road
Hammersmith, London W6 8JB
www.harpercollins.co.uk

Visit our authors' blog on www.fifthestate.co.uk

First published by Harper*Press* in 2008

Suzannah Dunn asserts the moral right to be
identified as the author of this work

A catalogue record for this book is available from the British Library

ISBN 978-0-00-725827-7

Set in Bembo by G&M Designs Limited

Printed and bound in Great Britain by Clays Ltd, St Ives plc

**Mixed Sources**
Product group from well-managed
forests and other controlled sources
www.fsc.org   Cert no. SW-COC-1806
© 1996 Forest Stewardship Council

FSC is a non-profit international organisation established to promote the
responsible management of the world's forests. Products carrying the FSC
label are independently certified to assure customers that they come
from forests that are managed to meet the social, economic and
ecological needs of present and future generations.

Find out more about HarperCollins and the environment at
**www.harpercollins.co.uk/green**

*For Peter Hunter*

'If God is pleased to grant her a child, things will take a turn for the better. If not, I foresee trouble on so great a scale that the pen can hardly set it down.'

SIMON RENARD, Imperial envoy,
writing to EMPEROR CHARLES V, 1555

ENGLAND, AT LAST, in view: a small harbour settlement crouched on the shoreline. And rain, still this rain, just as he'd been warned. Mid-August, but rain for the three days – and nights, long nights – they'd been anchored offshore. It wasn't as if Spain didn't have rain. Plenty of it, sometimes, and sometimes even in August; sometimes lasting all day, perhaps even several days, but then done and gone and the sun hammered back into the sky. In Spain, you marvelled at the rain, you sheltered, you endured it. Exuberant, it was: a visitation. Not like this.

This English rain wasn't so much falling as getting thrown around on the wind. It had a hold on the air; it settled over him and seeped into his clothes, skin, bones. He should go back below. Yet he stayed on deck as the ship moved forward. A huddle of harbour buildings and, beyond, to the horizon, greenery. *Pelt* came to mind: *pelts*; the land looked green-furred. Spain had green: from the subtle, silvered blue-green of olive and almond trees to the deep, dark gloss of citrus trees, and, in the middle, vines, the gentle shade of vines. Plenty of green in Spain, cultivated, trellised and terraced. This, though, here, this English green, looked relentless, creeping into the very lie of the land rather than gracing it.

1

Six weeks, he'd been told. That's all. Six weeks, at most, in England. The first ship home will sail within six weeks. Do the job we're sending you to do, and then you can come home.

England: a small, narrow island up off the edge of every-where else. A far corner of the world, where the sea turned in on itself, wave-wild, and the sun was cold-shouldered.

What were they doing, now, back home? Rafael closed his eyes to see the luminous shade of the courtyard, risked a hand off the rail to touch the little sundial in his pocket: just touch it, because of course it was no use, calibrated for a different latitude, and anyway there was no sun. He didn't know what time it was here nor there. But whatever the time back home, if not now then soon someone would be in the courtyard drawing water from the well: that particular, steady creaking of the handle. And even if the courtyard were otherwise deserted, there'd be the conversation of women behind the shutters: his mother, his aunt, his sister-in-law, and Leonor.

And Francisco, his little Francisco, who loved to crouch beside the well to pat the spillage. And if ever the filled bucket was unattended even for the briefest turn of a head, he'd skim it with his upturned palm, spoon it, let it well over his wrist and stream down his arm to splatter on the tiles. And then Leonor would call to Rafael to stop him, and Rafael would pick him up, having to brace himself, these days, against the strength of his son's reckless, over-eager lunge in the opposite direction.

Someone had made a mistake. That was what Rafael had heard. Someone senior on the Spanish side was supposed to have told the prince that his bride, the English queen, had provided for him; not financially (not a penny) but in terms of staff. A full household – hundreds of Englishmen – had been installed for him at court. The prince – ever-diplomatic – hadn't presumed that any provision would be made, so, despite meticulous planning for a smooth and inconspicuous arrival in England, he'd come with his own three hundred men, a month ago, to a palace which had very little room for them.

Various Londoners had been persuaded to take some in, it seemed. And now, Rafael and Antonio: belated arrivals, stragglers. Rafael didn't mind the change of plan. This initial inconvenience, yes, of course, he did mind: waiting to be allocated a host when they'd already suffered five days at sea and then the protracted journey overland in pouring rain. But on the whole, no. It wasn't going to cost – they'd still be fully provided for – and he'd rather lodge with a local family, he reasoned, than suffer the squeeze at court.

Antonio, predictably, did mind. No doubt he'd bragged back home that he'd be living in royal splendour. While Rafael waited at the office that had been designated to deal with Spanish matters, Antonio prowled around the courtyard outside, heedless of the rain, in search of commiseration with like-minded company. Which meant company other than Rafael's. How did he do it? – make Rafael feel as if he were his father. He did it all the time; he'd been doing it for the five years that they'd been working together: making Rafael feel middle-aged. In fact, Antonio himself was in his late twenties, by now; there were only twelve years between them.

Rafael had hoped they might be dealt with separately, but then it was, 'Rafael de Prado and your assistant Antonio Gomez.'

'Assistant': Antonio wouldn't like that. He worked for Rafael on Rafael's projects; he didn't 'assist'. Luckily, he hadn't heard. The Spanish official conferred irritably with his English, Spanish-speaking, counterpart before pronouncing, 'Kitson,' and offering his notes to Rafael, tilting them, indicating the name with a fingertip. Rafael made as if to look, but didn't; just concentrated on repeating, 'Kitson.' A relief: it wasn't so hard to say. At least he'd be able to manage the name of his host.

'A merchant,' read the official.

Out of interest, Rafael asked, 'Merchant of what?' but the official shrugged, making clear that he was done.

Fair enough. Rafael stood aside to wait to be fetched. He leaned back against a wall, wishing he could also somehow shrink from himself. He needed to bathe. He longed to bathe. His skin was – well, it was *there*; it was a presence, where usually he'd be unaware of it, be at ease in it. Raised and tight, was the feeling. His dear hope was that there were no other 'presences', nothing having made its own little journey across from a fellow voyager. It was inevitable, though, he knew. Whenever he went to scratch, he'd stop himself, suffer the itch, will it away, try to think of something else. He could think of nothing but water, though: warm, fresh water. He'd had more than enough of sea water. His hair was wild with sea salt and his clothes stiff with it. But fresh, warm water, to lose himself in. Half an hour in it, that's what he craved. The sea-journey had been bad enough, but now he ached from the wagon: there were jolts packed into his joints and he dreamed of soaking them loose.

Back home, it would be simple, he'd stroll across his family's land to the shrub-veiled pool at the bend in the river. He'd undress, then clamber over the rocks to meet the glare of the water and – this, he always relished – stare it down for a few moments before his surrender. He'd sit there on the rocks with the sunshine on his back. Still sitting, he'd ease himself forward for the drop and then – God! – the cold would snatch at him and crush him, but his shriek wouldn't surface because, like magic, the cold was warm. *Warm*! Warm all along. The trick of it. Tricked, and loving it. He'd wade and loll, gazing at the banks and feeling separate from the world, free of it.

Here, though, in England, in this chill, no one was going to strip off and brave a dip.

Two liveried men arrived, making scant eye-contact with Rafael and barely addressing him or Antonio. Between themselves, though, the pair shared plenty of comment, all of which sounded uncomfortably like complaint.

'No horses?' one of them asked Rafael; or barked at him, contemptuous. *Horses*, Rafael had to guess from the mime: the man exaggeratedly straight-backed, bobbing at the knees, fists paired and raised.

'No,' was all Rafael said. What he could've said, if it weren't forbidden to let on, was, *A thousand horses, and all of them destriers, no less; our Spanish ships sailed with a thousand war horses.* But none of them had sailed into Southampton; they remained moored offshore. The horses were for war with France; they'd soon be sailing on to the Low Countries, now that the wedding was done, as would most of the men and – rumour had it – the prince himself, keen to do his bit but, as a new bridegroom, having to balance expectations and demands.

Not Rafael, though. No soldier, Rafael. Do the job we're sending you to do, he'd been told, and then you'll be out of there on the first ship home. Last ship in, first ship back. Six weeks at most, they'd said. He'd need only two or three. Six weeks at most, he kept reminding himself. He kept it in mind while – Antonio in tow – he followed the two miserable-looking men out of the courtyard.

He followed them and then, behind a building, around a corner, there was the river, putting a stop to the land, reclining on it, fat and silver, brimming and gleaming despite the leaden sky. A thousand yards wide, he'd heard, and, seeing it, he believed it. Chilly though the waterfront steps were, Rafael was glad to be there. There was lots to see, from nifty wherries of oarsman and solitary passenger to painted, gilded barges, canopied and fabric-draped, each hauled by its own boat of eight or ten rowers. Two of these barges were idling close to the jetty, self-important liveried staff frowning at the steps in an attempt to lay superior claim while their passengers made moves to gather up their finery. Another barge had just departed, heading downstream, presumably city-bound, gathering speed, its silky banners frantic in the breeze. More serviceable barges lacked the canopies but ran to cushioned benches. One drifted near the jetty, one was disembarking, its sensibly dressed clientele trying to clutch cloaks around themselves while feeling for handrails and accepting helping hands, its four rowers resting, flushed, their oar-blades floating placid. One disembarking gentleman had two dogs with him, on leashes, their collars as wide as their slender necks; they slinked ahead of him on to dry land. Behind the barges, workaday boats jostled for position with their cargoes of hide-covered crates, their crews with rolled-up sleeves and heavy boots. Horses, too, Rafael saw to his surprise. Gliding into view was a vessel bearing five horses. All but one of them stood stock-still, on ceremony, noses raised to the breeze; the troubled one was giving fussy jerks of the head, and an attendant was doing his best to soothe. Wherries passed by, distantly, in both directions, their hulls glinting, the passengers hunkered down and the single or paired oarsmen hauling on the water. Amid all this, fishing boats were biding their time: a couple of dozen, he estimated, on this stretch. And everywhere were swans, some singular, many in conference, each and every one of them looking affronted.

Rafael envied the swans; momentarily forgetting the cold, he wanted to feel his feet like theirs in the water. Suddenly he was impatient to be on it, to feel it under him, buoyant, and to smell it, breathe it in, raw and fragrant. He and Antonio had to wait, though, for a quarter of an hour or so for a small craft – unpromisingly uncovered – to be brought to the steps, and their luggage to be hefted on to it. The three rowers had sweat-plastered hair despite the chill: clearly they'd been busy. To Rafael, they looked horse-faced – these long, flat English faces with big teeth, where they had teeth at all.

He wondered how he looked to them. Foreign, yes, undoubtedly, but how foreign? What kind of 'foreign'? He'd been attracting some stares on the jetty – he was aware of it – but that happened sometimes in Spain. There, though, it was because of the suspicion of Jewish blood. In Spain, he looked as if he was descended from Jews, as if he came from a family of *conversos*. But there'd been no Jews in England for more than three hundred years: would the English even know what to look for? Antonio had been attracting some interest, but that'd be because – despite his efforts to appear otherwise – he was with Rafael. On his own, he might be able to pass unremarked, here, his hair not far off blond.

Once aboard, they and their two liveried attendants were rowed upstream, heading north in the shadows of the water-front walls of Whitehall, the palace in which they'd had to while away the afternoon. The biggest palace in Christendom, Rafael had heard. A whole town had been razed just to make space for the tennis courts. It had been built by the queen's father, the one who'd had all the wives and killed some of them. The one who'd locked away his long-serving Spanish wife – the queen's mother – and turned his back on the Pope so that he could marry his English mistress. And now, twenty years on and against all the odds, time had turned and the sole, shut-away, half-Spanish child from that first, ill-fated marriage was queen and married, herself, to a Spaniard, and this palace was hers.

And England was hers and, like her, it was Catholic. That was the idea. Or, at least, the queen's idea. The problem was that the English people had other ideas, Rafael had heard. They weren't taking it seriously. At one church, last Easter, the sacrament was stolen some time between Good Friday and Easter Monday, so that, come the triumphant presentation, there was nothing, and the congregation laughed. No one would ever laugh in a Spanish church. No one would dare.

And just as the queen had been mistaken in her assumption that her people would take easily to the return to Rome, she'd also been mistaken to assume they'd welcome news of her forthcoming marriage. The ship had been full of it, on the way over: the appalling reception they were facing from the English people. Someone who knew someone who could read English said he'd seen a pamphlet claiming that thousands of Spaniards would be living and working in London by the end of the year. *Jack Spaniard*, it said, coming to rob the English of their livelihoods. According to someone else, snowballs had been lobbed at the dignitaries arriving at the palace with the marriage treaty. That particular scare-story had less impact because no one knew quite how serious an assault that was: did snowballs hurt? Someone from central Spain was consulted, and − to everyone's relief − found it amusing.

English women were shameless: that, too, Rafael had heard on the voyage, but he knew better than to believe what men said about women. He hadn't seen many English women, so far, and had had only fleeting glimpses as he and his fellow countrymen had passed through towns, villages, courtyards. What was striking about them was their minimal headcovering. Certainly no veils. He'd worried that he'd look at them, exposed as they were. Well, he *had* looked at them. He didn't know *how* to look at them: that was what it was. They'd looked at him and at his fellow countrymen, turned and looked, but as yet he'd never once been able to read the expression.

Like most Spaniards, all he'd ever known of England before the scandal of the philandering, excommunicated king, was King Arthur and his round table of knights. Back in his boyhood, he and his best friend Gil had lived and breathed stories of the English King Arthur. He'd forgotten those stories until he'd known he was coming here; but in his boyhood, as for so many Spanish boys, that for him had been England. Likewise for most of his fellow countrymen, he imagined. Now, though, he didn't seem able to remember anything other than a sword-bearing arm rising from a lake. A woman's arm, rising strong and unequivocal from the murk and weeds: *Here, have this*. Handy. Well, from what he'd already seen, England had no shortage of watery habitats. Ladies of the lakes could be a common feature, for all he knew.

He sniffed before he could stop himself. He'd noticed that everyone in England sniffed all the time, and now he, too, was at it. The prince, he'd heard, had had a dreadful cold at his wedding, within four days of coming ashore. Antonio's nose and the rims of his eyes were red-raw in the wind. He was dishevelled: there was no other word for it. How he must hate that. His near-blond hair, unwashed and damp, was dark; the feather in his hat, lank. Not that Rafael himself would be looking too good, of course, but he didn't expect otherwise. He didn't have Antonio's boyish charm. Mind you, Antonio didn't have Antonio's boyish charm, at present. And he was lost without it. It was how he won people over; everyone except Rafael, of course, no illusions about that. Here, so far, in England, it hadn't been working. Presumably just because he was Spanish, people here turned from it, refused it. It was interesting to witness, but Rafael shied away from gloating. Because, like it or not, they were in this — this trip, this escapade — together.

On the far bank, there was nothing but pasture. Some trees, massive but lopped for firewood. Well, they'd certainly need that, here. A few patches of cultivation — vegetable gardens, by the look of them, although impossible to see from the boat what was being grown — and an occasional orchard. Nothing much, then, south of the river.

When the river curved east, they were at last beyond the palace and the cluster of official-looking buildings. This, now, was residential, and what residences! He'd thought he'd never see anything to rival the finer houses of Seville — nowhere in the world was as rich as Seville — and having been told that the English were a Godless people, he hadn't expected such elegance. These south-facing houses had their own riverside landings and through the immense ironwork gates there he got glimpses of long, geometrically laid gardens, and statues, fountains and — defiant under the dull sky — sundials. In the distance, behind the riverside walls, were the buildings themselves of rose-red brick and their banks of twisted, towering chimneys.

As the boat came to glide alongside the city itself, Rafael's overriding impression was of the many, many chimneys in a haze of smoke. This time of year, the fires would only be for cooking. How bad would the air be in winter, when Londoners needed heat as well? Above it all, though, reared a Heaven high, needle-sharp spire. One of the men saw him looking, and gestured towards it, said: 'St Paul's.' He'd spoken grudgingly, but Rafael smiled his thanks for the information.

Standing to disembark, he turned to see an immense bridge downstream. Just the one bridge — all crossings elsewhere were made via the little wherries that had been cutting across in front of and behind their own vessel — but if a city was going to have just one bridge …

'Look at that!' he heard himself say aloud. It was made of arches: nineteen, he made it with a rapid count. Just as impressive, if not more so, was the street of many-storeyed houses that ran down its length. It was like a whole small town afloat on the river.

At the quayside, the two men engaged the services of a porter to assist with the rest of the journey, which was to be undertaken on foot. The cart bearing the trunks trundled off ahead — two near-misses of pedestrians before the first corner — and was soon gone from view. Rafael understood why boating was the preferred mode of transport. The streets were like tunnels: narrow in the first place but made narrower still — almost roofed — by extended, overhanging floors above ground level. Timber-frame buildings. There'd be a big risk of fire even without all the fireplaces these homes and shops would be running during winter. Almost every house was also, on the ground floor, a shop. Doors flew open in their path, admitting and discharging a considerable traffic of customers whose elbows bristled with baskets. Many of them were unaccompanied women. Almost every shop also had a trestle table outside, at which Londoners stopped — usually abruptly — to browse. He'd never seen anything like it: these people clearly loved to shop. As long as you had money to spend, this was the place to be.

Some lanes were paved, but many were lined with planks along which everyone had to process. Londoners were, of course, much better at it than he and Antonio. Londoners were good at it, they were practised, they'd learned to balance. Over-balancing meant sliding into mud and muck, and within yards his boots were in an appalling state. One of the liveried men shook him by the shoulder to get his attention and then clapped his own hands to his pockets: *Be wary of thieves*. Rafael nodded his thanks, but he didn't need to be told how to protect himself from thieves – he was from Seville. The problem was that he couldn't balance if his hands were in his pockets.

He saw beggars crouching in the muck at every street corner, barely clothed, bootless, and often with children. He presumed they were children, but there was nothing childlike about them. Small people. Pitifully small, with scabby scalps and claw-like hands. In Seville, there were beggars, of course, by the thousands, black and white, from all around Spain and from the colonies: they all came to Seville. But here, in London, it seemed somehow different. Worse. These people – the small ones, particularly – looked abject. Because they were cold, perhaps that was it. Perhaps because of the smell of roasting of meats, which seemed to be everywhere here but wasn't for them that couldn't help. Something he'd learned on the ship was that there was no charity in England. There was no one to do it; no monks, no nuns. There'd been no religious houses for the past twenty years, thanks to the old king. Nowhere for people to go in hard times but on to the streets. *I hate it here* sprang up in him and squeezed his throat. *I hate it, I hate it*. The choked air, the crammed streets, the pitiful children. How on earth was he going to survive this? Even a day of it, let alone six weeks.

A quarter of an hour or so later, they were in a quiet little street where there were no shops other than what looked like a glove maker's. The two liveried men consulted a note

produced from a pocket, waylaid the sole passer-by for confirmation, and then indicated to Rafael and Antonio that they'd
arrived. Rafael was finding it hard to get his bearings, the sun
hidden behind tall buildings and then behind cloud, but he
decided that the lane ran roughly north–south. All that was to
be seen of their destination was a high redbrick wall in which
was a solid wooden gate overhung by a sign of crossed keys. A
knock on the gate provoked the barking of some dogs and
summoned a man in a blue jerkin that was a lot less fancy
than the brass-buttoned, braided and crest-embroidered
finery of royal households, but nonetheless had the look of
livery. Tussling with two wolfhounds, he ushered the visitors
through into a cobbled forecourt and there was the house:
four-storeyed and newly built, ochre plaster and silvery
timber, glassed windows glinting greenish. There was a simple
sundial on the wall, a double decliner – north-east facing,
then – that'd be no use except on the sunniest of mornings.

They followed the porter and dogs towards the main, rose-
mary-flanked door of the house on which was a large, interesting doorknocker: the head of some beast, something feline,
a leopard. A rap of it got the door opened – and more pande-
monium with more dogs – but then someone else had to be
found to welcome them inside. And quite something, he was:
a tall, slender young man with hair like golden silk. All smiles.
Good teeth: just the one gap, but barely visible. The household steward, Rafael later learned. He made much of their
welcome to the household, not that they could understand
what was actually being said; but whatever it was, it was delivered with flair. Slick, was the word that came to mind. And
slick would definitely do, after a day of being fobbed off.

Rafael wished he could respond more fulsomely to it, make the effort to enter the performance, but he hadn't realised how exhausted he was until faced with this ebullience.

The man moved them swiftly to a staircase, shooing back the house dogs, up a flight and then along a rush-carpeted gallery – its walls papered, printed with a design in orange and turquoise – to more stairs, three flights of them. The room was small and simply whitewashed, with a glassed window but no fireplace, and the daylight was so weak that he couldn't immediately ascertain its aspect. Their two chests had been delivered. On the bed were two piles of bedclothes, folded. A truckle bed was perfunctorily demonstrated: for Antonio, Rafael realised with a lurch of despair; he, too, was to be in here. There was no desk. When the truckle was out, there'd be no room for one.

The steward was confiding something, speaking quickly and quietly, his eyebrows raised; he indicated the doorway, the stairs, perhaps the house beyond. Rafael felt this was an explanation and an apology. The house was full and this was all there was. Rafael was careful to keep smiling and nodding; Antonio, he saw, was staring moodily at the window. The steward wore the same blue as the porter, but better cut and better kept, and beneath it was a shirt of good linen, perhaps even Holland linen. He'd stopped speaking and was instead presenting one hand to Rafael, palm upwards; the other hand prodded at it and then at his mouth. Forking food? Then a sweep of the hand that had held the imaginary food, from the doorway: *Some food will be brought up to you*, Rafael understood him to mean. More smiles and nods. No mention of dinner. They'd be having dinner daily at the household. Lunch at the palace, dinner at the Kitsons', both at no cost: that was the arrangement, or so he'd been told. Could they have missed dinner? What time did these people eat? The steward was going, bowing out of the doorway, off to shower someone else with his abundant beneficence. They'd been dealt with.

Rafael sat on the bed – where else was there to go? – and felt he'd never get up again. Such a long, long day, it'd been; it seemed to have started days ago. And in a way, it had – thirteen days ago, when he'd left home. Two days to the port, five days sailing across the sea, three anchored, and then three travelling through England. And here he was, arrived; only just arrived, but ready now to go home. The journey was done – he'd done it, come to England – and now he wanted to go home. He had a home, and the very fact of it was compelling: home was where he should be. All he had to do was turn and go. Yet he felt adrift, and despaired of ever seeing it or Leonor and Francisco again.

Antonio said, 'I'm going out for a drink.' He spoke from the doorway; he hadn't come in any further. He didn't say, *You coming?* And of course Rafael didn't. He could imagine that there might have been a temporary truce on this first evening at the end of their very long journey. A grudging truce. But no, and he was glad, really, and relieved. They'd been in each other's company all day and – the horror of it – were going to be in each other's company all night. He said, though, 'You don't speak English.' Meaning, *You're Spanish.* And Spanish – as they all knew – wasn't a good thing to be, at present, in London.

No one expected problems from nobles and officials – they'd be well schooled in manners and they'd have jobs to do and be kept busy doing them – but the common people were known for their dislike of foreigners at the best of times, Rafael had heard, to say nothing of when their reigning monarch had just become a foreigner's wife. Their ruler: now someone's wife, and, worse, someone who wasn't just anyone but heir to the world's biggest empire. Who, in this marriage, was to obey whom? Should she obey her husband, or should he, mere prince in her country, obey her? But he was her husband, and how could a wife not obey? Well, with considerable ease, in Rafael's experience and, he bet, in the experience of a lot of husbands with varying degrees of happiness and success. But the Church, in its unmarried wisdom, saw it as impossible. A wife obeys a husband: simple as that. And, anyway, one day soon, this husband – amenable though he was reputed to be – would be ruler of most of the world, which was another reason, so the thinking went, for his wife to get used to knuckling under. They'd been warned over and over again on the ship to anticipate the Englishman's ambivalence and try to understand it. Play the grateful guest at all times and never rise to provocation because the English – Godless people stuck there on their island – are barbarians and we won't sink to their level. And remember, above all, remember that it's not for long. Six weeks and we'll be gone, diplomatic mission done. Until then, keep your head down.

So, how was striding into a London tavern and speaking Spanish keeping your head down? But, of course, Antonio had an answer, as to all things, unintelligible though this one was to Rafael. It was English, he knew: probably, *A jug of your best ale, please, sir.* Too fast, though, for him to grasp. They'd all learned some English during the voyage – greetings, pleasantries, a few crucial nouns – from English-speaking seamen, and Rafael had worked longer and harder at it than most, but what Antonio had lacked in application, he was clearly making up for in confidence. And so now here he was, ready for drinks with the locals.

Well, good luck to him. Left alone, Rafael lay back on the unmade bed. *This is so far from home*, came to him. *Leonor, this is so far from home.* She wouldn't want to hear that, though; she'd want to hear about the house. What could he tell her? *I'm in a grand house in London. Blue-liveried staff. Dogs, though, indoors.* In his mind, he walked himself back through the house, the way he'd come, this time taking note and trying to glance ahead. *Everything new, by the look of it: freshly painted panelling, the frames red, the insets gold. Tapestries with a sheen to make you blink. There's a clock just inside the main door, Leonor, and you'll know that I'll be going down there to take a closer look at that.* She wouldn't be interested in the clock; clocks were no interest of hers. He sat up, but laid his head in his hands. *Francisco, Poppet, the doorknocker's a leopard's head. Yes! Snarling, keeping guard on the house. I'll have to be brave, whenever I knock. And there are dogs, too, inside the house. I came here, to this house, on a river; it's almost as wide as you can see, and it's so busy, it's like a town in itself. Not just boats, but swans, hundreds and hundreds of them. And along the river are huge red houses like castles. Do you remember, darling, your 'purple house'?*

No, he wouldn't remember, and Rafael himself was surprised by the memory. Francisco hadn't mentioned his 'purple house' for a long time, perhaps a year or more, but back when he was two or so, if he liked something, he'd say he'd have it for his 'purple house'. *I'll have that in my purple house:* a little stool; an ornate-handled knife; a neighbour's donkey. No one but Francisco knew what or where this purple house was. Nonetheless, it was well furnished. Long forgotten, now, though. He'd moved on.

*What would I have in my purple house?* Rafael laughed to himself even as he was aware of being close to tears. These past thirteen days, he'd been shaken to the core by how homesick he felt: the savagery of it, its relentlessness. Dizzied by it, was how he felt. About to buckle. Hollowed, as if something had been ripped from him. His chest sang with the pain and he was confused and ashamed because he saw no sign that other men felt like this. Antonio certainly didn't. But, then, other men too would hide it, wouldn't they, so there'd be no knowing. He hadn't anticipated feeling like this. He'd often been away from home – sometimes for a couple of weeks – and had never enjoyed it, but nothing had prepared him for this. And because he hadn't anticipated it, he felt tripped up, tricked by it, taken unawares and thereby enslaved by it. He couldn't see how he'd get from under it, or how he was going to cope, to continue, from day to day. Common sense told him that he would, that it would lessen, but he didn't believe it. This homesickness was going to hunt him down.

He missed his little Francisco – God, how he missed him – and in six weeks there'd be so much more to miss, because he was growing so fast. A head taller at a time, he seemed. Rafael felt that his son's head came up to his chest now, even though he knew it couldn't be so – but that's where he felt the lack of him, that's where the hollowness was. That little head. Rafael longed to cup the back of it as he had when Francisco was a baby; take the weight of it, enjoy the fit and solidness of it in one hand. His little boy's hair, too: *his silly blond hair*, as Rafael thought affectionately of it. He longed to touch it, to relish its abundance. Not much of it was there when he was newborn, most of it had grown since – which Rafael found almost comical, and touching: all that busy, vigorous but gloriously oblivious growing that Francisco had done for himself.

What if something happened to Francisco while he was away? This was what had got a hold on him, these last two weeks. This was what was haunting him: the fear that he'd never see his son again. That he'd already seen him for the last time. A fever, a fall. An act of negligence by a servant, or cruelty from a stranger. An abscess deep in an ear, the poison leaking deeper. A cat scratch going bad, a loose cart wheel, a rotten branch, a misfooting on the riverbank, a kick from a horse … Anything or nothing, really: it could be nothing that would do it, in the end. *It happens.*

He longed to ask Leonor, *How do you live with this fear?* In thirteen days, he seemed to have forgotten how to do it.

But Francisco was so full of life, he was crammed with it and, if he were with him now, he wouldn't be sitting around like this. *Snap out of it*, Rafael urged himself. Stop this. For his sake. Because what kind of a father are you to him, to sit here like this, foretelling his death?

And it was at that moment that he saw the child. The door had been left ajar by Antonio and in the gap was a small face, a child, a boy of perhaps four or five years old. Huge blue eyes, serious expression. From behind him came a reprimand, 'Nicholas!' to which he reacted immediately, scarpering. The voice had been pitched to reach not only the child but also Rafael. And now, pitched even higher, for him alone, came a word he understood: 'Sorry!' The tone was cheerful, confident of acceptance, but no less heartfelt for it. He was across the tiny room in two steps. He couldn't just stay sitting there in silence: he should accept the apology. And make clear that he hadn't minded. On the contrary, any distraction was welcome, even a mute child.

Below on the stairs was a woman – a servant, judging from her simple linen dress and blue apron. She was poised to descend further, coifed head bowed and nape exposed. She was neither very young nor old. She was very pale. A plain, pale woman. Not plain in a bad way, though. Tall, long-boned and broad-browed: that's what he noticed about her. That, and how she touched the child. Over one arm was looped some fine fabric – clothing, probably, for repair – and her free hand was on the little lad's shoulder, ostensibly directing him down on to the step in front of her but, Rafael felt, less a shepherd-ing than an excuse for contact. He recognised the quality of that touch. Parental.

She looked up, saw Rafael, gave a surprised, 'Oh!' and a smile. It spoke to him, that smile, he felt, although it said nothing much, said only pretty much what you'd expect: *Kids, eh?!* That affectation of resignation which was in fact senselessly proud. He did it all the time, he knew, back home, back in his life. He would've loved to have been able to say to her, *Oh, I know, I know, my own little boy …* and he felt she'd have welcomed it. An easy exchange, unremarkable, but such as he hadn't had for weeks. The possibility of which, he realised, he'd begun to despair of. As it was, he returned the smile and said, 'It's fine, it's fine,' forgetting his English and speaking his own language. She understood him, though, he saw.

The next day, Rafael and Antonio had lunch at court – a whole separate sitting for Spaniards – before returning to their host, as arranged, for supper. Supper was served at five o'clock, they'd learned to their dismay. As such, it would follow their afternoon rest. They'd thought they'd stay at the palace for the afternoons – finding somewhere to bed down – but now they realised that, tide permitting, they might as well go back to the Kitson household after lunch and rest in the relative comfort of their room until supper. The problem concerned afterwards: no doubt everyone at the Kitsons' would return to work after supper for a few hours, but for Rafael and Antonio there would be the journey all the way back to Whitehall. And, again, there was the tide to consider. The cost, too, although the fare was regulated and reasonable. Rafael had been told he'd be fully provided for, but of course he'd come with some money in hand. Whichever way they worked it, there would be, most days, a lot of waiting around, some unanticipated expenditure, and two long return journeys on the river.

Not for the time being, though. Apart from a couple of site visits, Rafael didn't need to be anywhere in particular to do his work, although it would help to have space to lay out his drawings. In a couple of weeks' time, though, Antonio would need a workshop in which to execute the design.

Tiredness always made Rafael hungry, and, after a night of trying and failing to sleep in the same room as Antonio, who snored, his tiredness was beyond anything that an afternoon rest could have improved. And, anyway, it hadn't been much of a rest. The palace lunch had been so heavy that they'd been unable to face the river-journey immediately afterwards and instead they'd napped – or tried to – in the uncomfortably crowded room of friends that Antonio had made. Antonio had then suggested that they stay at the palace until the evening, skipping supper, making do with leftovers passed on from his new friends, but Rafael had insisted they both put in an appearance back at the house. He was going to have Antonio behave properly for once.

He regretted this stand of his, though, as they paused in the doorway of the Hall at five o'clock. Inside, there were tens of people already sitting packed together, while others hurried to step over benches and slot themselves down at the long tables. Clearly everyone knew his or her place. Even dogs, he saw to his horror: four, he spotted, nosing among the diners and receiving the occasional indulgent pat. Beyond all this, up on its dais at the far end of the room, was the elaborately set high table, as yet unoccupied by the householder and his family and their guests.

*Where do we go?* He sensed people staring, and no wonder: he and Antonio were conspicuous in their hesitancy. No overt hostility in the stares, he didn't think, but nonetheless difficult to take. He couldn't meet their eyes, there were too many of them; and even if he could have, then what? He had the distinct feeling that, if he smiled at them, they wouldn't smile back. They didn't want his smiles, they just wanted a good look at him: *stranger, Spaniard.*

And then he spotted the steward in the same instant the steward spotted him, but any relief was dashed when he saw from the man's fleetingly startled expression that he'd forgotten all about them. Even this supremely organised steward had no idea where they should go and – worse – was about to make quite a show of rectifying the situation. And here it came, the big smile and a scanning of the tables before 'Ah!' – raised eyebrows, raised forefinger – as if he'd known all along that it was there, indeed had reserved it, and had only momentarily lost sight of it: a place for them.

As they made their way towards the bench, Rafael saw the servant-woman and her son in the glow from a west-facing window. She seemed at first to see him, but no: her gaze merely touched his face before moving onwards unchanged. She was whispering, he saw, to her son. No one in the room was talking, but she'd said something fast and low, a mere scrap of words. She mimicked inexpressiveness but there was tension in her face. No smile now. The little boy's eyes were turned to hers. Rafael recognised that manner of hers, both distracted and emphatic: parental, again. She'd been making something clear: *I told you …*; or, *Didn't I ask you …*

Over the next few days, he found himself half-looking for her, because hers was one of the few faces he recognised in the household and the only one that didn't seem flummoxed to see him. He'd find himself checking whether she was around, and feeling safer – more at home – if she was.

In those initial few days, he was kept busy learning the ropes. First to learn was the journey to and from the palace, which proved easy enough. Then, at the palace, a place had to be found for him and Antonio to work. For this most basic of requirements to be taken seriously, he had to make various appointments with relevant personnel who would then turn out not to be the relevant personnel after all. In the meantime, they had to pass their time there in Hall with their fellow countrymen who were keeping themselves busy playing cards, making music and – those who could – writing home.

His other priorities were how to send letters home and how to get his laundry done. The first was being organised, he discovered, by the Spanish office that had been set up at the palace, although of course he didn't yet know how reliable they'd be. But the laundry remained a mystery. Having little English and even less confidence in it, he had to learn at the Kitsons' by watching, and that was how, on the first evening, he'd discovered where jugs and bowls of clean water were to be had. Where this water came from, he didn't know. There was no well in either the front courtyard or the rear; and although there was a very small walled garden adjoining the rear, south-west-facing courtyard, he hadn't seen anyone bringing a bucket in from there. He passed two wells in the streets close to the house on his way to and from the river, and he decided these were the sources, although he'd not seen anyone struggling into the house with containers. He could now wash himself – and be shaved at the palace by a Spanish barber – but the problem was his shirts. Even if he could properly wash them in a little bowl, where would he then dry them? His – and Antonio's – room was so tiny that they couldn't even air the layers of clothes that were dampened every day by the rain, and Rafael was conscious of smelling like a wet dog.

His supply of clean shirts dwindled: the need for fresh ones would soon be pressing. Despite increased vigilance, he saw no evidence in the house of any laundry. No hanging of it in the courtyards or from windows (and of course not, in this weather). Nor any sign of an actual laundry room: no wafts of steam, and none of those fragrances of hot liquid soap and boiled herbs. His searches – admittedly tentative, because he couldn't go barging down private-looking corridors or open doors – led nowhere. And Antonio was no use: he referred cryptically to an arrangement at court, the implication being that it was a personal one. He'd charmed someone to take in his washing.

Rafael could've made a stab at asking the steward if he'd known how to ask for him, but he hadn't managed to catch his name and he didn't know the English for 'Steward'. And every dinnertime for several days running, to his dismay, the opportunity to waylay the man would somehow disappear. So, in the end, he was reduced to hanging around at the foot of his staircase or near the kitchen, looking lost and hopeful: hoping that someone would step in and fetch the man in charge. He hated having to do it, this wide-eyed helplessness. The staff were too busy to notice him, or that's how they liked to appear. Busy or not, they were clearly reluctant to engage with him. And then, at last, after perhaps a half-hour of his hanging around, someone did fetch Mr Kitson's secretary, who spoke Italian. As if Italian could substitute. They were bogged down in language difficulties immediately, but just as he was about to try to mime the washing of his shirt, the pale woman approached them. The woman who'd smiled at him and – thank God – here she was, doing it again, looking attentive and keen to help, unlike everyone else. Rafael said, 'Madam, please,' and then asked her in his own language even though there was no chance of the actual words being understood: Was there a laundry in the house? Then the inevitable mime: he plucked at his shirt, before vigorously rubbing his hands together.

'Here? No.'

She indicated that he should give his shirts to her. 'To me.' She was *so* pale: her eyes were transparent and her skin had the luminosity of stone or weathered bone.

Whenever he saw her after that, she was carrying fabric and he wondered how he had ever missed it. She was no doubt a seamstress; she'd have been the obvious person to ask about laundry. Linen was what came to mind, now, whenever he saw her. Forget stone and bone. Linen: unfussy, durable, adaptable

Still nothing had happened at Whitehall to provide Rafael with office space, but at last he gained permission to visit the queen's private garden in which he was to site the sundial. He had no need of Antonio for this, and left him engrossed in a card game.

Doing as he'd been told, he entered from an orchard at the south, opening an unlocked door on to a vast gravelled courtyard. On his left, the eastern side, bordering the river, was the queen's private residence. These garden-facing windows would catch any afternoon sunshine, but today the building was blank-eyed. At the far end, facing south, was a double-storeyed, ornately carved and gilded gallery, on which was mounted a direct-south dial. No one would be inside that gallery seeking shade on a day such as this. The centrepiece of the garden was a white marble fountain: a portly, pouting sea-creature depicted mid-flex, craning skywards, its dribble clattering into the basin like heavy rain. Dark, less well-defined figures stood to attention here and there in other parts of the garden: topiary girls, full-skirted and small-headed. Wood-carved, pet-sized beasts postured on top of twisty-twirly poles: a green-and-gilded lion up on its hind legs, flourishing paws and fangs, and a long-muzzled, mordant-faced − which was to say English-looking − hound resting on its haunches. All very pretty, perhaps, but fussy. There were many raised beds − a bed of lilies, one of poppies, one of daisies − and areas of lavender bordered by rosemary, as well as similarly shaped areas of clipped grass. Nearer the fountain, the beds looked different. Curious, Rafael crunched across the gravel to them. The borders of these beds, too, were low-hedged, but contained more ankle-high hedging − two kinds to each bed − planted in a pattern to give the illusion of two strands intertwining, of being linked in a loose, elegant knot. He crouched and rubbed a piece of foliage to confirm: thyme. Thyme partnered with cotton lavender. Peppered around the knot to make up its background were low-growing, spiky pink flowers.

He glimpsed one of the queen's doors opening, and rose, ready for interrogation − Who was he? What was he doing? − but realised that he had no way of making himself understood.

Why hadn't he asked for a note in English to bring with him? The interloper was a solitary lady – absurdly richly dressed – and she hadn't yet noticed him. Closing the door behind her, she came no further, leaning back instead against the wall and tipping her face as if to the sun. For a moment, he too stood still, but then decided he'd better get on as planned. He'd have a look, first, at that direct-south dial.

His walking around the fountain alerted her to his presence, though, and she came towards him at a brisk pace – how she managed it in that dress, he didn't know. She advanced with authority; no wariness in this approach to a strange man in the queen's own garden. He braced himself. From her stature – tiny – he'd assumed she was not much more than a girl, but now he could see she was in early middle age, folds bracketing her mouth, a line between her eyebrows, and a dustiness to her pallor. He was surprised to have made the mistake, because she had none of the softness of a girl; her shoulders were sharp and movements abrupt. She was so English-looking: fireside-dry skin, ashen but flushed, as if it were scalded. The smallness of her colourless eyes was accentuated by their stare. Due to genuine short-sightedness, he judged the stare to be, rather than any attempt to intimidate him.

She was all dress, parading what must've been years of other people's close work, and all of it layered, furred, edged. She'd probably taken until this late in the day to get dressed. For all the effort, though, the result was disappointing. *Curtains*, was what came to Rafael's mind. Not just the fabrics – splendid, yes, but sombre – but also the lack of shape. She was dressed in the old-fashioned, softer-lined English style – no Spanish farthingale – and on her thin frame the clothes were shape-less.

She asked him something and, small though she was, her voice had no squeakiness to it; it was unexpectedly deep. And officious though her approach might have been, there was no unpleasantness in her manner. She'd sounded straightforward, no nonsense, which gave him some confidence. He greeted her and stated his name, hoping he wouldn't have to say much more. Surprisingly, she came back at him in what he recognised as Aragonese: 'You're Spanish?'

An English speaker of a Spanish language! He confirmed that he was indeed Spanish.

'Welcome to England,' she said in Aragonese, touchingly serious, which made him smile, although nothing similar came back from her. He wondered at her connection with Spain – she was so very English-looking, English-dressed, but her accent had been good and there'd been a naturalness in how she'd spoken. Not like an English person trying a few words of Spanish. Surely she did have some connection with Spain. She asked him something else but he didn't grasp it – he couldn't speak Aragonese. 'Castilian?' he asked her; he'd be able to converse in Castilian.

She shook her head, regretful. 'French?'

No.

'Latin?'

He could read Latin but had never been able to speak it.

In English, she said, 'I speak French to my husband – he understands French – and he speaks Castilian to me, because I understand a little.' She gave an exasperated roll of her eyes but, Rafael detected, she was proud of their complicated arrangement. She looked expectantly at him; he considered how best to convey what he was up to.

'For the sun,' he said in Castilian, gesturing – pointlessly – at the sky, then remembering the vertical dial on the gallery wall and indicating that instead. 'For the queen, from the prince.'

'Ah.' Interest – approval – shone in her eyes.

Then came an interruption: a second lady emerging from that same doorway. This lady was younger, prettier, altogether lighter, a breath of fresh air, and she was all a-bustle, giving the impression that she'd been following the first lady and failed to keep up: 'Oh!' – *found you*. She collected herself, exhaled hugely, a hand pressed to her breastbone to steady her heart, and then she dropped into a deep curtsey.

Rafael understood at once. His own heart halted and re-started with a bang, his blood dropped away then beat back into his ears. Time had taken a wrong turning and was away before he could retrieve it and make good; he'd never, ever be able to make this good. He couldn't believe what he'd done. He simply couldn't believe it. He *wouldn't* have done it: no one could, *no one*, not even a child. Especially not a child: a child would have had an instinct. No one but he could have been so stupid. What exactly was it that he'd missed? He'd missed something clear and simple, he'd been busy thinking of some-thing else, perhaps too busy translating. All he could think, now, was that, despite the finery, she'd seemed so ordinary. Her face was ordinary, and she spoke ordinarily. But, then, what did he know of how a queen would look and speak?

What now? He had no idea, absolutely no idea how to save himself. Everything – courage, imagination – failed him and he stood there like, he felt, a small child. She'd known, hadn't she: she'd known that he had no idea who she was, and she hadn't enlightened him. How, though, really, could she have maintained her dignity while she enlightened him? She was talking cheerfully to the other woman, the new arrival – 'Mrs Dormer', she called her – indicating Rafael as she did so. Mrs Dormer's eyes had a mischievous glint. She knew. So, it had been obvious. It was that bad. Even though she hadn't been there, from the distant doorway she'd somehow guessed from his demeanour – presumably from his lack of deference – that he hadn't known he was in the presence of the queen. He longed for her – for both of them – to go, and then perhaps there'd be the tiniest chance he could pretend to himself that it had never happened. He would never, ever tell anyone. Would they? He wasn't sure of the merry-looking Mrs Dormer. It was a funny story, to her, and he sensed she liked a funny story. He'd have begged her then and there, if he'd known how. If she did tell, what kind of trouble would he get into? *I'll get sent home for this*: it flashed across his mind, lifting his heart.

Both women were waiting on him, now, politely interested. He did his utmost to look as if he were of service. Everything had changed: he was no longer a sundial-designer being waylaid by some woman, but a man being granted a personal audience by the queen of England. And he did what he should have done at the beginning: bowed fulsomely, abjectly, all the time horribly aware of the merry-looking lady witnessing it. Graciously, the queen was declining to acknowledge that anything had been amiss; she continued speaking, wishing him well with his work. She looked up into the sky and a note of apology came into her voice: '… no sun here …' she was saying. And then they headed back to the door, the queen leading the way at a jaunty pace.

Watching her go, Rafael felt a pang. She'd seemed so pleased that he was Spanish, but what, until now, had Spain ever done for her? Her Spanish mother had been set aside by the king in favour of a mistress, and she herself – an only child, twelve years old – had been taken from her, for ever kept from her and disinherited. And what had her uncle, the Spanish king, done? He'd expressed his concern and sympathy, his disgust and outrage, and he'd done so time and time again for years and years. But what had he actually done? And then, during her little half-brother's reign, she'd been persecuted for her religion, prevented from practising it, harassed, hounded and vilified, and what had her uncle done? Expressed more concern and sympathy, more disgust and outrage. She and her mother were just women, after all; and it was just England, after all. He could never have gone to war for them.

Watching her go, he found it hard to believe that she was the woman over whose accession to the throne, he'd heard, there'd been such jubilation: such jubilation, it was said, as had never before been seen in England. She'd spent most of her life shut away but then, when it mattered, the English people – making much of their sense of fair play – had rallied and championed the old king's eldest daughter as rightful heir. Rafael had seen her as ordinary when she'd stood talking to him, but, also, he now saw, nothing could be further from the truth. Her bearing, as she walked away, was regal.

Like an aunt, though, she'd seemed to him. A maiden aunt, spry and assiduously interested in him, with a no-nonsense voice and clothes of excellent quality but no flair. Somehow girlish but with no youthfulness. An eldest daughter, the dutiful one, no one's favourite; well respected but not loved. No children of her own, and now past childbearing. But none of this, now, was the truth, he reminded himself. She was thirty-eight, he knew: just in time, was the hope. Hence the marriage. She was no longer a maiden aunt but a newlywed with a husband – her respectful nephew – who was eleven years her junior.

He didn't mention the encounter in his letter home. It would sound ridiculous, unbelievable, and he didn't want those back home to doubt him, didn't want to add to the distance between them. His letters should be like whispers in their ears. If he told them that he'd spoken with the queen, they would – as he envisioned it – take a step back in surprise and confusion.

And so, instead, it was more of the same: the shocking weather, the unfresh food, the shops, the dogs. He'd been going to tell Francisco about there being a boy of his own age in the house, but had changed his mind. He'd been thinking of the little boy as a kind of friend, almost, for Francisco, before realising there was a risk – however ridiculous – that his own little lad would see the English child as a threat, as a potential competitor for his father's affections.

Rafael wasn't expecting letters in return: six weeks was the estimated delivery time to and from Seville. He'd be home before he could get any post. He'd probably be home before they got his missives, but he wrote just in case. There could be a delay, sea-journeys being as they were. Or sea-journeys being as they were, the worst could happen, and at least then they'd have word that he'd been thinking of them during his time away. At least Francisco would have something of him.

Francisco's preoccupation in the months before Rafael's departure had been death. He'd discovered it. Some of their conversations on the subject had been wonderfully weird, Francisco once excitedly considering, 'What shall I have written on my grave, Daddy? What would you like on yours?' Mostly, though, of course, they'd been distressing: *When you die, Daddy, and Mummy dies, I'll have no one left to love.* In that instance, Rafael had tried to explain that it often wasn't quite like that. 'You'll be old by then,' he'd dared to hope, 'and you'll have your own wife,' wondering with a pang if that would indeed be true, 'and your own children.'

Rafael's fear was persistent: that the worst might've already happened to his son, but that he didn't yet know it. A choking on a grape. The yanking over of a cauldron of boiling laundry. And Rafael not there to hold him, to try to ease his terror and his pain, not there to wash him before they wrapped him up and parcelled him away for ever. He couldn't yet know if something had happened. For six whole weeks, he wouldn't know. For six whole weeks he'd carry on as usual, eating and sleeping and sailing on the river, mindless, oblivious and unforgivable.

The household staff made much of looking busy, put upon, stretched – more, Rafael guessed, than was warranted by the actual workload. Mostly men, they were, and mostly liveried, which didn't help him learn to distinguish them from one another: grooms, watchmen, footmen and clerks. Rafael's family was probably no smaller but served more than adequately by a handful of staff who seemed to have all the time in the world. Those first few days in London, he longed to encounter the insouciance of his mother's maid, Maria, or the sleepiness of Vicente, the stablehand. Cook was the exception, back home, but that was just Cook: no one gave his rattiness any credence, and Rafael began to think even of him with affection.

One of the Kitson grooms limped: that one Rafael recognised. One of Mr Kitson's clerks was blind in one eye. One of the lads who served at dinner was a redhead. As for the Kitsons themselves, Rafael tried to get an idea of who they all were. They were easy to spot, sharing a certain foxy-faced look. The family was well endowed with girls: a pack of them, of all ages, and all, it seemed, assigned to looking after one another, so that one of them was almost always rounding on another with exaggerated patience or haughtiness. Sometimes, inevitably, their ill-fitting poise would slip. Once, he glimpsed one of the girls rushing up the central staircase, feet jabbing at the treads, her skirt held high, her scarlet-clad ankles and calves revealed. Another time, he saw from his window a Kitson girl swipe viciously at a smaller one who dodged, laughed in the face of her companion's fury and skipped away. There were only two Kitson boys. One was nine or ten years old and walked with the aid of two sticks.

The other was several years older, with a long face and big ears and a permanent stare into the middle-distance. Sometimes he'd cover those ears and shut his unfocused eyes and rock. He kept close to the lady Rafael knew to be Mrs Kitson, or to a sister who appeared to be the eldest of the pack. The girl was old enough to have dropped the airs and graces affected by her sisters and sometimes, from across the Hall, she gave Rafael a timid smile, for which he was grateful.

He didn't need the presence of the Kitson boys to remind him to be thankful for Francisco's perfection. Back at home, he'd sometimes found it funny: it'd seemed *too much* – perhaps that was what it was – so that sometimes, seeing it, he'd feel a laugh welling up. Incredulity, he supposed it was, but it felt like a laugh. So precarious, though, it seemed now, that perfection.

There were three other young men in the household who were clearly well-to-do, not staff, but didn't share the Kitson resemblance and, anyway, were too keen, too polite and too watchful of themselves to be members of the immediate family. At dinner, they served the high table. Rafael couldn't fathom who they were or what the arrangement with the Kitsons might be.

At the palace, a Spanish lad had got himself into trouble and had had his earlobe bitten off in a fight with an Englishman, according to Antonio. 'Clean off,' were Antonio's words.

Rafael doubted that there'd been much cleanliness about it. 'A fight?'

Antonio looked expressionlessly at him. 'There are a lot of fights,' he said.

But that was at the palace, where Spanish and English were shut in side by side. In the city, Rafael was beginning to feel more confident, braving some local exploration. To and from the river, he began to deviate just a little from his route: down Lombard Street and then Abchurch Lane, perhaps, or St Nicholas Lane, instead of St Swithins Lane. Or down Walbrooke into Dowgate. Up St Laurence Pountney Hill. The English might not like foreigners but there were foreigners here nevertheless, running their businesses. Word had spread among Rafael's fellow countrymen of French button makers, Dutch shoemakers, an Italian hatmaker, a Genovese glove-perfumer. These people were managing to live their lives here unmolested. Still, Rafael walked fast with his head down, his hat low over his face, avoiding streets from which tavern noise came, turning from streets in which he'd have to balance on planks. These precautions afforded him a limited view of London, of course. He saw few sundials – hardly surprising, given the climate – and none was innovative: nothing more unusual than a decliner. He noticed the forlorn remains of shrines: stripped empty, often stuffed with rubbish. Something else that struck him – head down, listening more than he dared look around – was how much the English talked: they never seemed to stop; they even talked to the dogs they took around on leashes, even to cats on top of walls. For all this talk, there was never any flow to it that he could hear; hard and sharp, the words sounded to him.

The river was an easier place for Rafael to be – not only on it, but also on the quayside. There, he could stop and stand, facing south, soaking up whatever sunlight there was, and take his time to look. Breathing space. Once, he watched the dazzling royal barge being towed downstream. On that occasion, he could enjoy the luxury of being just one of the crowd.

If he wasn't at or en route to and from the palace, nor in the Kitsons' Hall for dinner, then he was up in his gloomy little north-east-facing room. That was where he spent the evenings. Downstairs, the Kitsons entertained themselves and their guests as the trestle tables were cleared and stacked away, music played and dancing attempted. Staff finished their various duties and then retreated to the kitchen, Rafael presumed, to gossip and play cards. Up in his room, having written home – a little, each evening, towards a weekly letter – Rafael would work on calculations, work on his design. He also spent a lot of time gazing from the window: hours, he spent, doing that. St Bartholomew's Lane was below with nothing much to it, just houses, but linking Threadneedle Street and Throgmorton Street, so there was always someone passing through. Sometimes more than someone: gangs, probably apprentices on the loose, and, to judge from the whoops and kicking of a ball, good-natured enough, but he was very glad not to be down there. Later on, he'd see the Kitsons' guests leaving, as comfortable defying curfew as anyone in any other city he'd ever visited, their way lit for them by torch-bearing boys.

His little window was glassed and had a curtain, for which he was grateful. No shutters, though, and he missed them – the window looked odd, to him, without them. Exposed. And in general, around the Kitson house and on the houses along his routes, he missed their sounds: the clunks and gratings as a household stirred at the start of a day and then as it settled down at the end. When he'd had enough of staring into the dusk, there was the mere rasp of curtain rings along a pole. Dusk, in England, took for ever. Worth watching, it would've been, if there'd been a sky to see, if there'd been light enough to cast shadows. But as it was, it just hung around outside, damp, like something mislaid.

From time to time in any evening, though, came something that made it sparkle: the booming of church bells. Sometimes his floor would shake with it, and he'd get down there to feel it. There were three churches just beyond the end of St Bartholomew's Lane. A hundred in the square mile of London, he'd been told. For a Godless country, that was a lot of churches.

If Antonio wasn't back by the nine o'clock curfew, he wouldn't be coming back and Rafael would doze in the near-dark before waking to darkness and lighting a candle by which he'd get ready for bed.

Nights, he missed Leonor. Waking, he'd remember how, on his last morning, Francisco had climbed into bed and laid down beside him, thrown his rag-rabbit into the air, caught it, turned over and gone back to sleep.

In his second week, he got a bad cold. The surprise was that it'd taken that long, as all the Spaniards he came across had already been laid low. Especially Antonio, who had lolled around for days on end, hugging himself and barely raising his eyes, refusing to do the river-journey back to the Kitsons, imposing instead on friends at the palace. Well, now Rafael understood. For two days, he stayed at the Kitsons', stayed in his room except at suppertime. Then the worst of the cold shifted, but only down to his throat where it stuck, itching, causing a cough which inflamed it further, particularly at night. After several days and nights of this, he was taking his place for supper when a cup was placed in front of him on the table. He swivelled to see the pale woman: a flash of a smile from her, her fingertips to her throat and a forced cough, *It's for your cough.* And then she was gone – stepping back and away across the room – before he'd begun to thank her. He was touched, but mortified that his cough had been so noticeable. Under the faintly contemptuous glances of his neighbours, he raised the cup to his nose but was too blocked still to be able to smell it. He took a sip: honey, he detected, and something sharper. Two more sips and complete relief: something he'd stopped believing was possible. Enough remained in the cup for him to take it to his room and he got his first good night's sleep for almost a week.

The following evening, the woman did the same and this time he was ready to thank her. The evening after that, too, and the one after that. But the next one, he thanked her as usual and said, 'It's good, now,' and, smiling, raised his hand – *Enough, thank you* – which she must have understood because that was the last of it.

He still felt rotten for much of the time, because of indigestion. There was so much meat in England and so little else. Meat, even on Wednesdays, Fridays, Saturdays, and even in the court of this Catholic queen. Clearly she was bringing back only some of the Catholic ways. The Kitson family went to Mass, but everybody did now that the queen required it. There was no other evidence of their Catholicism. Rafael didn't know if he knew much about Protestantism. He knew that a Protestant priest would speak in English, not Latin, which he found hard to imagine: it didn't seem, to him, to be a language for wonders. And Protestants believed they could talk to God, he knew: offer up their every hope and grievance and He'd hear them, He'd listen to them. They debated the contents of the Bible, too, as if it were up for debate and by anyone.

Rafael had been going with the Kitson household to Mass at St Bartholomew's on the corner, but he missed a few days when he had his cold and, afterwards, didn't resume. He realised that if anyone marked his absence, they'd assume he was attending Spanish Masses at the palace. Likewise, his fellow countrymen, if they considered it at all, would assume that he was going to Mass with the Kitsons. At home, for years, his attendance at church had been the bare minimum. Church distracted him from God – that was how he felt – and perhaps this was because of the gloom of the buildings when – he was sure of it – God was in light. He didn't know how his brothers could bear it, that gloom, the two brothers of his who were priests. He'd feel God's presence sometimes when he was riding, or in the garden, or making calculations, and often when he glanced at his son. The feeling was always both awesome and intimate. It was a feeling he hadn't yet had in England.

When he was young, he'd talked about that feeling with his friends and many of them had felt the same. The Spanish Church, though, would judge it heretical; so now, older and, he hoped, wiser, he was careful to keep it to himself. He, whose family, Jewish-looking, Jewish-named, had no room for error.

During one of his visits to the Kitsons' local church, he'd glimpsed the pale woman. She'd had her eyes closed, as did many people – but they were dozing, he was sure, and she was biting her lip. He saw there was a vigilance about her.

Towards the end of the second week, Rafael was advised by an official in the Spanish office to abandon his project. The strain on the prince's budget – two households to support, the one he'd brought with him and the one his bride had assem bled for him – meant that there was no guarantee that Rafael would be paid, nor even that he'd be reimbursed for what he planned to spend soon on materials. 'But you must've known,' Rafael objected. The prince had been in England for a month. 'You could've stopped me coming.'

'Not *me*,' the official replied with a shrug, '*I* didn't know you were coming.'

Rafael had known that very few of his fellow countrymen were working. Duplication of any Englishman's duties was to be avoided. In deciding this, Spanish officials had been trying to keep the peace. Sit tight, everyone had been told, and passage home will soon be arranged.

Rafael had no doubt that the problem in his particular case would be resolved in his favour. In the meantime, it cost him nothing to continue with his work, so he wandered in the direction of the queen's garden. It was a raw morning, and he'd assumed no one would be there but, opening the door in the wall, he saw he was mistaken: *she* was there, the queen, at the fountain, accompanied by the mischievous-looking Mrs

Dormer. His heart clenched, squeezing the breath from him, and he backtracked immediately. He'd claim, if questioned later, that he'd taken a wrong turning. To his dismay, though, she'd seen him, or − short-sighted − she'd seen *someone*, and was beckoning. A whole-arm beckoning, it was: enthusiastic, unequivocal. Yes, she was mistaking him for someone else. Wouldn't her smirking companion put her right? He didn't know what to do. There was no choice, though. He couldn't disobey. He'd have to accept that he'd got himself into this − *How?* it was not like him to be incautious − and he'd have to see it through.

How, though, to approach her? He couldn't just stride over there. How else, though, would he get to her? And where − while he was walking − should he look? Surely he shouldn't stare into her face; but wouldn't it be disrespectful to fail to meet her gaze? And crucially: when, exactly, *where*, should he bow? Now, in the doorway? Or when he was closer? Or both? And how much closer? And how many bows?

But there she was, gesturing with cheerful impatience. So, in the end, he just did it, putting his trust in her accepting him as a bumptious Spanish peasant, and walking over to join her. He stopped at what he hoped was a respectful distance and bowed deeply, but she was already speaking to him in English: 'No sun, Mr Prado.' She said it anxiously, with only the briefest, most reluctant of skyward glances. Hard to imagine what kind of harvest could come from a summer such as this. He wondered again: how did the people here survive? They'd be going hungry, next year, and they didn't look in great shape − to say the least − even now.

Nor did she. Her small, watery eyes were pink-rimmed. It was said that she worked very hard. Rafael recalled hearing that she'd appointed a huge council of men – any English nobleman who had any claim, regardless of religious persuasion – and insisted on listening to each and every one of them, more than thirty, on each and every issue. If her extraordinary openness to him was anything to go by, he could believe it.

She said, 'My husband is a good man.' Good to have arranged the gift of the sundial, he took her to mean. She glanced at Mrs Dormer with something nearing a smile – a softening, a shyness – to which the lady responded with her own dazzler. Bashfully dipping her gaze, the queen repeated, 'My husband,' as if to listen to it, to hear it. To relish it. Rafael was surprised by such girlishness in a woman who'd been unmarried for almost forty years. He'd been assuming that this marriage of convenience was a personal inconvenience for her, just as it was for the prince. Word was that, when she'd come to the throne, she'd resisted her council's suggestion that she should marry. Hardly surprising, given the fate of her unfortunate mother. Everyone in Spain knew that the prince had had to leave behind a mistress, his wife in all but name. Did the queen know? The prince's job, now, was to be attentive to his new wife, and he'd be taking it seriously. Rafael didn't envy him his duty. For all the queen's openness, there was something off-putting about her. Not her looks, despite what everyone said; nothing so simple. It was perhaps her openness itself, he felt. An over-eagerness.

He wondered how – as heir to the throne – she'd got to such an age and not already been married. The prince was an old hand, he'd been married and widowed. Eleven years her junior, but already second time around for him. Then Rafael remembered that she hadn't been heir: she'd been a disinher- ited heir, which was worse than no heir at all. A liability. Who'd have wanted her? How everything had changed for her in just one year. So much change so late in life. This once- sidelined spinster was now wife of the man who would one day be the most powerful in the world.

She was peering at him. 'Do you have a wife, Mr Prado?'

Yes, he was glad to tell her. 'Leonor.' Her name came to him like a cry, which he forced down to be a lump in his throat. What would Leonor make of this? Being discussed by the queen of England. That'd be some gift to take back with him: *The queen asked about you.*

'Children?'

'One, Your Grace: a son, Francisco.' If Francisco were present in person, he'd be frustrating his father's efforts, cling- ing to his legs, refusing to look up.

'Francisco,' she echoed, appreciative. 'And how old is he?'

Three, he told her.

'He's little.' She sounded surprised, and asked, bluntly, 'How old is your wife?'

Taken aback, the English word eluded him; he found himself raising his hands and doing four flashes of all his fingers.

'Forty?' She turned, chatting animatedly, to her compan- ion. He felt he knew why his answer pleased her: Leonor had had her first baby in her late thirties, the queen's own age. The queen, though, looked so much older; she could easily be ten years older than Leonor. She turned back to him, held him in that pale stare of hers. 'I'm thirty-eight,' she said. She placed her hands squarely on her belly and said, matter-of-fact, 'Pray for me, Mr Prado.' As queen, she could expect an entire population to be praying for her, but he understood that she was truly asking it of him and he was honoured. Then she and her companion were going before he realised, and he had to do his bowing in her wake.

Again, Rafael refrained from making mention of the queen in his letter home. He'd tell Leonor when he saw her. *We spoke about you.* He could see, in his mind's eye, her habitual expression of humourful disdain, the scepticism with which she always faced him. He'd insist, *No, really*, and watch her making up her mind whether to believe him. That watchfulness of hers: that cautious, clever look. The tilt to her chin, and the hard little mouth with its crookedness so that it slipped whenever she spoke and more so when she smiled. Which made her smile seem partial, reflective, wry. She almost always looked amused, but Rafael couldn't remember ever having heard her laugh aloud. When he'd first ever seen her, she'd been standing with her arms folded, and that's how she almost always stood, how she seemed to be most comfortable although it didn't look comfortable to Rafael. She held herself separately, seemed to be appraising – a look to which he hadn't warmed, at first – but he'd learned in time that this wasn't so. On the contrary: more than anyone else he knew, she suspended judgement.

She'd arrived in Rafael's life as the bride of his boyhood best friend. Gil, a doctor's son and a doctor himself, now, had gone away to study and returned home with a bride. So far, so predictable. But with her tightly folded arms and half-smile, she wasn't the kind of woman Rafael had expected Gil to bring home; Gil, who asked little of life except that he be in the thick of it, offering a helping hand. Rafael didn't know what to make of her. The women in his family simultaneously indulged him and brushed him off, as they did with all men. Leonor, though, took the trouble to talk with him. Well, sometimes. Her talk was of nothing much, for much of the time, but that was what made it special. The women in his family talked to him to organise him, cajole him, or set him right: they had aims in their dealings with him. Leonor meandered, passing the time of day, her gaze idling on his, her slate-hued irises sometimes blue, sometimes green, grey, even almost amber. Occasionally, she'd speak more seriously – religion, politics – and say things that, in Rafael's experience, most people didn't dare say, but never provocatively, never carelessly. Always properly cautious, she was. But then she'd seem to be gone from him for perhaps as long as several weeks at a stretch, even though in fact she was there, around, arms folded and gaze unflinching.

If she didn't suit Gil, Rafael often wondered who'd suit her: who would he have imagined her with, if he hadn't known she was married to Gil? Someone older, he felt, someone reserved. He wondered what she and Gil saw in each other. Something, though, that was for certain, because once, years into their marriage, he spotted them kissing in the grove behind their house. Slipping away unseen, he nursed his shock, because it wasn't what he'd have expected of them.

He'd fallen in love with Leonor. When? For a while, the question preoccupied him, he felt he owed it to his helpless, hopeless loving to be able to account for it. And then he accepted that he'd been searching for an excuse: she'd always been her, he'd always been him, and thus he'd always loved her, even when he hadn't quite liked her, even when he hadn't been quite sure of her.

How did he live those years of unspoken love for his best friend's wife? There was no art to it. He worked hard and was away a lot, eventually, with his work. He lived from breath to breath, and hard at his heels were the doubts, the fears: what did she feel for him, and what did she know – or suspect – of what he felt for her? In one breath, he'd dread that his longing was an open wound; but in the next, he'd be congratulating himself on his subterfuge. Each and every heartbeat trapped him between a craving to see her and a desperation to avoid her. He loathed himself – of course he did – but sometimes there was also something like pride, because sometimes the secret that he carried inside himself as a stone was, instead, a gem.

And Gil. How had he felt about him? Well, he'd felt all things, over the years, and often all at once. He felt close to him, his boyhood soul mate, in their shared love for this woman with the hard-folded arms and cool eyes. He felt distant from him, too, though, as the husband of his beloved, which was who he'd become. He pitied Gil his treacherous best friend. And he resented him, of course he did. But he'd never wished him dead. No, he'd never done that.

In the early days, to keep himself going, Rafael allowed himself the luxury of imagining that he and Leonor might just once allude to their feelings for each other being deeper than they should be. For a time, he thought that'd be enough, but that was before he caught sight of her in the grove and witnessed the hunger in her kissing. From then on, for a while, nothing was enough and he stopped at nothing in his exploration of the life that they might have had together. Getting into bed, he'd find himself thinking about whom they might have entertained that evening, if they'd been married, and what they might have remarked to each other when alone again. And longing to see the look in her eyes as she reached around to unfasten her hair, last thing.

At the end of his second week, Rafael arrived home for supper one afternoon with Antonio to find the house being packed up. Just inside the main door, three men were taking down a tapestry: two of them up on ladders, the third supervising from below, and all three absorbed in a tense exchange of what sounded like suggestions and recriminations. Rafael might have assumed that the huge, heavy hanging was being removed for cleaning or repair – although no tapestry in the Kitson household looked old enough to require cleaning or repair – had he not noticed the packing cases around the hallway. Some were fastened and stacked, others still open. In one lay household plate: platters and jugs, the silverware for which England was famed. In another, cushions of a shimmering fabric. Towering over the cases, resting against the wall, was a dismantled bedframe, the posts carved with fruits and painted red, green

and gold; and on the floor he spotted – just as he was about
to trip over it – a rolled-up rug.

One of the men glanced down, eyes rheumy with a cold, as
if wondering whether he had to pack the two Spaniards as
well. At this point, the pale woman appeared, hurrying as if
she'd been looking for them: a purposeful approach. 'Mr
Prado? Mr Gomez?' Some kind of announcement was going
to be made, it seemed, and, to judge from her expression, one
that would give her pleasure. She spoke, indicating the boxes,
then herself, a touch of her fingertips to her breastbone. Rafael
missed it, and looked to Antonio for translation. Antonio
looked dazed, still catching up with her. 'She's the house –' He
frowned, and then it came to him: 'She's the housekeeper?'

She was. A skeleton staff was staying behind, of which she
was the backbone, the housekeeper. Later, Rafael would learn
that the Kitsons lived for most of the year at their manor in
the countryside and, like many of their friends, had only been
at their townhouse to witness the splendour of the royal
newlyweds' entrance into London and the elaborate pageants
held in the streets to celebrate it. They'd ended up having to
be patient. The wedding had taken place at Winchester
Cathedral just days after the prince had come ashore at
Southampton, but the royal couple's progress to London
thereafter had been leisurely, taking almost a month.

Now, though, in the first week of September, festivities
over, the Kitsons were heading back to their manor. In Spain,
the land was for peasants: that was the unanimous view of
Rafael's fellow countrymen. Something, then, that he had in
common with the English: the dislike of towns and cities, the
preference for open expanse and woods.

The first evening after the Kitsons' departure, he arrived back alone. Antonio was using the departure as an excuse for his own absence – as he saw it, he no longer needed to play the part of the guest. Not that he'd ever really done so. Rafael took it to mean the contrary, considering himself obliged to show support for the pale woman who'd been left almost alone to cater for them. He knocked on the door – wielded the leopard's head – and was disappointed to hear that one of the dogs remained in residence. The pale woman opened the door, dodging the animal; the boy, too, was behind her. The woman wasn't quite so pale – flushed and somehow scented – and Rafael guessed she'd been cooking. He wanted to apologise for having interrupted her, but didn't know how. She looked behind him. 'Mr Gomez?'

'No.' He didn't know how to say more.

She shrugged, seemed happy enough to give up on him, and stepped aside to let Rafael in. He noticed the bunch of keys on her belt: all the house keys, he presumed. She said something that sounded concerned and, frowning, touched his cloak. Said it again: 'Drenched.' *Drenched.* Then something else, faster, and a mime of eating, a pointing towards the Hall.

Having hung up his cloak, he went along to the Hall and, self-consciously, took a place at the single table alongside the others: the porter who'd let him through the gate; a man who he was fairly sure was one of the grooms; and a quite elderly man whom he'd seen around but had no idea what he did. And the dog, of course. The old man was talking to the others – dog included – and didn't let up when the pale woman began bringing in the dishes. Rafael rose to go and help her, but she shook her head and then he saw that she had the child in tow as helper. When an array of dishes was on the table, she helped the boy on to the bench and took her place beside him. After Grace, the old man resumed his chat and the others took him up on it, although the child kept quiet. Clearly, mealtime silence was only for when the whole household was in residence. Perhaps they were catching up on a day spent mostly alone.

Eventually, Rafael felt he should say something. 'Very good,' he said to the woman, indicating the spread, even though it was yet more meat – poultry of various types – served as usual with the jellies which he guessed were made from berries of some kind, whatever kinds they had in England. She frowned and shook her head, and he understood her to mean it wasn't her doing – this food had been left by the cook for them. But to this, he smiled back his own dismissal: the food was well presented and that would have been her doing; there was still plenty that she'd done. And this time, albeit with a small show of reluctance, she allowed it, bowing her head. To follow the meats, she fetched a bowl of something sweet, causing much excitement among his fellow diners. Usually there wasn't anything sweet, just the soft, wet cheeses. This was a sweetened, fruited cream with the unmistakable, delectable flavour of strawberries.

When the table had finally been cleared, Rafael wondered what he should do. Usually, he'd go to his room and work on his design, but surely it would be rude to walk away openly from this small gathering. The woman indicated that he should join them on cushions around the fireplace – in which no fire was lit – and so he did, only to find to his embarrassment that both the porter and the groom were excusing themselves. The old man took a heap of cushions and lay back immediately for a sleep, and the dog muscled in. The woman seemed to have produced from nowhere an article of clothing to adapt or repair, and her little boy began working on another, unpicking stitches for her. Rafael felt profoundly awkward: he had nothing with him, nothing to do. Pretend to doze, perhaps; perhaps he should do that. He had a cold and was conscious, in the silence, of his snuffling. But then the woman spoke to him: 'Spain, England,' and she drew a horizontal line in the air with her index finger. 'How many days?' She laid the fabric in her lap and held up both hands to display her fingers: 'Five, six, seven …?'

'Five,' he said. 'Five days.'

She looked appreciative of the answer — that he *had* answered — but then didn't seem to know what to make of it, didn't seem to know if a five-day sea-journey was long or short, or indeed longer or shorter than she might've guessed. There was nothing to say.

He indicated her son: 'Four, five years?'

'Four.'

So, he'd been right; and of course, because Francisco was almost four. 'Big,' he said, careful to sound impressed.

Looking at her boy, she shrugged with her mouth as if considering. She was being modest; the boy *was* tall, and — Rafael saw it — she was pleased he'd noticed. Sad, too, though — Rafael saw this, too — if only for a heartbeat: a fleeting sadness, perhaps at her little boy growing older and leaving his infant years behind. 'Nicholas,' she said. Rafael repeated it with obvious approval. 'My son,' he said, making a fist over his heart. 'Three years. Francisco.'

'Oh!' Her eyes lit up, and she looked as if she'd like to ask more. Instead, though, a small gesture, and unconsciously, Rafael felt, a reflection of his own: a brief, steadying touch of her own hand to her own heart. Which rather touched him.

'Rafael,' he said, tapping his chest.

'Cecily,' she reciprocated. This, he hadn't expected, and suffered a pang of anxiety that he'd pushed her into it. 'Madam' would've been fine. Again she looked expectant and he guessed that he was supposed to repeat it, to try it out, which he did and to which she looked amused although it had sounded all right to him.

After that, he'd felt relaxed enough to excuse himself and go up to his room to fetch paper and charcoal, and for the following couple of hours in Cecily's company he sketched and half-worked on ideas.

Subsequent evenings, this became the routine, sometimes with him working at the table, sometimes on a letter home. The old man, Richard — and dog, Flynn — would sleep, and Cecily would continue her work on a gown. Fine wool, it usually was: definitely not her own. 'Frizado,' she said, once, holding it up for him to see and relishing the texture between her fingertips. Another time, 'Mockado,' and another, 'Grogram.' Later, every evening, though, she'd put her work aside and then, standing up, standing tall to stretch, she'd reach to the small of her back to release her apron's bow with a tug. As it dropped away, she'd swoop it up, giving it a shake to release any creases and looping it into a couple of easy, loose folds. Then she'd reach into the linen basket for the little unassuming roll of undyed linen in which were pinned and pocketed her own special needles and threads.

The first time, she'd held up a needle, presented it to him although it was so fine that it vanished in the air between them, and said, 'From Spain.' She said it with a depreciating little laugh: there wasn't a lot they could talk about and this was the best she could do. For his part, he'd tried to look interested. What did interest him was that she'd made the effort to find something they had in common. That was what mattered; not the actual, invisible, though no doubt very good needle. She turned it in the air: 'Very, very good,' she assured him, eyebrows raised and head tilted in a parody of earnestness which he then mirrored so that she smiled.

Also in that linen pouch were floss silks of various colours. Her method was to lay them on the dark glossy tabletop to make her selection. The skeins were greens and blues, reds and yellows: the greens from fresh and bud-like to velvety fir-blues; the blues from palest lunar glow to deepest ultramarine; the reds from cat's tongue rosiness to alizarin; the yellows from the creaminess of blossom to the confidence of lemons and the darker, greeny-gold of pears. The best needles might well come from Spain, but everyone knew the best embroidery came from England.

Rafael would watch Cecily choosing her colours. She'd feel her way along the range, not touching: fingers walking above the row, rising and falling as if idling on the keys of a virginal. Then – yes – she'd pick one up, pleased to have made the decision but perhaps also a little regretful, Rafael detected, to have committed herself. The selection would be hung over her finger, unregarded, while she made the next few choices, then she'd drape them all in the fold between thumb and forefinger to trail across her palm. That little handful she'd lift into the light, whatever remained of it, sometimes even leaving the room, presumably in search of what was left of it. The scrutiny involved a slow turning of her hand one way and the other, then a flip so that the skeins could dangle free and light run the length of them. The final test was a single strand concentrated in a tiny loop, like an insect's wing, which she'd press to the embroidery for consideration against what was already there. From what he could glimpse, her design was of some kind of beast – stylised – prancing or pawing inside a geometric border. Her brilliant colours were so unlike those in which his designs were realised by Antonio. His and Antonio's colours were incidental: ochre tints in marble and patinas on bronze. And her materials, lax in her lap, were so pliable in comparison to theirs, which needed tackling.

Whenever he was too tired to think, he sketched what he saw in the room: the immense fireplace and, in detail, the Tudor roses carved into it; an expanse of wall-panelling and its delicately carved frames; sections of the decorative plaster-work on the ceiling; several floor tiles of differing heraldic designs; and the table clock from all angles. One evening, he began sketching Nicholas: unapproachable Nicholas. And perhaps that was why, the dare of it. Nicholas: approachable only like this, in surreptitious glances from across the room. And, anyway, Rafael found himself thinking, *he stares at me*, from that first evening, from the doorway, and ever since. Nicholas had never yet spoken in Rafael's presence, nor smiled. What he did – all he did – was stare. There was no blankness to that stare, it was full of intent: *Leave me alone.* Whenever their paths crossed, Nicholas stared Rafael down; stared until Rafael – smile abandoned – looked away.

Not now, though, for once. Not when the boy was relatively off-guard, weary at the end of the day and wedged
under the wing of his mother. He was kneeling beside her,
playing with a tin of buttons. Well, not playing. Play must
have been his mother's intention – 'Here, look!' – and he was
obliging her to the extent that he was doing something with
the buttons, but all he was doing was gazing at them as he
dabbled his fingertips in the tin. Rafael had considered him
an unnaturally still child – never running around, always
clinging to Cecily – but now he noticed how much the
apparently motionless Nicholas was in fact moving: chewing
his lip, and shifting his shoulders – one, two, one, two – in a
strange, rigid wiggle. The poor boy was so taken over by this
restlessness that there was nothing of him left for button-
playing.

Francisco would be lost to those buttons, he'd love them.
He'd line them up on the floor, transforming them in his
imagination into something else, creating a drama for them
and probably talking them through it. He was always occupied. What he was actually doing might well not be clear to
an observer. He'd be sitting straight-backed with that downward incline of his head, his attention on his hands, and his
hands busy.

Cecily shifted on her cushion and her son's gaze snapped
up to her. However unwelcoming those eyes were to anyone
but his mother, there was no denying that they were extraordinary: huge, almond-shaped, and a proper blue, not what
passed for blue in most eyes here in England but was really an
absence of colour, a mere shallow pooling of what passed for
light.

Francisco's smile was famous, lightning-quick and light-ning-bright, all eyes and teeth, almost absurd in its intensity. People would laugh aloud when first faced with it, and turn to Rafael, incredulous and celebratory: *What a beautiful smile!* Truly it was a gift: such a smile could never be learned. Rafael recalled it from Francisco's earliest days: Leonor turning around to walk away, and there over her shoulder was the baby and in a flash that cheeky, laughable smile. Nothing withheld, nothing watchful or measured in it. Such a smile anticipated no knock-backs, no caution on behalf of the beholder, nothing but the absolute best in response. It was wonderful to witness and Rafael understood the seriousness of being the guardian of it.

Naïvely, he'd not intended Cecily to see his sketch of her son. But on one of her trips from the room with her silks, she glanced over and exclaimed. Instantly, though, came a hesitancy, as if it might have been presumptuous of her even to have recognised the subject. Rafael sat there with it in his lap, helpless, exposed. Was it a gift? Just because that hadn't been his intention … It was a gift, wasn't it, this sketch of her boy. Had to be.

'Nicholas,' she said, sounding amazed. 'Look.' And then that hesitancy again: to Rafael, 'May I?'

He handed it to her, and she knelt beside her boy to show him. 'It's you.'

He stared at it, no less wary than when confronting Rafael himself, studying it, intent and grave, as if looking for something, before surrendering it back to his mother. She received it with a slight reluctance. In turn she went to hand it to Rafael, but he declined with a smile and a raising of his hands.

He hoped to strike the right note – a glad giving up of it, but not too dismissive of it, either – but didn't know that he'd been all that successful. She withdrew gingerly, looked for somewhere to place it and laid it face-up on the table, where it seemed, to Rafael, vulnerable.

The following evening, he sketched Cecily's hand; not the one busy with the needle but the other, the steadying one, her left. The one on which she wore a wedding band. And he wondered: was she a widow? He'd been presuming so, but maybe there was a husband working away somewhere – perhaps for Mr Kitson, abroad, or at the country house. Rafael hadn't a clue as to the ways people lived and worked here in England. Perhaps it was normal for spouses to live – to work – apart. If she was a widow, how long had she been bereaved? The child was only four. Clearly she'd had him late in life, and Rafael wondered if there were others, elsewhere, grown up. Rafael imagined opening the conversation: *You know, my wife and I, we only ever had the one, and late.* They had so nearly not had him; he had so nearly never happened.

There would become a graininess to the dusk and soon they'd see that it'd already happened: the lovely, velvety mix of light and dark would finally have lost balance in favour of darkness. However hard Rafael tried to see the moment happen, he never succeeded. It was, he knew, in the nature of it: it had to happen unseen or it couldn't happen at all. This evening, as on all others, they'd been sinking into the shadows, letting themselves and the room be taken. But soon Cecily would get up and begin lighting candles, and the candlelight would gently scoop them up, set them apart and make them observers of those shadows.

He could see how unscarred her hands were: unburned, uncalloused; no signs of hardship. Certainly she endured none in this house. She was a seamstress who didn't do the laundry; she shopped for food rather than pulling it from the soil or kneading or cooking it. But she'd have come from somewhere. She'd have survived things; there would have been things to survive, there were always things to have to survive. Had she always lived and worked in houses like this? There was no trace of her personal history on her hands, except for the marriage. It shone, the evidence of that. How long had she been here, gliding through this household, fabric over her arm, and ready when required to claim the favoured position of housekeeper? For ever, said her demeanour, but – Rafael felt   a little too deliberately. The child gave her away. That child wasn't at home, here.

Rafael concentrated again on his sketch. There was plenty for him to do, from the fan of bones across the back of the hand to the indentations on the knuckles. His own wife's hands, by comparison, were small and featureless. Not that he'd ever actually sketched them, but, then, he didn't have to, he knew them. Dainty, was how he'd thought of Leonor's hands, if he'd thought anything of them at all, although the realisation surprised him because he'd never thought of *her* as dainty. She was small, yes, but strong.

Prettily bejewelled, was what he remembered now of Leonor's hands. Cecily's wedding ring, her only ring, was loose. It moved as she moved her hand, dropping back towards the knuckle and revealing a stripe of pallor. She was fussing Nicholas's hair now and Rafael could almost feel the reassuring clunk of that ring – its solidity and smoothness – as if on his own head. The slight resistance of it, its switching back and forth. He wondered if her feet were like her hands, long and distinctly boned. And then he wondered what he was doing, wondering about her feet. The dusk must be addling him. He wasn't thinking of her feet, of course: what he was thinking of was proportion and line. Because that was what he did, in life. In his work. Angles. She had begun to walk around the room now with her taper, bestowing glowing pools, and he let himself think of the strong arches beneath those soft-sounding feet of hers.

Then she took him utterly by surprise in coming up and looking over his shoulder. No escape.

The surprise, now, was hers. 'My hands?'

He cringed. 'Yes.'

She looked down for a while longer at the drawing, then began to look at her own, real hands – raising and slowly rotating them – as if for comparison. As if seeing them when before, perhaps, they'd gone unremarked. But also as if they weren't hers. He said, 'I'm sorry.'

'Oh! – no.' The briefest, faintest of smiles to reassure him. Then, tentatively, the tip of her index finger down on to the paper, on to a stroke of charcoal, where it paused as if resisting following the line. Then back, locked away into a demure clasp of her hands. She gave him another brief smile, this time as if in formal thanks. This sketch, he didn't offer her. It was just a study, after all. A technical exercise. That's all it was.

Thereafter, chastened, he made a show of sketching the far end of the Hall, rigorous in his shading, frowning at his efforts. Cecily had returned to her embroidery, her son was drowsily stroking the dog, and the old man rattled with

snores. When Rafael judged an acceptable interval had
elapsed, he made his excuses. Cecily's upwards glance was
dazed from the close work she'd been doing and – reminded,
herself, of time having passed – she switched that glance from
Rafael to Nicholas, to check on him. And there he was, fallen
asleep. Rafael hadn't noticed, either. He wasn't surprised,
though: the child had quite a nasty cold. Cecily huffed, exasperated: he'd have to be woken to go to bed.

Rafael slammed down the impulse to offer to lift him. It
would be too familiar of him. But it must have occurred to
Cecily, too, because now she was looking at him as if she
didn't quite dare ask. He'd have to do it, then; but here came a
flush of pleasure that he could do something, could offer her
something. Still mindful, though, of overstepping the mark,
he gestured: *Shall I . . .?*

Her response was a hopeful wince: *Could you? Would you
mind?*

He set down his sketches and charcoal, convinced that he
was going to do it wrong, do it awkwardly and wake the
boy, who'd be alarmed to find himself being pawed by the
Spanish stranger. Approaching him, Rafael sized him up,
deliberated how to ensure least disturbance and greatest
lifting power. Cecily fluttered around him as if offering
assistance, but in fact doing nothing of the kind – although
there was nothing much she could do except wipe her son's
nose. Rafael crouched, slotted his hands under Nicholas's
arms and drew him to his chest. 'Come on, little man,' he
found himself soothing, just as he would with Francisco. The
boy offered no resistance and Rafael nearly overbalanced.
Righting himself, he strained for the lift, bore the weight

then settled him, marvelling how the little body could feel both so unlike Francisco's and, somehow, at the same time, identical. His heart protested at the confusion. Breathing in the muskiness of the boy's hair, he nodded to Cecily to lead the way.

She led him from the Hall to a staircase and up the narrow stone steps to a first-floor door, opened the door, ushered him inside, and drew a truckle bed from beneath the main bed. He made sure not to look around – that would be improper – as he lowered Nicholas on to the mattress. Nicholas frowned, turned on to his side and drew up his knees; Cecily bent over him, wiping his nose again and then busy with blankets. Rafael retreated, risking a glance back from the doorway and getting a preoccupied smile in thanks. She'd be staying in the room. He made his way to his own.

The next day, visitors arrived: Mr Kitson's secretary – in London on business – with four smartly dressed men whom Rafael didn't recognise. They, too, talked all through dinner, but just amongst themselves, perhaps on business matters, which left Rafael's usual crowd in respectful near-silence. Suffering the beginning of Nicholas's cold, Rafael was content to sit back. He listened not for the actual words but to the sounds, and he found that he was beginning to be able to distinguish between those sounds: yes, there were the blunt ones, particularly concerning things to hand – the food, and the dog, in whom they all took an interest as if it were a child, in fact in place of any interest in the actual child – but then they'd turn into conversation which had more flow, and Rafael would catch notes of French and Latin. It was a rag-bag of a language, English.

They'd gone by the following suppertime. After that meal, Rafael retired as usual to the cushions alongside Cecily and her son, and Richard — the old man — and dog, to sketch from memory the front elevation of the house, for Francisco. *This is where I'm staying. This — up here — is my window.* After a while, it occurred to him that Cecily might be watching him: occasionally there was a quick lift and turn of her head in his direction. Once, he'd managed to meet her gaze but she'd glanced back down, expressionless, as if hoping to get away with it. Having sketched her, he'd unsettled her, which he was sorry to see. She was anxious to know what he was up to, to see if she was once again his subject. But it would be too open an acknowledgement for him to take the initiative and show her his drawing. Instead, he took to putting it down every now and then in what he estimated to be her view, while he blew his nose; and then, when that didn't seem to have worked, he laid it aside while he paced to stretch his aching legs. After that, there were no more surreptitious glances.

Later that week, he found himself dabbling at the cleft between the thumb and forefinger of her left hand. In isolation, the fold wouldn't be recognisable: just a smudge of charcoal. Nothing, really. A space.

There was something about her brow, though, with its broadness that he'd noticed when he'd first seen her. There was something appealing about that. The eyes wide-spaced, unlike so many English faces, which tended towards the pinched. Hers was an open face. He half-sketched, doodled, seeing how little she had by way of eyebrows or eyelashes. Cursory and incomplete, they were, as if only the briefest attempts had been made at them. He had to be so very light with the charcoal to draw their absence.

He could see some of her hair, even though he wasn't looking. It reflected light – but whether it was golden or silvery, he didn't see. Women's caps here were placed back to reveal middle partings and hair sleek to the head. In Spain, there was never a glimpse of hair: just foreheads, high and bare. Leonor wouldn't sketch well, even if he dared try. Spanish women were generally soft-faced and doe-eyed, but Leonor had a sharp face with small, slate-coloured eyes, and her mouth was hard, thin-lipped, slipped sideways. He adored that cussed little mouth, a glimpse of it never failed to give a kick to his heart. The memory of it, even. Her hair was plain brown and her complexion sallow, which suggested she was delicate when in fact she was anything but. A trick, that. She was no classic beauty, but still Rafael was captivated by her.

That night, for the first time in a long time, he thought of Beatriz. She'd been his mother's maid and she'd seemed to him, aged fifteen, to have been in the household for ever. But it had probably only been two or three years, and she was likely no older than he was. He'd never looked at her: that was the truth. Not like that. She was just there, his mother's maid. Later, he puzzled how he'd missed that she was so extraordi-nary-looking with her pale face and amber eyes. Her hair – an abundance of tiny copper curls – he couldn't have known about.

One afternoon, while he was sitting in the garden, she approached him, coming up close as if curious. She bent to look into his eyes, and held the look. His worry was that he'd done something wrong and been discovered, because there was a knowingness to her expression. There was nothing for him to do but look back at her, and wait. He'd never before looked into her eyes – of course not – and he was intrigued by their colour. Not a colour that he'd ever seen in anyone else's eyes, nor even imagined possible for eyes. *Amber.* Then she had her fingers in his hair, lifting it back off his forehead, away from his face, as if he had a fever. He was suddenly conscious of her laced-up bosom, so close. The easing of his hair from his scalp was causing him a physical stirring of the kind he'd felt before – no use pretending otherwise – but never in direct response to someone's touch. But then she was gone, across the garden, back towards the house.

He knew something. He was suddenly in possession of a knowledge, he felt sure, that was going to make all the difference to his life: a touch – the mere touch – of a woman was all that mattered, was reason enough to be alive.

From now on, he hungered for her presence. That was all. He was sure she'd come to him again; he understood that was what she'd wanted him to know. And a couple of days later, she did come to him. In the garden, again. She stopped as if he'd called her to a halt, which he hadn't. And gave him that same look, albeit from a distance. He was to come to her, then. Her stillness reminded him of childhood 'catch', the pause before the dash. His blood beat inside his ears, great giddying thwacks. When he reached her, he didn't know what to do; he didn't know what it was that he was supposed to do.

Washed up, he was, there before her. *Her face.* The linen band of her cap, its edge proud beneath his fingertips; the tiniest drop down on to bare skin and along to the scarcely perceptible well of one temple. The rough silk of her eyebrows. Folds of her nose, one side and the other. Crest of her lips, its resistance. Then the lips themselves, the drag of them in the wake of his fingertip, his complete, so-slow circle. *Her lips*, their fingertip-breadth, as if made for this.

They opened, those lips, just a little, just enough to catch his fingertip in her front teeth: the very lightest of bites, very smallest of threats. The serrated edges of her teeth and the unevenness of their set. And then her tongue, a burst of soft, wet warmth.

He withdrew his fingertip, but only because he wanted to put his own tongue there against hers, just inside her lips. Her breath was hot, which he hadn't anticipated, and musty. The tip of her tongue lifted his, and he was surprised by its strength.

Fearing he was about to disgrace himself, he took his mouth from hers, but within a heartbeat he was prepared to take the risk and was back there. Suddenly, though, she pulled away, was on her way across the garden, and only then did he hear what she must have been listening for: footsteps. Into view came the kitchen boy with a handful of herbs. All Rafael could think was how he and Beatriz could continue. It was as urgent as if someone had stopped his breath.

When he next encountered her in the garden, she did the stopping and looking but then moved off and he realised he was to follow her. She led him through the gate into the woods; and from then on, that was where they met. She'd take

off her cap and shake free her wonderful hair. The cap was all
she ever took off; he never saw her less than fully dressed.
They'd lie down and kiss; she'd lie on him and he'd be all too
aware of the pillow of her bosom. They lay pressed together,
pushing against each other to get closer still. After a week or
so of this, she did reach underneath herself to unlace him, but
he assumed that she was merely making him more comfortable. She'd have known that he'd never dare do it himself in
her company, so she was doing it for him, allowing it, tolerat-
ing his indecorous state.

It never occurred to him that she might do anything else to
relieve him. That was for him to do, later, alone. One day,
though, during the kissing and after the unlacing, when she
was sprawled on top of him and pushing downwards, there
was some give and he realised he'd gone a little way inside
her, somehow. Both hardness and softness, was the sensation.
His initial reaction was that something had gone wrong, but
then – almost instantly – that, no, something had gone right.
She was already settling herself down on him; he was already
a little further inside.

It became what they did. He lived to do it. And whenever
they did it, he thrilled to their perfect fit, relishing it. After a
while, she'd gasp and tighten her grip on his shoulder. The
first time she'd done this, he feared he'd hurt her, and he
stopped moving, but she pressed down harder, pressed him to
follow her and he got the idea, which in turn brought on his
own response.

This moving of theirs was always done as if accidental, incidental to their kissing. He played along in creating that
impression, but alone, in his dreams, he did nothing else: no

kissing, even; just this moving, and more of it, ever faster. Afterwards, he'd feel that this might in some sense be a betrayal of her, to think of her like this; but he didn't particularly care. He certainly didn't care when he was doing it. If he could've got away with binding her to his bedposts, he would've done so. He only took care not to hurt or distress her so that she wouldn't stop doing it with him.

Looking back, as an adult, he was able to acknowledge this, appalled though he was. To understand it, almost, even: a fifteen-year-old boy. Given the chance, Francisco would probably be the same, and Rafael didn't think there was much he'd be able to do about it.

Beatriz never so much as addressed him during this time: they never spoke. They never had. In that respect, nothing changed.

He had no idea, at the time or since, as to whether she'd had liaisons with his brothers, all or any of them. She might've had. Gut instinct said no – his pious brothers? – but, then, it would, wouldn't it. And the pious ones are probably the worst. In retrospect, he suspected she wasn't a virgin. He wouldn't have known it at the time – he knew nothing, at the time.

How long did it go on? He hadn't kept track; it was something that was happening, it was his life. Months, anyway. And then one day, his mother, with Beatriz at her side, informed the family that her maid would be leaving the household in three days' time to go home to her village and get married. She knew, she said, that everyone would wish to join her in offering their congratulations – and so they did, amid expressions of regret at the impending departure. And Beatriz nodded and smiled her own shy thanks for the congratulations and the regrets. *Married?* There'd been no talk of marriage. But, then, of course, there'd been no talk at all. So, Rafael accepted it. It was something servants sometimes did.

There was something he'd no longer be doing, though, and the prospect was dire. He tried to get to see Beatriz, but she seemed always to be in his mother's company. He waited in vain in the woods and then suffered more vigils in the garden. But the three days passed and there he was, standing with the rest of the household to wave her goodbye. And she didn't look at him. And if there was ever mention of her again, he never heard it. But, then, why would he? Servant-talk was for women. Only twenty-four years later and more than a thousand miles away, feeling uneasy and contrite, did he find himself wondering about her departure, about what she'd been going to and why.

Some evenings, Antonio deigned to come back to the Kitsons and then everything there was different, there was conversation. Lively conversation. Between him and Cecily. She often found him funny: she did a lot of laughing and, to Rafael, her laughter sounded genuine.

He made no attempt to listen – catching no more than the odd, uninteresting word, such as *you, the house, London, in Spain* – but watched Cecily sitting straight, concentrating on sifting comprehensible words from Antonio's accent. She'd often respond, and sometimes ask questions; but despite engaging with Antonio in these conversations more than she ever did with Rafael, she gave less of herself, he felt, than in their own stilted exchanges. Her hands, for instance: Rafael noticed how for him they were always moving, raised and given up to the effort to show him what she meant, whereas for Antonio they stayed in her lap.

And Antonio was useless with her son. Rafael suspected he was useless with children in general – he was the type, he'd see them as competition for attention. It was hard to imagine how that could be so in this particular case, but anyway Antonio made no attempt to include the boy, not so much as an occasional glance. Rafael often made the effort to smile, fat lot of good though it did him.

It was after an evening – and a night – of Antonio that Rafael decided to ask Cecily for help. He felt able to ask for it, now, for his final week or so, especially as the Kitsons weren't going to be around: 'It's possible …? Antonio, me: two rooms?'

She frowned to indicate that she was thinking, then gestured for him to follow her. They went to the main staircase and up the stairs, along the gallery to more stairs – different from those to his old room – and along another, narrower gallery to yet more stairs. No sign of life anywhere, of course: everyone gone. Everything gone: patches on walls where paintings or hangings had been, and scuff marks where there'd been benches or chests. The child had come with them, but didn't run ahead as Francisco would have done. Francisco wouldn't have cared that he didn't know where they were going. Indeed, that would be it, the game of it: running ahead with an ever-increasing anticipation of being called back. This child, though, skulked in their wake, the fingertips of one hand – Rafael could hear – trailing along the walls. Ahead, Cecily was both dissolving into the dusk and shining in it.

She stopped at a closed door and she took a key from her belt to unlock it, opened it, stood back to reveal the room. A good size, was Rafael's first impression. Big bed and two oak chests. North-east facing, though, again, to his disappointment. Cecily was saying something quickly, indicating the bed, her hands raised and then falling. Bed hangings, he assumed, of which there was a notable absence, but her tone was cheerful and he guessed she was saying that she could find some. He was keen to accept the offer and to show his gratitude. There was no question: this room would do fine, hangings or no hangings, and even north-east facing. What mattered, frankly, was that Antonio wouldn't be in it.

Having enjoyed success with this request, Rafael decided he should tackle the lack of something else that would make the remainder of his stay more bearable: fresh drinking water. Beer and ale failed to quench his thirst, particularly when he had a cold – and he'd had a cold more or less ever since he'd arrived. Drinking from the conduits in the streets, or the wells, or the supplies delivered to the house by water-carriers: all these, he knew, were emphatically advised against. He longed for the well at home in the courtyard, the delving of its bucket into the chilly, drenched folds in the deep-down rock; longed to hear the song of the crank and the applause of stray droplets on the tiles. If there was a safe source of fresh water anywhere in or near London, even if it was at a price – and he felt he'd pay any price, he'd find a way to pay any price – then surely Cecily, as housekeeper, would know. But when he did ask, the evening after his success with the room, she was horrified at the suggestion and at pains, as far as he understood it, to persuade him that he should never be tempted.

She did seem to gauge his desperation, though, because she very kindly fetched him an earthenware jug and beaker from which she mimed taking a sip and enacted being taken aback: *sharp*, she was telling him with the backwards jerk of her head, her lips pursed, eyes big with blinks. Then a slow smile: the drinking of this sharp liquid, she was showing, was ultimately pleasurable. Refreshing, she was saying. Thanking her, he accepted the jug and beaker. 'What is it?' he asked, although he wasn't sure that he'd understand her reply.

Something apple, she said.

He'd half-understood. 'Apple?'

She raised her hand – *Wait* – and disappeared for a few minutes before there came again the rasps of her skirt. Rafael recognised that sound from whenever she was busy around the house. Never footsteps: the soft soles of her shoes were muted on the flagstones. She appeared with something in the palm of her hand: a small, apple-like fruit; like an apple, but much smaller. *Something* apple, she insisted, but it was no word that he recognised. He sipped the juice. Her mimed recoil had been accurate, although she was right about it being refreshing. Sour, was what it was, and he could imagine that some people could develop a taste for it. She was watching him closely, so he made much of his approval.

He also craved olives: the rub of their flesh on his tongue, the challenge of their bitterness. Word among his fellow countrymen was that they could be had, in England, and had been spotted on top tables. His further enquiries, though, were countered with shrugs and mention of markets. He didn't know the whereabouts of the nearest market – he was still barely deviating from the one route to and from the river. One day later that same week, he asked Cecily: 'Is it possible?' and showed her a handful of coins to establish that the forthcoming request wouldn't impose on her housekeeping budget (because who knew how expensive they'd be): 'Olives?' He'd taken care to learn the word. He'd had to: it bore no relation to the word in his own language. Nevertheless, disappointingly, a fair few attempts were needed before she understood him. She tilted her head to one side and then the other in her efforts to catch it. When she did, though, she was enthused, forgetting herself and chatting on at him without regard for his incomprehension, which amused him. He heard *market*. Then she made as if to push his hand away: she'd buy them. No, no, no, he insisted. What's more: 'Can I go?' he asked her, meaning, *Can I come?* but only knowing *go*. 'With you?' He'd surprised himself by asking, but suddenly he'd quite fancied a little expedition in the relative safety of her company, and he could shop for presents to take home for Leonor and Francisco.

So, that's how they came to be at the door together, one morning in September, both in their near-black cloaks: the bruise-hued, affordable version of black. His was short, Spanish-style; she was attaching little metal hooks to the hem of hers, presumably to keep it above the mud. Baskets were mustered at their feet. She had tried but failed to persuade her son to stay home. That's what Rafael had heard, as he'd come down the stairs: her tone low, emphatic, but then fractured, as if she were struggling – physically – to extricate herself, and at the same time a cry from the child of protest or desperation.

When Rafael reached the foot of the stairs, the child was there and dressed for coming with them; and Cecily looked shame-faced. Defeated.

Rafael was reminded of Francisco's latest tactic for protest. It had been a relatively new ruse – of perhaps a couple of weeks – when he'd left. He wondered if Francisco was still doing it: the declaration, *I'll never be your friend!* And a declaration was definitely what it was: haughty; quite a performance. No wheedling, no anger, but, on the contrary, calculated, cali-brated: Francisco throwing down the gauntlet, albeit with a flash of humour in his eyes. And indeed, in all but the most trying of situations Rafael had – secretly – found it funny, although the source of humour wasn't those knowing eyes but the mouth. The pout of extraordinary proportions, imitated from who knows where and executed without finesse.

He enjoyed walking with them, but it wasn't for long. At the end of the lane they turned right and ahead, in the distance, was the market. The Chepe, she called it. Cheapside. The sun was cloud-covered behind them, casting no shadow. He was glad he hadn't braved the trip alone. They were drawn into the crowds, a queue shuffling along the boards over the mud. Passing them were those with better boots or no boots at all to lose, braving the muck, and those on horseback or horse-drawn, their horses tetchy. Stepping surefooted around and through all this were traders bearing trays of wares. And thieves, too, Rafael knew: they'd be around. Cecily had her son by the hand, and Rafael marvelled at their balance. But although Nicholas was doing well, a little boy could only be so adept and Cecily was visibly tense, guiding and supporting him, her basket banging her hip.

There were butchers' and fishmongers' stalls, which had Rafael reeling, alongside enticing bakers' stalls. Cecily favoured a particular baker, buying two loaves. There was a spice stall at which Rafael would've lingered if he'd had the chance. Next to it, no less pungent but less pleasant, were rounds of cheese and small blocks of butter. In some of the blocks were flecks of leaves, perhaps herbs. Cecily stopped and they endured some buffeting from the ongoing crowd until they established a footing and she could request one of the blocks, free of leaves. Salted butter, Rafael suspected: he'd only had salted butter in England and, despite rarely having butter at home in Spain, was missing fresh. Cecily bought no cheese, which didn't bother Rafael. He found cows' milk cheese bland, compared to the sheeps' or goats' cheese that he ate at home.

Then came sacks of grains to step around, and barrels of wine, malmsey and sack from Spain; then crates of apples and buckets of flowers and herbs placed to catch the eye of Londoners with no gardens of their own. A potions stall was proving popular, causing a bottleneck. Further on came stalls of cloth and carpets. Leather, too, and rolls of ribbon, coils of rope. Rafael glimpsed a small table devoted to quills, and glanced away from one that bristled with birch rods. A girl edged past him with a tray on which were rolling a lot of tiny bells, presumably for hawks. Then he spotted a little boy – around the same age as Nicholas – with a gingerbread man: a well-dressed boy, being led by one hand, and, in his free hand was his prize, at which he gazed, captivated. Rafael wondered how anyone – however new to the world, however small and unknowing – could be in thrall to such a clumsy depiction of a figure: head, pair of eyes, arms, legs. Yet it did the trick, always did, never failed. Who hadn't once been vulnerable to the charm of a gingerbread man?

Nicholas, too, had spotted the boy and his gingerbread man, and Rafael was struck by the hunger in his stare. Not so much a physical hunger as a yearning to be bestowed upon. To be granted something special – and a frippery, no less – for himself and himself alone: for the decisions as to what to eat (head, first, or legs?) and when (all now, or save some for later?) to be all his own.

But there was Cecily's tightening of her grip on her son, too, Rafael noted: her making clear that there'd be no dalliance with any gingerbread man on this busy, provision-buying trip. No time for it, nor money, probably, either. And there was more than that, Rafael guessed: the concern that if she gave in on this one occasion, Nicholas would expect her to do so in future. As a parent, Rafael understood. Of course he did. What took him completely by surprise was that his heart went out to that surly little boy.

And he had the freedom of not being Nicholas's parent: he could enjoy that freedom. Moreover, he was a visitor, a guest, so he *should* bestow. It all made sense. This was something he could do. He halted Nicholas with a hand on his shoulder; and, as he'd intended, Cecily sensed the sudden resistance and faltered, too. Turning from them, he pressed his way to the nearby confectionary stall where, while being served, he kept his talk to a minimum – a mumbled thank you – and the baker, busy, didn't look twice. So, he'd managed that, and now there remained only Cecily's possible disapproval to face. If she did disapprove, he'd understand – and apologise – but he'd beg for her understanding in turn: *See his little face, Cecily,* and *Let me, just this once.*

If she was disapproving when he returned, she had the grace not to make anything of it, giving him only that anxious, reproachful look which said, *You shouldn't have,* but which he took to be no more than dutiful. She was careful to enthuse for Nicholas, 'Look at that! Isn't that lovely!' but then prompted him, 'What do you say?'

Rafael hadn't foreseen that. Should have, perhaps, but hadn't.

'Say thank you.'

Rafael was conscious of his smile dying on his face, his heart scrabbling in his throat. This — Nicholas under duress to speak to him — wasn't what he wanted. It wasn't why he'd bought him the gingerbread man, although no doubt this was how Nicholas would now see it. Rafael shook his head, but Cecily wasn't looking.

'Say thank you to Mr Prado.'

The boy looked up from the gingerbread man and, wide-eyed, regarded Rafael. He looked trapped. His mother was losing her patience. 'Nicholas!'

'Please, no,' Rafael implored Cecily, but it sounded like nothing, just a politeness. Was she trying to make a point? Rafael didn't think so. Her manner was blithe, suggesting that she was accustomed to conversation from her son and had forgotten or never noticed — was it possible? — that he didn't talk to Rafael or even in his presence.

'Nicholas! Please! Say thank you to Mr Prado!'

*No,* Rafael found himself willing him: *Keep your silence.* And then a jolt, a realisation that he'd been wanting this since he'd arrived: for the boy to be cornered, humbled, made to acknowledge him. Yes, he had. He, a grown man. He flushed with shame. 'Please, Cecily, no,' and his hand was on her arm. And it worked, she stopped, albeit with a huff of indignation and, at Nicholas, a look of fury.

She stalked off, and Rafael followed her to a stall of dates, dried figs and olives. The olives were still in brine, they'd not been put into oil, but they'd be better than nothing so he bought some. He was contemplating buying some dates and figs for Cecily, dried though they were. At the neighbouring stall, she was asking for some oatmeal. Taking the paper cone of oatmeal from the stallholder, she turned around, expectant, and asked, 'Where's Nicholas?' Rafael did the same; turned around to look and even to ask someone behind him, although there was no one he could ask. He turned right around, twice, his gaze sweeping both close up and further away. No Nicholas. How could there be no Nicholas? There'd be a simple explanation for his momentary disappearance. They just weren't looking in the right place. Cecily, though, was already demanding of everyone: 'Where's Nicholas?' No one was answering, of course. A couple of people shuffled to one side, making way, self-conscious, unsure what was being asked of them. She began shouting Nicholas's name: no more questions for bystanders but a direct appeal to her missing son. Dismay and disbelief flared inside Rafael, even anger. *You wouldn't dare, would you? You wouldn't dare run off. Not here. Here, of all places.*

He heard himself shouting, too, but what he heard was his accent. He was hearing himself as others heard him, and he saw them looking. They were turning around not because of the commotion over a lost child but to trace the source of the accent. A liability to Cecily, he was: people were looking at him rather than looking for her boy. His anger switched to them: *stupid* people, stupid *English*. Then Cecily's eyes were briefly on his and he saw the terror in them and knew it as if it were his own. One of them would have to stay in case Nicholas returned. 'You stay here,' he said to her, even though he knew it would be agony for her, that her instinct was to go, to search. But he couldn't have said, *I'll stay, you go*; he couldn't have said that. He'd spoken first, and there was nothing else he could have said. She began to object but he shouted her down – '*For Nicholas*' – and span away before she could stop him, shouldering his way into the crowd, checking with a glance every stall, every alleyway. It was his fault: yes, his fault, for having given Nicholas the gingerbread man. Rafael hollered his name over people's heads, and did it defiantly, making the most of it because the boy couldn't fail to be struck by the accent, to recognise it, to look up, to give himself up.

How could anyone ever get anywhere in this crowd, let alone get lost? A four-year-old boy couldn't have gone far. But, then, the opposite was just as true: a lost person would never be found in all this. And suddenly, ridiculously, Rafael's fear was for himself, turning on him, rearing up and making a strike back at him, because what if Cecily hadn't listened? What if she didn't stay, but abandoned her post at the grain stall to go after her son? Face it: that was where she was going to go, after her son. And then he, Rafael, would be lost. She'd find her son and go home, relieved, while Rafael was here among the wily traders and the beggars, unable ever to find

his way back to the house. That was what he felt, even though
he knew it was mad. He was mere streets away and he could
ask, even if it was in fractured English, or he could head down
to the river and find his way home from there.

*Ridiculous*, he told himself. *Focus*, he ordered himself, but
everything was in his way: baskets and boxes and barrels, boots
and the hems of cloaks, dogs, horses' haunches. *Focus, focus.* He
was failing at this. He was failing a little boy who'd be terrified. He was hopeless on the boards, tottering along, and he
didn't know the lie of the land, didn't know where Cheapside
led, didn't know which alleys were dead-ends. And couldn't
ask anyone anything. He should never have charged off,
acting the big man. Cecily would have been swifter and
sharper.

He'd gone far enough in one direction; Nicholas – or
anyone who *had* Nicholas – couldn't have got any further in
this direction in the time. The other direction needed to be
checked, double-quick. He began barging his way back,
aiming to sneak past Cecily so that she couldn't see that he
hadn't yet found her son. But when he got close to where he'd
left her, he saw she wasn't there. *She wasn't there.* He glanced
around, checking. Definitely not there. But the panic he'd so
feared didn't come. He'd wait for her; he'd suspend his search
because someone had to be here for Nicholas if he found his
own way back. She must've reached the same conclusion as he
had: that she could search better. He took up his post by the
stall. She'd recovered her wits and set off, and good luck to her.
She'd find him, Rafael suddenly knew she would. And only
then did the blindingly obvious occur to him: Nicholas wasn't
a child to get lost. Nicholas, of all children. If he'd gone, it was

deliberate. And if he'd gone somewhere, the chances were that Cecily – when she'd had a moment to think about it – would know where.

And she must've done because – thank God, thank God – they were back within minutes and Nicholas looked fine. There was no triumph in Cecily's expression, though, nor relief. Only weariness, as if she'd been having to do something she really hadn't enjoyed. Fetching him, that's what she'd been doing. Not finding him, but fetching him from somewhere. The child stared at Rafael as he usually did, and took a bite – his first, Rafael saw – of the gingerbread man's head. Nothing was said by way of explanation.

Later, though, back at home, Rafael asked her, or tried to: 'Nicholas ...' at the market '...' *where?*' How he hoped to understand her reply, he didn't know. Not that it was a problem, because all she did was shrug. Implying that Nicholas had been nowhere in particular and she'd been lucky enough to come across him. Rafael didn't believe her.

By his sixth week in England, at the end of September, his design was long finished but there was still no word on the likelihood of future payment nor, at the very least, the covering of the costs of stone, brass, wood, paints and goldleaf that he and Antonio needed if they were to go ahead with construction. He was visiting the Spanish office daily, but it was besieged with complaints and disputes between Spaniards and Englishmen. In any case, numerous officials had claimed to have no record of his ever being contracted to produce a sundial, and his original contact was in Spain. He demanded to speak with someone − anyone − more senior, but assurances that this would be arranged had so far come to nothing. He had a letter from his original contact but no one at the office ever showed much interest in reading it. The implication of their indifference was that circumstances weren't as had been envisaged and what might have held, back in Spain, no longer held now, here, in England.

He didn't know if he should give up and press instead, now, for his passage home. The promised six weeks were up. But these relatively junior officials, distracted and exhausted, might well be mistaken and, if and when the situation calmed down, it was Rafael who'd have to answer for the sundial project having been abandoned. He didn't know if he could leave Antonio to build it later if called upon − he didn't know if Antonio would agree and, if so, what retainer he'd expect from Rafael, nor, crucially, if he would be capable of the work. Antonio was an excellent stonemason, but Rafael had had an unexpectedly long time to work on this design and it surpassed anything he'd ever produced. He'd planned a structure as tall as a man, comprising eighteen hollowed scaphe dials: horizontal, equinoctial, polar and vertical; inclining, reclining and deinclining. Antonio would have to be trusted to select and spend wisely on a range of materials, and to subcontract the brasswork, carpentry, painting and gilding. Moreover, he'd have to be able to follow specifications far more complex than any he'd previously encountered. Rafael would hate to have to leave any job less than perfectly done, but especially this one, his finest ever design. On the other hand, the design itself was done, and what did he care about how it

might look here in England? This was no country for sundials, and there was no one here he wanted to impress. Of
course he'd like the queen to have a good dial, but if it did fall
short, she'd know no better.

He was still at Whitehall every day for lunch. *Turning
English, I am,* he'd joke bleakly to himself: interested in
nothing but eating. The English drank, too, but their thirst for
beer went way beyond what could politely be termed an
interest. Rafael was eating the fare on offer at the palace only
because there was nothing else for him to do, nowhere else to
go, and no food affordable or available elsewhere until suppertime. And if there was news of any ship heading home, he
wanted to hear it.

While they ate and drank, the English gossiped: so claimed
Rafael's acquaintances. A nation of gossips, the English, with
nothing important to say but never shutting up. But what
Rafael heard at lunch one day in late September was definitely no mere gossip. This was official, this was news, and, as
such, was something for him to take back, that evening, to the
house. He hoped no one had already reached Cecily with it;
he wanted to make a gift of it for her. Good to be able to offer
her something, for once: she, who'd been so generous to him
with the fruits of her household labours and so ready with
friendship. He suspected – to his shame – that he'd so far been
a bit of a misery around the house. Well, this evening, he
would step indoors with a genuine smile.

On the palace's riverside steps, handing over the regulated
fare to the boatman, he avoided eye-contact as usual, but he
detected less animosity, he was sure, and a boatman – never
backwards in coming forwards – was a good indicator of the

general mood. The good news was good for everyone, and already, it seemed, the English were softening towards their visitors. He took no chances, though, acting invisible, gaze averted to nowhere in particular and face expressionless – something he'd become good at, as had most of his fellow countrymen. The art was to look blank but with no hint of nonchalance which could be mistaken for the fabled Spanish arrogance, rumour of which had circulated long before any of these Londoners had ever actually seen anyone from Spain, and which was persisting despite their very best efforts.

Rafael's sole essential expense were these boats, daily, to and from the palace, and on this occasion – as on so many others – he was having to afford it alone. With the likelihood of informal celebrations at the palace, Antonio had decided to stay late. How did he afford it? – complaining long and loud of lack of money but usually finding enough for an evening of beer. Winning it or borrowing it, he must be. He wasn't getting it from Rafael, although of course he'd asked. But if Rafael himself hadn't been paid, he couldn't pay Antonio.

'There's the money for materials,' Antonio had objected.

'It's for materials,' Rafael had insisted.

Antonio laughed. 'Oh, come on,' he derided, 'you know it's not going to happen.' And he'd tried again: 'Lend me some.'

Unlike Antonio, Rafael had been going very carefully with the money he'd brought with him. Everything but boats was having to wait. No repairs to his boots until he was back home. It was the same for all the Spaniards he knew, they were all broke. They could only try to keep up appearances until their departure.

Antonio would need to be in luck with his lenders, today; there'd certainly be some celebrating, tonight. Spanish talk, all this afternoon, had been of the return to Spain, and it was excitable talk, now, in place of the usual despondency. The job was done: the queen was pregnant. The prince could go; at last, he could go and get on with the war against France. Because that had been the deal, hadn't it? The plan. And if the prince was going, so was everyone else. Soon, this Godforsaken backwater would be behind them: that's what people had been saying. Rafael wanted to share their optimism but, settling himself in the wherry, he recalled how, that time, the queen had said *My husband*, and he wasn't sure she'd ever been in on any plan for him to leave.

But *home*: he'd been saying the word to himself all afternoon, compelled to savour the weight of it as if it were treasure. That was all he'd done with it: think it, just that one little word, never daring to look inside it, to summon memories of home, for fear of what? Well, breaking it: that's how it felt. Leonor and Francisco were held inside that one word. He didn't dare rush at it. Didn't dare hope too much. Shouldn't tempt fate. Others, though, were happy to throw caution to the wind. *Let's run for our lives*, he'd heard someone laugh, at lunchtime, unashamed to admit it. Relieved, in fact, to voice it. Declaring the English as savages. The Spaniards had done their bit, played the perfect guests – courteous and solicitous – but for their pains had been overcharged and swindled, jostled and jeered, even pelted, spat at, attacked and robbed. These past few weeks, Rafael had been warned about gangs operating breezily in broad daylight. Last week, two Spaniards had killed an Englishman in self-defence and had hanged for it. Rafael was only surprised that there hadn't been more deaths, what with so many people – Spanish and English – having armed themselves, with even women and children tucking knives into their belts. He'd bet that most of the passengers on these boats were carrying a knife. Not him, though. He had tried, on the recommendation of the prince's officials that every Spaniard should be prepared to defend himself, but he'd found it a distraction. His fear was that he could have ended up with it being used against him. If it had come to it, his preference would have been for a punching and kicking, not a knifing. Some choice. He still made sure to go nowhere but the palace and back, by the most direct route. Even if everything was about to become better, he was so sick and tired of it. Home: was that really so much, now, two months on, to ask? *Please just get me home.* He was holding Leonor and Francisco in mind like a lifeline.

The prince was said to be considering cramming all his men into court lodgings, for safety, until they could leave. *We'll be a sitting target*, despaired Rafael, staring over the sludge-coloured, wind-jagged water. For as long as he had to stay in England, he wanted to stay with Cecily. She made it bearable. His only regret at leaving this place was that he'd be leaving her to a long, hard winter. Despite there having been no summer, winter was blowing in. The air had never been warm, but he realised in retrospect that there'd been a softness to it where now it was unrelentingly hard-edged. No prospect of respite, either, now. In August, there'd been the hope – albeit in vain – that the weather would improve. But here, now, were the last days of September and England had drifted too far from the sun.

He shuddered to think of this narrow, northern island marooned in December, January, February: the damp cold, the drenched half-light of which he'd been told, the darkness by mid-afternoon. Thank God he wouldn't be here to see it. But Cecily would. And the cold and dreariness would be the least of it. Winter was pouring into England on top of a disaster of a harvest and there'd be little food from now on, for a long time. Imports, yes, for those who could afford them, and surely that would include the Kitsons, but there would be little variation in what could be shipped in. A year, almost, of food from barrels: salted, desiccated. And this was the second such year.

People were saying the coming hunger was God's punishment for the English having turned from Him. The harder the English had turned from the Catholic Church, the worse their harvests. That was how the queen understood it, everyone said. Rafael envied her the sense of purpose that such belief gave her, the cause for optimism, the belief that there was something she could do to restore God's benevolence. She'd have crucial work to do, as she'd see it, in restoring England to Rome, and Rafael doubted she'd be deflected. He remembered how she'd laid her hands on the flat front of her gown and said, 'Pray for me.' The gravity with which she'd said it, the acceptance. Faith. And God had willed it: that's how it seemed. He'd given his blessing to her marriage: that's how she'd be seeing it, and so would most people. A scrap of a thirty-eight-year-old woman, now expecting a baby. She'd had faith when it seemed hopeless, and faith was all she'd ever had – she'd never taken to arms, never butchered her adversaries, but she'd triumphed, this woman who, for decades, had been disregarded. This woman whom time seemed to have passed by. She'd been steadfast and, against all the odds, decades later, her time had come. God was on her side: that was certainly how it looked.

Back at the Kitsons', by the door, was a spider – crab-like and stippled – in a web on one of the rosemary bushes, and Rafael kept his distance from it as he knocked with the leopard's head. The news he had for Cecily was the best possible news for this country of hers. Nothing could be done about the lack of harvest, but at least the prospect of an heir would bring some stability. At least – at last – there'd be that. An heir would mean no more of this changing back and forth every few years: Catholic, Protestant, Catholic. It would mean an end to the muddle that England had been in for twenty years. And an heir would sideline the sister – the self-regarding sister – who everyone agreed was trouble. 'There's news,' Rafael said to Cecily when she'd opened the door and he'd sidestepped the excitable dog, 'good news.' He felt conspicuous, as if he were about to give a performance. He checked, first, 'You know it?' *Perhaps you've heard it already?* But no: her look was blank. Not blank: open and attentive, that was how it was, as usual. He felt a pang, the sweet ache of recognition, because he loved it, that look of hers. He'd hated having to come to England but there had been this unexpected gift of Cecily, of having met her.

The door was closed behind them when he said, 'For the queen, a baby.' His first surprise was that she didn't seem to have understood him – her expression unchanged – but then came a tilt of her head and she queried, 'The queen?' The second surprise was her tone, which was unlike any he'd ever heard from her. Sharp. But he could appreciate that she'd find it hard to believe what he'd just said – it was unexpected news. His stomach prickled with panic, though, because now he had the job of persuading her that he spoke the truth, a job he hadn't reckoned on. 'Yes,' he confirmed, but careful to echo her scepticism, 'a baby,' and shrugged expansively, inviting her to join him in his amazement but to accept it: *God moves in mysterious ways.*

Still nothing from her – then, 'You believe it?' This, too, was new: a challenge. He'd assumed it would be easy to bear this news, but there was something he wasn't doing right. She was right to question it; he should have been better prepared. To come with such big news and not be able to back it up: he wasn't doing right by her. Struggling to respond – what was English for 'announcement'? – he cast around and had to settle for, 'The queen says yes, and the doctors.'

She challenged him further: 'Has it been *announced*?' She'd never before spoken to him like this, her eyes wide and unblinking, quite fierce. And there'd be no breaking into a smile, he sensed, when she'd had it confirmed. He was out of his depth: what was going on here? He hadn't witnessed any reactions other than relief and happiness. Protestants would be concerned at the prospect of a Catholic heir, even though they had no need – this queen was famously tolerant – but Cecily wasn't a Protestant; he'd seen her at Mass. Or was she a Protestant? But this reaction of hers felt personal, a very real wounding. Not a matter of doctrine. Why should news of another woman's pregnancy so unsettle her?

*Has it been announced?* – she'd made clear there must be no misunderstanding, demanding of him an unequivocal answer.

Fair enough: it was important news, it should be got right. But he'd never seen this steeliness, before, in her. It thrilled him even as it distressed him, because only moments ago he'd been thinking he knew her, and now this, now this: more to know. He did as she required and answered her just as definitely as she'd asked: '*Yes.*'

She took it. Didn't answer back. Gave nothing back.

'It's good news?' He cringed to hear how pathetic he sounded, how clueless, how wheedling. He needed her reassurance that he'd done something good in bringing her this news. He needed her to tell him what he'd done wrong. Instead, she pretended that nothing had happened. 'Yes, good news.' Her voice was higher than usual, striving to sound casual. 'Very good news.' Adding insult to injury, she threw up her hands and let them drop back with a slap in an expression of surprise. Pretending that it was the surprise that had unnerved her. She dismissed him with a tight little smile that didn't reach her eyes. And then she turned to walk off. Just like that. Well, he wasn't having it. He seemed to have offended her and he couldn't make amends until he knew what was wrong. He had wanted so very much to be the bearer of good news. 'Cecily,' he protested, and he'd taken her arm before he realised. He couldn't believe he'd done it, but then, because it was done, he didn't let go. Might even have tightened his grip. She turned harder away. '*Cecily.*' Nothing, though, from her; so, in desperation, he took her downturned, turned-away chin and raised it, turned her face to him. His heart was wild, he was unable to breathe. His touch to her chin was so light as to be almost no touch at all, but for all her reluctance she came with it. Still, though, that refusal to look at him – a very delib-

erate, furious turning away of her gaze – but he saw that her
eyes were red and his heart clenched with the shock.

'It's good news,' she said: a mere repetition, because she was
trapped into it.

Chastened, he released her, and only then did she look at
him, composing herself and repeating, 'good news,' but only, he
knew, to make clear that there was to be no discussion. It was
then, though, that she touched his arm, just a dab of fingertips
to his sleeve, in what he took to be reassurance – *It's not you,
Rafael; it's not your fault* – and he, himself, veered towards tears,
brimming with relief. Her turning from him now had no
urgency; she went ahead into the house, to her tasks, leaving
him still wondering what he'd done. Perhaps she was mourning
her own missed opportunities in life; perhaps it was that.

During the following weeks, her mood didn't improve. There
was a sadness about her. For a long time, though, this had been
a sad country and perhaps she'd been like this for a long time
and he'd not seen it, perhaps because he hadn't watched her as
closely as he now did. He feared she was ill but saw no signs.
Maybe she'd been keener to hide her melancholy from him,
before; but now, knowing him better, didn't bother. Life must
be hard for her, he reasoned, alone here in this house with her
child. Widowed. Well, he knew all about widows: he was
married to one.

Six weeks at most, he'd been told. The first ship home, he'd
been promised. Well, the first ship home had already set sail,
more than a week early: the Duke of Medina-Celi's, with all

his men. Rafael's problem was that he was no one's man. But, he told the Spanish office, he was prepared to travel on anything, on any trade ship to anywhere in Spain. And now that the six weeks were up and they were still unable to give him word on the likelihood of the sundial being funded, he reckoned he was entitled to leave. They'd look into it, they kept telling him: this, from officials who couldn't see beyond the man waiting next in line to complain.

Cecily embroidered in the evenings without looking up, biting her lip, working at the stitching rather than taking pleasure in it. They'd never been able to converse much but there'd been an openness where now, he felt, she was closed to him. Once, even, she cried. He'd taken it to be the usual English sniffing until, with a jolt, he'd realised his mistake. At the time, he was sitting at the table, writing what he'd once again assumed to be his final letter home. He stared at the wet scratches of ink, wondering what to do. What to say. Anything would almost certainly embarrass her, but he couldn't sit there ignoring her distress. He couldn't bear it. A simple, *Are you all right?* would be knocked back, he guessed, with a mere, *Yes, thanks*. He managed, 'Cecily? Something happens?' *Has something happened?*

Surprised into looking up, she thanked him for his concern with a quick, dutiful smile through obvious tears. 'Oh, no, nothing. But thank you.' Then she was back to her needlework and he was helpless, at a loss. Nothing for it but to turn his attention back to the letter in front of him. He'd still had no replies because Leonor was expecting him back any day. Don't write, he'd been telling her, because I'll be back soon. For a month, now, he'd been saying that.

Most days, lately, if the rain looked to be holding off for long enough, he'd been out walking. Word was that the streets were safe since the breaking of the queen's good news, and indeed he met no trouble, just glances from the curious. Walking helped him to feel less trapped. Odd, that he should feel free in the crammed lanes, jostled by shoppers, dodging beggars and pedlars of baked apples, sidestepping spit-roasts. Kept on his toes, he was, though, which was what he needed. Well-to-do streets ran alongside bad, and he never knew which he'd find until he made the turning – although he never made the same mistake twice of turning into Fleet Street, with its open sewer and hellish-looking prison. Some areas were charming: the cheese kiosks in Bread Street; the bookshops around St Paul's. The cathedral itself, though, he avoided after his first visit. Hundreds of keen-eyed Londoners milling around in the nave, clearly conducting dubious business deals: no place for an onlooker. From the streets around St Paul's, he would often head downhill to the river where he relished its lustre and the sudden, unexpected openness. The breeze working his eyes to a shine, he'd watch men in the distance riding the supple back of that body of water to make their living: garrulous boatmen, and stoical fishermen. In the shallows, sometimes, oxen quenched their thirst under the eye of their herdsman. And downstream was London Bridge: the span of arches, and towering, timber-intricate houses. Though he loved the look of it, he'd never dared go on to it, let alone across, knowing from Antonio that the south bank teemed with taverns and brothels. It was where the bear-baiting happened, too, and in August a bear had broken free and savaged a man.

Late afternoon was when he did his walking: no later because dusk – and with it, curfew – was coming so much earlier. Despite the chill and the clouds rolling dense and dark like smoke, there was something in the autumn air of which he couldn't get enough. He breathed it deep and tingled with it. A sharpness, at which his body tightened in anticipation. The season was turning; he'd never before experienced a turn as hard and fast as this. The prospect of winter appalled him but his body was alive, animal-alive, to its coming.

He got sick in October, and languished for two days with a bucket, lying in his bed watching half-hearted daylight drift around his room, and thirsting for fresh, sun-sparkled water. He missed Leonor. Even by her own admission she was a poor nurse, but that was what he longed for: the laughable incompetence of her nursing. Her good-natured failing. When he did get downstairs again, Cecily and Nicholas were nowhere to be seen and the men were fending for them-selves in the kitchen, living on bread and cheese, until each of them in turn disappeared for a couple of days. When Cecily reappeared, she moved gingerly for a day or two and her eyes were shadowed. So she, too, had been ill, and probably her boy, also.

He was back at the Spanish office as soon as he was able, to be told of a distinct possibility that he and Antonio would be setting sail within a fortnight. Details would be forthcoming in time. Progress indeed, and the two officials who broke the news seemed confident, even cheerful. His hopes soared.

Around that time, the house filled with spiders. There was no season for them in Spain and, at home, they were rarely inside the house, but at the Kitsons' it was as if they were answering a call. They seeped from nooks and crannies, and wherever he turned, it seemed, there was one crouching, beast-sized, on the wall. Sometimes they looked blind, stunned to detect themselves in the open; insensible and just as likely to dash forwards as away. Other times, he saw them as watchful and malign, biding their time, the exaggerated crook of their legs posing the threat of a sudden drop. He hated that they came from the dark. He hated their clambering across walls like taunting fingers, and their frantic prancing over folds of fabric. And their silence: give him the rowdiness of the mice in the roof, any day – at least he knew they were there. Spiders could be anywhere, and, at the Kitsons', often were: on the back of his curtain, even, and once clinging inside his cloak.

One evening, Cecily lifted some cloth from her basket and a black blotch dropped from it to skitter into the shadows of the fireplace. Recoiling, she and Rafael then shared a self-conscious laugh of relief. Poking nervously at the other fabrics, she said, 'It's lucky, you know, to find a spider in your wedding dress.' Did she mean she'd found one in her wedding dress? Was he supposed to ask? He didn't – didn't dare – and then the moment had gone.

Some evenings with Cecily were better than others, and some were almost as they'd previously been. One evening, unexpectedly, she spoke as she selected a thread: 'Bear's ear.' She'd addressed no one in particular. Her son – practising tying knots – didn't seem to register it, and Richard was asleep. Rafael queried, 'Bear's ear?'

She was startled by his misunderstanding. 'No, not from a bear's ear,' with an unsure laugh. She held up some silk floss, taut between her hands. 'The colour: "bear's ear".' So he laughed, now, too. She scrabbled in her linen pouch for another skein, drew it free and dangled it in the air: 'Dove.'

'Dove,' he repeated, approvingly. He knew *dove*.

That seemed to please her. One more, a pink: 'Lady-blush.'

'Lady …?'

'Blush.' She patted her cheeks, raised her eyebrows.

Oh. He smiled. *Blush*.

She put them back, then pointed into the pouch at another: 'Pound-citron.' She was matter-of-fact, now. Another: 'Brazil.' A last one: 'Isabella-colour.' Then, busying herself back with her embroidery: 'My father was a wool merchant. We lived on a farm.'

A wool merchant, a sheep farm. Big business. The annual shearing, and wool-winders descending, setting up camp while they cleaned the wool and packed it for bringing to London for grading and packing again for export. The year-round busyness of a farm, too, not just with the ploughing and sowing and harvesting, but the endless ditching and weeding and repairing. Back at the house − as at any manor house − the brewing and egg-collecting and cheese-making, candle-making and butchery. And there'd have been an office for the collection and collation of tithes and rents, and the keeping of accounts. Big money in English wool. How, then, had she ended up here? Hers was a valued and responsible role in the Kitson household, but all the same she was a servant.

'Your father?' she asked him.

'Doctor.'

She nodded in approval.

'And one brother, a doctor.' He refrained from saying the other two were priests.

'But not you.' She said it with a smile.

'Not me.' He returned the smile. She knew what he did for his work, but he worried that she didn't fully understand why he wasn't working here. He wondered if he should try explaining it again, but she was asking, 'Your father …?' Full of concern: asking if his father was alive.

'No. But my mother, yes.'

'Oh.' Careful: sympathy for the death of his father, thankful that his mother was alive.

'You?' he dared.

She lowered her eyes, shook her head. 'Fifty-one.'

He had to grasp the number itself before he could recall the English sickness of 1551, the closing of the ports in his country to ships from hers. 'I'm very sorry,' he said, and she glanced up from her work in acknowledgement of it. And then that seemed to be it, for the evening: no more was said.

Later that night, Rafael recalled Francisco's very first encounter with the notion of death: how his little boy's reaction had shaken him. *But people don't want to die!* – his outrage, his distress had been immediate and unequivocal. How had he known? He'd never been told, it'd never been discussed – he was three years old – but he knew.

It was something everyone knew.

Cecily's countryside childhood came up again when, a few days later, they went blackberrying. Rafael was delighted to be asked along. Quite an occasion, this trip, to judge from her bustling preparations. The morning was glorious, the first in all the time since his arrival. Richard was to drive them. 'Up to Shoreditch,' Cecily said. Even Nicholas looked pleased at the prospect, but no one matched the dog's excitement: he was first into the cart, and no one admonished him.

Richard drove along Threadneedle Street, then Bishopsgate Street. From up in the cart, Rafael could occasionally see over walls into gardens. Many of the houses and other premises up this way had small gardens – some with simple sundials, which, for once, were of use – and even little orchards. Fruit trees, he glimpsed, and vines; other climbers, too, and rose-bushes, poppies and pinks, although none were in flower. Francisco went through a phase of picking flowers for Rafael, the smallest flowers he could find and a solitary bloom at a time. *I've got you a flower – look! – I've got you a flower, Daddy.* A solemn bestowing, a little drama: a gesture that he could make. *Oh, thank you, Francisco, that's lovely, that's really lovely, thank you.* For several months, the house was littered with those single, spindly stems and their tiny, wilted flower heads, and Rafael was forever having to judge when Francisco had lost interest in them so that they could be tidied away. He didn't always get it right, this betrayal of his son.

*Where's the flower I gave you, Daddy?* Or, *Hey! Who threw my flower away?*

Francisco came to suspect him, he was sure, or half-suspect him, incredulous though he must have been at his father's disregard. He turned watchful; it was harder and harder for

Rafael to manage to get rid of those flowers. By the time of
Rafael's departure, Francisco wasn't looking at flowers; they
held no interest for him. The stakes were higher, there was so
much more he could do, his world was so much bigger and
faster.

Approaching Bishopsgate, they passed a site which looked
as though it had been a religious institution. It was derelict –
doors broken down and windows gaping, gates taken, roof
tiles missing and timbers exposed – but some reconstruction
had begun with two ladders propped against a wall and a pile
of new bricks in one of the courtyards. Cecily caught his eye
and read his mind: 'No' – shaking her head – 'for rich people,
a big house.' And he understood this was no re-establishment
of the religious order, but a residential conversion.

Traffic through the Gate was heavy, not only with vehicles
but a flock of geese being driven to market. Whether there
had been anything on the Gate – bits of bodies, traitors'
bodies – he didn't know, he'd avoided looking. Beyond the
gatehouse, the roadside remained built up. One cluster of
well-ordered buildings just outside the Gate seemed to cause
particular interest, Cecily and Richard gazing at it. 'Hospital,'
Cecily told Rafael when she realised he was watching her,
and Richard tapped his head. 'Bedlam,' Cecily said. Rafael
glimpsed a big stone sundial wedged out from a wall to make
it direct-east: no need for the maker to have calculated the
angle of declination.

He saw none of the archery practice that he'd been told
happened on the land outside the walls. Too built up, here, for
that. Gradually, there were fewer buildings at the roadside.
Cecily closed her eyes. Rafael loved to see her like this:

relaxed, in sunshine. He loved to be riding along with her. Eventually they arrived at what had probably once been a village quite separate from London. 'Shoreditch,' Cecily announced.

Flynn was first out, bounding from the cart and stretching himself on the warm ground to soak up the sunshine. Cecily showed Rafael the fruits to pick, the blackberries, and he was keen to do his best for her. There were thorns and he'd have to be wary, too, of nettles. He found the hedges themselves interesting, made of different kinds of vegetation. 'Whitethorn,' Cecily told him of the one that seemed to be the most common. He liked it that she wanted to tell him. When he looked closely, he saw that in some places the branches had been trained horizontally to give a sturdy weave. 'Plashing,' she called it. There were other fruits, too, less prevalent, as small as the blackberries but smooth, spherical and blue-black. He indicated them to Cecily: *These?* Should he pick these? 'Blackthorn,' she said of the bush, 'Sloes,' of the fruits, and shook her head: 'November.' The same – 'November' – for something more tree than bush which she called Bullace, and which, he saw, bore fruits with identical blue-black frosting but oval and bigger, like tiny plums. *November:* she'd held his gaze for a heartbeat when she'd said it, he felt. By November, he'd be gone.

The sun laid down its light, piling it down in a rich silt. Back home, sunlight was thin and sharp and on the attack from overhead. In this slanted illumination, trees cast webs of shadow. Sometimes Rafael's own shadow took him aback, bringing him up sharp: so distinct, it was, and compact, solid-looking, advancing with confidence. The sun blessed his face, his shoulders, his back. The trees fizzed with breeze; a bumblebee hummed like a bow dandled on a string. Both Nicholas and Richard were industrious. Cecily's face had some colour, Rafael saw. *Lady-blush*.

The day should have been perfect, but Cecily was tense because the yield was poor. Apart from the scattering of plum-like fruits, blackberries were the last before the long winter, she told him, and should have been plentiful. She didn't like other pickers near, Rafael noticed, which was because they were competition but could also have been because many of them were so obviously armed, firearms slung over their shoulders. Whenever anyone else was around, Rafael kept quiet, kept his head down. He was even less protected, he realised, than in London. Had Cecily realised it, too? Did she see him as vulnerable, up here? He hoped she didn't, and he hoped he hadn't been foolish to come.

Whenever he glanced up, London was there in the distance, all spires. A city of churches, yes, but invisible from here were the ruins of some and the ransacked look of others. Seeing him pause to take in the view, once, Cecily confided, 'I don't like London.'

He was surprised. she'd never even hinted at it. 'No?'

She merely shook her head.

'You prefer …?' He waved a hand around: open country-side.

She considered how to reply. 'I come from far away,' she said, eventually, in that careful English with which she spoke to him.

'Me, too,' he said, and then they both laughed. He'd have loved to have asked her more, if he'd known how. And she'd taken it as a joke, his coming from far away, but he, too, had grown up in the countryside. Three miles from Seville, although he'd gone to school there and his father had worked there, as did all his brothers.

His brother Pedro's working away every day in Seville was what had enabled his wife, Jeronima, to have her affair. Rafael tried not to think of it, but that night after the blackberrying, he was unable to stop himself.

Jeronima had had a playful smile but seemed to play with no one except, of course, her two adorable little girls. From everyone else in the household, she was pleasantly aloof. She'd been living alongside Rafael for five years by the time he was nineteen and he still knew nothing about her. But why would he? – he was a nineteen-year-old lad and she was an elegant woman in her mid-twenties, a wife and mother.

One Sunday, he'd fallen down some steps, leaving him shaken-up and bruised, his ankle twisted and swollen, and his mother had allowed him to stay home instead of going to Mass. He was in his bedroom, lying on his bed and thinking nothing much, as he often did. Thank God that was all he'd been doing, because suddenly his sister-in-law was in the doorway. He hadn't known she was also at home, didn't know of her own indisposition; he might have been told, but he wouldn't have listened. She was in her nightgown, her hair down, and there was that smile of hers. She was inside his room and locking the door. He sat up, startled, puzzled as to what she'd want with him, but somehow she was already sitting on the edge of his bed, leaning over and kissing him. The touch of her lips, her tongue to his: the physical effect was immediate and he felt both strong and helpless. What was she up to? Some kind of a game. Must be. A game he didn't quite get. He would, though: in a second, he would, and then it'd be over, and they'd be sitting back from each other and laughing. Until then, she was his sister-in-law. Her mouth was on his. Two compelling reasons for shutting up and doing as she required.

Her mouth was different from Beatriz's: that was what he was thinking. And she was scented: something floral. How clever, to be scented like that. Artful. Floral-scented and fine-boned: the bones of her back rippled beneath his hands. She was beautiful, he realised. She was utterly beautiful and he'd been blind to miss it.

But what was she doing? His sister-in-law, this glorious woman, rose, moved beside him – still with the smile – and then lay against him, comfy as a cat, before easing him over on top of her. A game, a joke, all soon to be revealed but, until then, indulged in. She was so warm. He'd forgotten about the warmth of a body and how intoxicating it was. He played along: kissing her, lying on top of her. With pleasure, yes, but merely playing along. Not to say that he wasn't aroused – of course he was, but he practically always was, although never before pressed against his sister-in-law. He hoped against hope that she hadn't noticed: if this was a game, he didn't want to spoil it.

She eased him on to his back and knelt beside him, began unlacing him, unbuttoning. As if this happened all the time. She didn't actually hum, but it was that kind of unlacing:

brisk, no fuss. Perhaps this was going too far: it occurred to him to resist, to put a halting hand over hers, but it was done before he could and, anyway, she was his sister-in-law and it wasn't his business to halt her. That's how it seemed, to him. It wasn't his business to do anything other than comply. And be glad about it. His state was now obvious to her, but she didn't seem bothered. On the contrary, she pulled her nightgown up over her head and dropped it to the floor. *Naked*. No: some kind of lower garment – he didn't dare look but glimpsed it – which was untied by a tug on a knot or bow, and then that, too, was on the floor. And then she was naked, she was naked. He'd never seen breasts before and hadn't anticipated that they'd be beautiful: but these, this pair, the swell of them counterbalancing her bony shoulders, and the delicate buds that were her nipples. But suddenly she was back beneath him: he was lying on top of her, afraid of squashing those breasts. Her legs felt strong; he hadn't thought of her as having strong legs but, then, he hadn't thought of her legs at all, just those long, pretty skirts of hers. And then he was inside her and then it was all over. She looked up at him with humourful exasperation – a ticking-off – but held him there anyway and, for some time, moved rhythmically against him, just a little, as one might run a spoon around an empty dish to scoop every last trace.

Eventually, he was too small and soft even for that, and she was up, getting her clothing back on, and that was when he saw the blood. She saw him see it (he'd not have mentioned it – what on earth would he have said?), which was when she spoke for the first – only – time of the encounter. 'No babies,' she said, cheerfully, which of course he didn't understand. In fact, he misunderstood, thinking that the blood had happened then and there as a result of a failure of conception. Conception – the possibility of it – wasn't something he'd considered.

And then she was gone, back to her own bed, to lie propped against her pillows, to be found there by her husband when he returned from church. Rafael stayed on his bed, sticky and bloodied, needing a wash. There was muck on his bedcovering. He was appalled. His *sister-in-law*. He'd be struck down. He'd seen his sister-in-law naked, let alone all the rest that'd happened. He'd let her do it, he hadn't looked away and hadn't stopped her. Had she gone mad? Was that what it was? Some weird female madness of which he should've known, against which he should've been on his guard? She'd hate him for it, for not bringing her to her senses. He'd failed her. He could've helped her and he hadn't. And now, when she came to her senses, she'd tell on him.

He prayed then and there, over and over, eyes squeezed shut, giving himself up to God. And yet, and yet … his own blood beat everywhere in him. He was alive, alive; alive as he hadn't been since Beatriz had gone. He'd seen Jeronima as she was, whereas, before, he'd been blind, he'd been blind to this wonderful creation of God. He knew something, he knew something which had to be known: the same feeling that he'd had with Beatriz. He'd done the same as he'd done with Beatriz, but faster, harder, hungrier, with a naked woman shamelessly open to him.

There was no question of her coming to him again. It'd been an accident, that once: he knew it. She hadn't been well. It was to be a treasured memory. Every night, he'd relive it, experiencing great pleasure that somehow gave him no pleasure at all.

One day, though, in view of the rest of the family but not their earshot, she sidled up to him − causing him some physical discomfort − and asked him if he knew of her friend Mariana's house. He did. 'Meet me there,' she said, naming a date and time. Unbelievable though it later became to him, he still didn't get it: he imagined she wanted him there for a confrontation, for an apology from him. He'd done a terrible wrong and she knew it − oh, did she know − and now she was calling him to account for it.

So, he arrived at the house in trepidation. He was lingering close to the gate, not knowing who to ask for, when she called to him from a window. 'Let yourself in,' she said, and indeed the gate was unattended and unfastened. The main door was also unlocked, and she called again to him when he was inside: 'Up here.' He climbed the stairs and there, in a bedroom, she was, smiling her pretty smile in greeting before turning her back on him: 'Would you unlace me, please?' As if this would come as no surprise to him at all. As if this was what he'd come here for. He complied incompetently because he was shaking and because he'd never done this before: unlaced a woman's gown. She was patient, standing very still. Later, it occurred to him that perhaps she'd been savouring it, that unlacing, and that he could have enjoyed making the moment last. At the time, he wondered if he should object. *Say something*, he told himself. Say, *Jeronima, I really think* … But *what?* What did he really think? He wasn't thinking, he was unlacing a woman's gown. He wanted her free of that dress. No: 'want' didn't cover it, didn't nearly cover it, came nowhere close; she *had to be out of that dress*. She had to be naked and he had to be inside her.

*It's going to happen.* His anticipation was so keen that it hurt him to breathe; he could have been the one with the ribs in lacings. His heart was reeling and he loved her, how he loved her and her clever finding of this house for them, and he'd have done anything for her, then, anything that she asked, it didn't matter what: he'd atone afterwards. He'd been busy atoning for weeks and he'd go on doing so, he'd double his efforts, really he would, *but afterwards.*

Once she was unlaced, she undressed herself in that businesslike way of hers and indicated with a flap of a hand that he should be doing the same. There was blood again, he saw: he saw it in that undergarment, a slash of it on a wad of linen, and assumed that she bled all the time and was unable to have more children. He didn't even know quite where that blood came from. He didn't understand until later in life that she'd been calculating about when their liaisons could take place. At the time, he was surprised that she exposed herself to him like that: she, with her elegant dresses. But she'd had to; she did what she had to, and wasn't precious about it.

He marvelled at the shape of her: the perfect breadth of her hips, a perfect span. If he'd put his hands up into the air in front of him, that'd be the span: it was exactly what a span should be. Her bottom, too, its beguiling flatness and broadness: how astounding for it to be hidden, usually, under a gown. She should walk everywhere naked: yes, she should.

She'd taken a square of thick linen from a bag and placed it on the bed; she got up on to it and reclined, her eyes on his. He didn't like standing there naked, so he hurried to join her. His skin on hers: the heat of it. Her scent. She said, 'We don't have long,' but that wasn't going to bother him.

She made no sound other than an appreciative hum from time to time. There came no intake of breath as Beatriz used to do, but that didn't concern Rafael, he'd half-forgotten that it had ever happened and assumed it to have been a peculiarity of Beatriz's. When he'd finished, she lay there, eyes closed, smiling as if she were facing springtime sunshine. 'Tomorrow,' was all she said.

Tomorrow? No time for atonement, then. That'd have to wait. Tomorrow would be a continuation of this same misdemeanour. It hadn't yet finished. Atonement was for later. For now, it was suspended.

The second time in that room, she stopped him just as he was about to get started, her hands firm on his shoulders, and commanded, '*Slower.*' And he got the idea: he must give her time. He began to learn to do that. A little, at least.

There was a third day but then nothing for weeks. Those weeks were unbearable. He couldn't look at her; he feared he'd explode. Once, he approached her; he didn't say anything – when *had* he, ever? – but presented himself there at her side, placing himself at her mercy. 'Next month,' was all she said. He had a sense that she was genuine, that she was giving him her word. She expected him to understand and he didn't, but he accepted it. He began putting the hiatus to good use when, reliving their encounters, he made himself practise taking it slower, making it last longer. *You want slow? I'll give you slow.*

Or, at least, try to.

He didn't know – never even wondered – how she'd managed to arrange for them to have that bedroom. That was her business. His business was to get there. They never spoke about what they did. He didn't know that there were words for it, that you could tell a woman what you wanted to do to her and she, too, could say what she wanted to do, and that alone, somehow, would make it happen, as if casting a spell. Jeronima never made a sound except for an occasional half-breath of a laugh, but she lay there beneath him, open to him in a way he hadn't known with Beatriz, and she liked to lie there afterwards, too, for quite a while, in that same manner. *Abandon.* He came to deride the memory of Beatriz: angry with her, even, for having given so little of herself, for having stayed clothed. All those times, it could've been like this. Because Jeronima was quiet, he had no fear that he was hurting her, however hard he went at her; and it was then, when he was losing himself, that she'd breathe that half-laugh, as if he were faintly endearing, perhaps a little ridiculous.

Atonement was ever-deferred. Rafael felt he was blessed; he had been given something against all the odds. Their liaison being out of wedlock and her being married to his brother: details, mere details, and inconvenient ones. They weren't doing wrong; they were in fact doing right: celebrating life, the wonder of God's creation. They were in the crux of it, they *knew life.* And, anyway, it was secret, and a secret harmed no one. He assumed that it would last for ever. It was at this time that Gil brought home Leonor as his wife. Rafael was happy for him although also sorry for him that this wife wasn't anything like Jeronima: beautiful and long-limbed and languid. Leonor was short and stocky and serious. He couldn't imagine Leonor doing what Jeronima did, lying on a bed with that spring-sunshine smile.

But then it happened: it stopped. Jeronima had promised next month as usual, and as usual he was trusting to her to arrange it and summon him. He didn't keep count of the days, just basked in the certainty that the time was coming. After a while, he began to suspect that the interval had been longer than usual. He made himself wait a week longer before seeking her out. 'Not possible,' was all she said. She said it regretfully but refused to be drawn, turning and walking away. *But you made it possible before*, he wanted to shout after her: *what's different, now?*

He never did find out. Practical considerations, probably, because six months later — six utterly joyless months — she came as usual with her smile to ask him to meet her in the afternoon. But by that time he was in love with Leonor. Newly and dramatically lovelorn, he refused to contemplate love-making — as he now wished to think if it — with anyone else. 'I'm sorry, I can't,' he told her, and, to make sure she understood: 'Jeronima, I can't do it any more.' If she was going to put it down to revenge or to newly discovered moral qualms, he was going to let her. He was that callow.

Now, twenty years on, he wondered what it had been about, for her. Had she ever — before or since — taken other lovers? Nowadays — in her forties, a mother of six — she'd probably not have the time or energy. She'd been unwell, too, for a long time, after the birth of the last child. But when she was younger, it couldn't have been just Rafael, could it? Or could it? He'd been convenient: in the same household, and young enough to pretend to himself that he didn't know better; and as Pedro's own little brother, he'd had almost as much at stake in keeping the secret. Reasons enough, perhaps, for her to have gone for him. But she couldn't have enjoyed the sex very much – he was old enough now to admit it. He hadn't really known what he was doing: there couldn't have been much for her to enjoy. Yet she'd still done it, month after month. Could she really have been that bored? Stuck miles from Seville as Pedro's wife and sole daughter-in-law of his mother, and mother herself of those two little girls with others almost certainly to come, she could have felt that trapped. That desperate for something to happen, something that was *hers*. To feel alive, while there was still time. That, now, he understood. What pained him was that he'd never once considered the risk she was taking. If they'd been discovered, he'd have been in deep disgrace, but she would have lost everything. She would have lost her children.

November. Rafael's October departure hadn't taken place because the selfsame officials who'd been dismissive of his claim that he was in England to build a sundial had – for no reason that Rafael could ascertain – changed their minds and written to his original contact for clarification. Rafael despaired, because how long before word came back? Six, eight weeks? He considered writing, himself, to put the case for abandoning the project after so long – but, then, if the sundial remained unbuilt, he'd almost certainly remain unpaid. Over two months, now, and still no satisfactory talk of compensation. He'd had to dip into the fund he'd intended for materials. He'd had to hand some over to Antonio. Not enough, in Antonio's view, of course, but at least it was something. If by any chance the sundial did go ahead, he'd modify his design so that it was less expensive to build.

Preparations were under way at the palace for the festive season and word was that this was to be a big one, there being not only the birth of Jesus to celebrate but the coming birth of a prince. Here and there, in smaller courtyards, under canvas canopies, pageant-screens were being built and painted: brash heraldic designs, lush landscapes, swirling seascapes. Once, Rafael saw a dozen or so people being fitted for costumes of some kind around a heap of feathery, glittery wings.

From memory, he sketched those people and their fluttery pile for Francisco; and in the accompanying letter he asked Leonor to write back, confiding that he didn't think he'd be home until after Christmas.

The prince still hadn't left and now, for form's sake, he'd have to stay for Christmas. When Christmas was over, though, it would be too late because the queen would be well into her pregnancy and then how could he go? How would that look? His wife, heavily pregnant for the first time at almost thirty-nine, and old anyway for her years. Rumour was that the prince was as desperate as his subjects to go, and Rafael could believe it. England remained hostile, he was no nearer being crowned king, he had been drained of his funds, and, no doubt, pined for his mistress. Rumour had it, too, though, that the queen wouldn't allow him to go, which Rafael could also well believe. Because, if the prince sailed away, when would he return? It had taken long enough to get him here in the first place. He'd delayed, arriving almost two months later than expected, and offered no convincing explanation. But now, in the queen's understandable view, he was happily married and expecting a baby, so why on earth wouldn't he want to stay? To share the joy, all being well, or to comfort his wife if it wasn't. And – purely practically – if the very worst happened, he should be in England to take over. There was something else, too, Rafael thought, which was no less important: how would it look to the people, if he didn't stay by her side? How would it look to the world? Cynical people in a cynical world, and she'd know very well they were watching.

Whenever Cecily asked after his progress with arrangements to return home, he described his disappointments as best he could, and she was sympathetic. *I'm so sorry, Rafael. How silly, this is so silly.* Once, she sighed, 'You must …' and shrugged. *Despair? Miss your family?* And once she said with a sheepish smile, 'But I don't want you to go,' and although she said it lightly, as if it were nothing, as if making a joke of it, he sensed – to his surprise – that the sentiment itself was no joke, and he was touched. His own smile flared in return and he said, 'Thank you,' and he wanted to tell her he'd miss her, too.

It was true. He couldn't imagine why she'd miss him – he was a burden, another person to cook for, clean for – but he loved her company. He was comfortable in her company, although if he'd voiced that it would have sounded nothing much, which didn't tally with how it felt. And indeed that was how he'd have considered it, previously: something that other men might say of their wives. Leonor's presence, though, he'd never found particularly comfortable; Leonor's company was many things, but never comfortable. He enjoyed himself in Cecily's company even when they were doing nothing. Perhaps especially when they were doing nothing. He felt understood by her, even though he was able to say very little. He'd never experienced that before with a woman. Hadn't known it was possible. The way she looked at him: *direct*, which was not to say that there was anything improper in it. On the contrary: the way she looked at him was clear, uncomplicated, like no woman in Spain ever did.

Like all his fellow countrymen, Antonio was complaining of the delay in their return, but although he'd be missing Spanish sun and food, and he'd be glad to escape the hostility in England, there was no one in particular to whom he'd be going home. There were no ties to have been damaged by his absence. And he was managing to live his life here in England largely as he'd lived it in Spain: friends, fun. He would emerge unscathed from this adventure, which was all it would be, for him, soon. Those from whom he'd been winning or borrowing money were running low, though, and were less keen to part with it. He was having to come back more often to the Kitsons' in the evenings. Infuriatingly, he was suggesting by his manner that this was actively his choice and – worse – that they should be delighted that he was gracing them with his presence.

It was during these evenings alongside Antonio, though, that Rafael became aware of how his own English had improved. To his surprise – and pride – it was better, now, than Antonio's, perhaps because Antonio had been spending so much time with Spanish-speakers. Unlike during the first few weeks, Rafael understood everything that Antonio said in English, or was trying to say, and could even help to translate. With his new-found confidence, he found he was taking more chances and, in turn, learning even more. It was only on Cecily, though, really, that he tried out this blossoming English.

He took care never to mention the queen to Cecily, even though he didn't know why he was avoiding doing so. He'd seen the queen, once, at the palace – with her entourage she'd passed by in a loose-fitting gown which was laced at the back even though she was only three months pregnant. She'd walked tall, despite her diminutive stature. He'd been reminded of when Leonor was pregnant. Rafael had been ready to see Leonor pregnant in the first year of her marriage to Gil, even though he'd wondered with trepidation how he'd feel. More of what she was might be revealed to him, he'd felt. She gave so little of herself, it seemed to him; but, pregnant, she'd have no choice over that, would she? And that, he was keen to see.

But it hadn't happened. Two years, and nothing. Then two more years, then two more. Gil did talk about it; he was never one to avoid mention of what was important, he was an open man. But there was nothing, really, to say. *God's will. It could still happen. There are compensations. I feel for Leonor.* Just what Rafael expected him to say. If Leonor ever had to allude to her childlessness, she shrugged her bony little shoulders, downturned her mouth, slid her gaze away as if to dismiss it. Gil was expansive with children, but, then, he was expansive in general. It wasn't for show. She was the opposite, but that, too, was how she was, and it worked just as well. She didn't talk down to children. But, then, she didn't talk down to anyone. She wouldn't have known how. Her way with children, as with everyone and everything, was quiet and cautious.

December the second, a Sunday, mid-morning, and Rafael was trying to decide if he should set off for Whitehall. Weekends were no different from weekdays in that lunch was provided, but — both weekdays and weekends — he was taking up the offer less and less often. It was a toss-up: lunch, but two bitterly cold river-journeys (and recently, for five days, the decision had been made for him by the freezing of the river); or no lunch but a fireside in the Kitson household. He was always keen to escape the clamour of the household — a week ago, the Kitsons had arrived back in residence for Christmas — but his clothing was inadequate and he couldn't afford to have anything new made. Perhaps he could have borrowed a heavier cloak — Cecily might have been able to arrange it — but he didn't want to draw attention to his predicament. Indeed, he was under orders not to. They all were. Some Spaniards were owing money here, there and everywhere, and were merely keeping up appearances until they could settle their debts.

Despite the return of the Kitsons, he'd managed to keep his room. At least there was that. No one had troubled him for it, which he suspected was Cecily's doing: she'd found him the room, and perhaps she'd kept it for him, either by keeping quiet or by arguing his case. It was something else for which he was grateful to her, and he was careful to savour the privilege despite the chill, for as long as he could. Which wasn't very long. He'd seen no fireplaces in any of the smaller rooms, and his was no exception. Firewood in England was in short supply, apparently, even for families like the Kitsons. So he'd sit in his stone-cold room, dressed in all his clothes – every last article of clothing that had come to England with him – and wrapped in his blankets, working on designs and calculations for as long as he could bare his hands. Then he'd wrap his hands, too, in his blanket and sit for a little longer, gazing from the window. And then he'd have to give up and head for the kitchen, do his best to look sociable. The servants congregated there and tolerated his presence even if they didn't invite him to join them in playing cards. Cecily was often there and always smiled at him in greeting, but from across the room.

He was increasingly bothered by a tooth. Only a matter of time, now, before he would have to afford the barber-surgeon. He hadn't mentioned it in his letters to Leonor: it was a tooth, that was all. He hated how it laid him low. *How are you?* he asked Leonor in his letters. It was something he'd rarely asked her in person, because he never got an answer, not a real one. *I'm fine, Rafael,* but said pointedly, the implication being, *Why? Why are you asking me? What is it, exactly, that you want to know?*

It was his brother, Pedro, who'd be asking her, reading the letter aloud for her. Pedro would have to write her replies, too, and Rafael wondered if that was why he hadn't heard from her.

Mid-morning on this particular Sunday, he glimpsed from his room more people than usual down in the lane. Scraping some ice off his window, he watched them all going in the same direction, brisk and taciturn. Something was going on. Something important, by the looks of it. Children were being led by the hand, and people who were less able than others were being helped along. He expected it to peter out, whatever it was, but instead, while he watched, it gained momentum. A crowd, it became: a small crowd. He made a snap decision to investigate, and was buoyed up by it: into his cloak and down the stairs in a blur of steps.

For once, he hadn't anticipated the cold and the sting of it up his nose was a shock, throwing tears into his eyes. The attention of the crowd was on its destination and he slipped in, unnoticed. He moved fast to shake off the bone-crushing chill. No clues as to where they were headed; he was listening hard, but these people knew where they were going and had no need to discuss it. Just the occasional, hoarse, cold-hollowed chiding to a child: *Come on, keep moving.* The English not gossiping, for once, and sober, too: nothing from them but their raucous sniffs and chest-cracking coughs. Occasionally, Rafael saw that he himself was seen – *Spaniard* – but the glances barely touched him: observed, he was, but considered irrelevant. Being inconspicuous in England was more than he could ever hope for, but he'd gladly settle for being unworthy of a second glance.

He was quite a way down Cheapside – every breath still sorely cold, the cold delving into his bad tooth – when he realised: St Paul's was where they were headed. Of course: he should have guessed. Something was going on at St Paul's, some preaching at Paul's Cross: that was all this was. It happened, he knew, on Sundays, this preaching outside St Paul's to hundreds of Londoners, although he was surprised that so many were attending on a day as cold as this. Glad to give up on his little adventure, he half-turned — but the crowd had built behind him and he saw there was no way back.

No way forward, either, because everyone was coming to a standstill. Rafael was nowhere near the cathedral yard. As soon as he stopped walking, the chill claimed the soles of his feet, his toes. The rest of him was faring better from being hemmed in, but there was the stench of so many people and he barely dared breathe, afraid that he'd retch. He tipped back his head for air. No sky, no sky at all: just cloud. Cecily had said something, the previous day: *too cold for snow*. Could it possibly be too cold for snow? She'd sounded as if she knew what she was talking about, but how could it be? But, then, he knew nothing about cold, about snow.

How long was he going to be stuck here? His stomach whimpered — he cringed — and someone's answered, then someone else's. The frozen insides of his ears felt as if they were splitting, and the pain stabbed again into the unsettled tooth. Suddenly, though, something was happening: a stirring in the crowd ahead and instantly all around him, but for a breath or two he didn't get it, couldn't grasp it. Then he did, just in time — they were kneeling. Gathering themselves to get to their knees down in the ice-splintered mud, each and every one of them. He hurried to do the same. Around him, eyes were closed and hands clasped. Absolution: they were being absolved. The bishop, way ahead at St Paul's, was granting them absolution.

A few days ago, England had officially been returned to Rome and here were the queen's subjects asking for forgiveness for ever having strayed. In the past — if Rafael was to believe what he'd heard – some of these people had made their protest by hurling dead dogs into churches: that was how low they'd sunk. Now, they'd come to the cathedral in their hundreds – thousands, even, perhaps – to offer themselves up. The end of twenty years of strife: that's how they intended it, he saw from those composed, closed-eyed faces, and he knew he should feel moved, but he felt uneasy. It wasn't that he doubted the crowd's sincerity. It was the sincerity that was the problem. The solemnity. *Not English*. The silence of a crowd, a kneeling crowd, Rafael knew only too well from Spain, where the Inquisition had been the teacher of it.

The queen had dissolved the Church of England, finally succeeding in having her father's Act repealed. Word was that she'd cried with relief there on her throne. No tears when she'd been declared queen, nor when she'd been crowned; but ending the Church of England, she'd let the tears come and hadn't wiped them away. For this, she'd told her noblemen – and only this – she'd become queen. For this, she'd stayed in England and not run to Spain, for all those desolate, dangerous years. For this, God had preserved her and made sure she'd triumphed. *This*: the righting of a terrible wrong, the undoing of the actions of a man who seemed to have gone mad and damned his people. She'd saved them. It was done. With God's will, she'd managed it.

Her men had been moved to see her in tears; moved in fact to line up, later, every last nobleman in the land, each with a torch, and bear their long banner of flame from Westminster to Whitehall. There, they'd knelt to beg her forgiveness for ever having gone along with the Reformation. Which of course she granted without hesitation, not being a woman for grudges and being keen to believe the best of people. And here, a few days later, England's people were doing the same, doing their own version: coming to St Paul's and kneeling in the streets. As if, Rafael thought, that would be all it would take. Perhaps it would.

December the third was Francisco's birthday, his fourth, and the sky itself bestowed what would have been the best possible birthday present if only he'd been there to see it: *snow*. As he woke, Rafael knew that something had befallen the world. The silence beyond his window had a thoroughness to it and his room was faintly but evenly illuminated. Outside, everything had turned clean white as if a spell had been cast. He ached to have Francisco beside him to see it; imagined him spellbound, first, then avid and already halfway to the door on his way downstairs. *Come here, little man, let's get you properly dressed up.* Rafael had resolved not to do the usual on his son's birthday, but to mark it somehow – go somewhere, do something – and now the problem was solved. He'd take a walk in the snow.

The sound and sensation of each footfall was utterly new to him, though he imagined walking across some kinds of sand might be similar. The cold was there but didn't attack him as the wind often did; it had lain down and rolled over, exposing its soft, spectacular underside. Every branch, every twig – the smallest thing, a nailhead on the gate, a knot in the grain of the gatepost – was edged with snow. Everywhere, it had done its delicate work. But the day was busy doing its work too and already there was an unevenness of cover, itself glorious, complex and intriguing. *This is for you, Francisco*, Rafael kept thinking, looking around. Who else would it be for, on Francisco's birthday?

But Francisco wasn't here to receive it and its extraordinary presence made much of his absence. Rafael was getting tired, having to tense every step against slipping, and, tired, he was getting cold. He gave up and headed back to the Kitsons', to the kitchen and – he hoped – a warm drink.

Huddled in a corner with the cup of spiced milk that one of the kitchen boys had been so kind as to fetch for him, he was aware that no one there knew it was his little boy's birthday. Not even Cecily, who was elsewhere. In that respect, Rafael had his son all to himself. He wondered what Leonor was planning for Francisco on this special day, all being well. *All being well*. Even if all was well, Francisco would be lost to him, he feared, in that he'd have forgotten him, by now. Oh, he'd remember the name – Daddy – and he'd remember that there had been a daddy, someone who'd been Daddy, but nothing more specific, Rafael suspected. 'Daddy' would be referred to, plenty, he imagined, today – *Daddy'll be thinking of you on your birthday* – but he doubted that would make him any more real to Francisco. Sitting in the Kitson kitchen, he burned to insist on his reality to Francisco: *I'm here; here I am; here*. But *here* would mean nothing to Francisco.

Rafael's own birthday was eleven days later and he self-consciously abandoned it. Slipping free of it, was how he chose to think of it.

Christmas came and passed with Rafael ill in bed. For a day and a night of which he was only dimly aware, fever shook him like a dog shakes its prey. His skin felt blistered; the touch of the bedclothes hurt him. *I'm dying, I'm going to die, here, so far from home*, but he didn't feel how he might have expected to feel: no rage, nor any yearning. *So this is how it ends*, was all he had the strength to think. He accepted it. Had to. He'd been writing a letter home and he hoped someone would forward it. That was all, really, that he wanted. He wasn't up to wanting anything more.

After perhaps a day or two, Cecily came into his room, but he didn't realise it – not properly – until later. He'd experienced it and remembered it as a dream. She'd drawn back his bed-hangings a little and had talked to him, but he hadn't understood or even tried to understand what she was saying. Later, during a half-waking, he noticed beside his bed a jug, some bread, and what looked like a piece of bark. He touched it: it *was* bark. Presumably she'd noted his absence and had come to check on him. She shouldn't have: she shouldn't have risked contagion. But he was too tired to think any more of it, other than that he must've looked a mess and seemed ungrateful, and collapsed back into sleep.

Some time during that night, he did drink the juice. His thirst raging, he returned to it several times, his body soaking it up, not needing the chamber pot.

Cecily came again, probably a day later, and this time her knock on the door and her opening it – having had no word from him – cracked into his sleep. But it was as much as he could do to open his eyes, and she would have to accept that. He did want more juice. Perhaps she'd just replenish his supply and leave him as she found him. She wouldn't need to wake him. Indeed, she should go as quickly as she could, get herself away from danger. She came to the bedside, spoke from the other side of the hangings: a tentative, whispery call of his name. Twice. Then a twitch of the hangings. 'Yes,' he replied, finally, and, as he'd hoped, she let the hanging drop. She didn't go away, though, he knew. She said his name again and this time there was no question in it; it was gently firm. She required him to respond. He moved the hanging – just so she'd know he was attentive – but was careful to keep himself in shadow. She held something in the opening; it was that piece of bark. 'Rafael,' she urged, and now he paid it some attention – intrigued, albeit faintly. She crouched down, her face level with his; he held his breath, he knew it would be foul. 'Rafael,' she said again, and mimed chewing on the bark. Chewing, definitely, rather than eating: a deliberate gnashing of her teeth. Then, before he could have done anything about it, her hand was on his forehead and quickly to one stubbly cheek, and she was making a sound like disapproval: *fever*. In spite of himself, his skin sang at her touch. *Do that again.* With a flourish of the piece of bark – *Don't forget* – she rose, saying there was more juice for him, and he murmured his thanks.

Her visit had unsettled him – he couldn't get back to sleep – so he did end up chewing on the bark. It was something to do. There was a sweetness to it, which he would never have expected. When he surfaced from his next doze, he felt marginally better, and thereafter kept up with the bark.

Cecily came daily, and despite his fear of the risk at which she placed herself, and the awkwardness of those brief visits of hers, he lived for them. Her coming into his room while he was in bed made for a delicate situation, with which she dealt by saying almost nothing, just bringing more juice, more bark and a little more food each day, and checking his fever – that quick, cold touch of her fingertips to his brow, his cheek – but keeping her judgement on it to herself. For his part, he'd lie almost totally covered by the bedclothes, taking care not to move: making as little physical impression as possible.

She sent someone else – a boy – for the chamber pot, which, luckily, he was hardly having to use. A bowl of water was also replenished, so Rafael could rub his teeth with a freshly wet cloth.

The days were barely days at all, the darkness in his room almost day-long: in that sense, he was missing nothing. What he did miss was the chance to check at the Spanish office for post, and he felt sure, increasingly so, there was a letter from Leonor waiting there for him, although he couldn't guess at what it would say.

Eight or nine days had passed before he felt able to get up. Depressingly, it took all his energy on that first day to sit, stunned, on the edge of the bed. Several times he did it, though, determined to build up his strength. The second day, he got to the door to intercept Cecily, to head her off. He'd been waiting for her – it wasn't as if he had anything else to do – and, at the door, handed over his jug and plate before receiving the fresh offering. He smiled but didn't meet her eyes, horribly aware of how bad he must look. He intended a proper wash, later that day, but ended up back in bed, asleep. The following day, he did wince and gasp his way through an ice-cold wash, and then managed – with a couple of rests on the edge of the bed – to dress. The day after that, he tried to go downstairs, sitting down once on the way, even if he did then turn around and – with more pauses – come back. He wasn't yet fit to be seen: he needed a shave.

For the shave, he'd have to go to the palace. The next day, he reached for his cloak – and discovered its new, much heavier lining. Fustian. Cecily's doing; *must be*. He touched it in wonder and profound gratitude. Not only had she risked infection but she'd thought to do this for him.

He couldn't go to thank her until he'd had the shave; so, he slipped from the house. Despite the new cloak-lining, the cold hit him like never before and he reeled, close to tears and shocked by his feebleness. The river-journey – the walk, even, to the river – was going to be impossible for a day or two more. He almost whimpered aloud with helplessness and frustration. He'd have to chance a local barber. What would a local barber do? Cut his throat? Well, let him cut it. What he did care about was that he couldn't go for his letter. Impossibly far away, it was. To his own letter, which he was carrying, he'd added, *I wasn't well but I'm fine now.* As soon as he'd realised that he wouldn't be home in time for Christmas, he'd sent Francisco a drawing of London Bridge. Francisco wouldn't have got it, yet, though – if he got it at all, if it didn't end up shipwrecked and dissolved into sea water. Two days of sitting on Coldharbour Steps, it had taken Rafael; he'd got in as much detail as he could. What he would really have loved to send Francisco, though, was a fragment of ice from a puddle. *Look, Francisco, see? Hard water.*

He entered the first local barber's shop he came across and the encounter was fine: the barest exchange of words and a brisk, skilled shave before the yielding of a couple of Rafael's precious coins. Leaving the premises, he was ready to face the world and Cecily, of course, was whom he went to face first. She was in the kitchen, sewing, her boy nestled up to her. 'Ah!' – she seemed surprised and delighted to see him, so much so that he wondered if his recovery had perhaps been in doubt. She was full of praise – he knew from her tone – for how well he was looking, which only served to make him self-conscious as to how truly dreadful he must previously have appeared. He displayed the lining of his cloak: 'You?'

She played it down: she'd had some spare, he guessed her to be saying, as she shook her head and indicated a pile of fabrics at her side. He thanked her profusely, telling her in his own language – but with an arm towards the door – how much easier it was now to be outside. 'Thank you,' he said again, 'thank you,' and she glowed even as she shrugged it off.

Christmas had been and gone during his illness but the Kitsons wouldn't be tackling the journey back into the countryside until the worst of the winter weather was over. At his first supper back in Hall, Rafael saw that the young men who usually served at the high table weren't there and their duties were being undertaken by the blond steward and a couple of ushers. Sitting at the high table, though, were three young men who were definitely Kitsons. So, *they*'d been away somewhere – serving at high table in someone else's house? – but were home now for the Christmas season; and the boys who served at the Kitsons' had probably gone in *their* turn back to *their* own homes. What a peculiar arrangement, Rafael pondered. Why wouldn't a family want its own sons around?

A couple of days later, the three Kitson lads were gone again and the usual servers were back. Rafael had wondered if he'd see other changes now that winter was biting hard, but there were no obvious shortages of food in the household. Less bread was left over at the end of meals than he remembered from when the full household was last in residence, but that might have been because the cold was making everyone hungrier. He suspected that the pottage wasn't quite so thick, but it was spicier as if to hide the fact, which made it tastier. On the whole, though, and especially since his illness, Rafael longed for simplicity, for clarity on his palate. At its best, English wintertime food had taste packed into it, simmered long and hard, but this only had Rafael craving the crispness of something fresh-picked, or the rough and readiness of sausage, the melting milkiness of goats' cheese, the honeyed gentleness of orange-steeped ground almonds. And an orange itself: how he'd love to nestle the tip of his thumb into an orange, to lever and split it and breathe in its scented gasp.

Thinking of an orange was in itself a luxury, he knew — there were plenty of people in London who couldn't think beyond necessities. More of them gathered at the back gate at the end of the day than he remembered from the Kitsons' last time at the house, and he noticed the paucity of leftovers that the kitchen boys took to them. That was where the Kitsons' shortages were: at the back gate. That's where they were beginning.

Inside, hospitality was stretched among more guests than they'd previously had. There'd been musicians when the Kitsons were home in the summer, and of course they'd stayed for supper, but now they had women and children with them, all of whom had to be fed. Not that there was any sign of a grudging reception. Everyone was graciously provided for. When the Kitsons' doctor came to dine during the first week of January, he was accompanied by his wife, five children, and an elderly lady, presumably his mother or mother-in-law. A couple of evenings later, one of the business associates who had come to dine with the Kitsons' secretary in October brought a nursemaid for the youngest of his children and she ate while the child slept in the crook of her arm.

Cecily didn't have to shop for provisions when the whole household was in residence. Some food had come with the Kitsons from the country house and anything else was being fetched by the kitchen boys. He heard someone, sometimes, leaving the house before dawn and returning an hour or so later, still before sunrise. Cecily's household duties had changed back to those she'd had when Rafael had first arrived. They'd reduced in scope but not in volume, to judge from the fabrics with which she was swamped whenever he saw her. That was when he saw her at all. In the full household she was less conspicuous, and he missed her.

In the second week of January, a servant came to the kitchen to tell Rafael that a man from the palace was asking for him at the main door. Rafael translated this into just one word: *home*. Was this it – his call home? The Spanish office must have heard back from his original contact and either he'd been absolved of his duty to make the sundial, or he was required to build it after all, but either way he was going home, be it now or, at the most, in a month or so. He began to shake more than he'd have believed physically possible, every breath shattered. *Home.* Then, though: could this be bad news from home? He'd still heard nothing from Leonor, and wasn't this what they'd do – call him in to have the bad news broken to him? The fluttering inside turned upside down and hammered at him.

He hurried to the door and demanded of the liveried lad: What did it concern, this summons? No response, save a shrug. Who, then, was asking for him? Shrug. Rafael gave up, didn't have time for this; just, 'Now?'

'Now.'

One minute, Rafael told him, and dashed upstairs for his cloak; but when he came back down, the lad was gone.

Rafael didn't know if the Thames was frozen. Two days ago, the boatmen had been smashing ice around the quays and breaking paths in it to a central, free-moving channel. How else would he get to the palace? He ran down to the river, puddles crunching underfoot and the wind scouring his face, his way lit by little icicles on protruding first storeys. Boats were moving, he saw as he got to the quayside: fewer of them, and with scant custom, but there was traffic.

Initially, he felt nothing on the wherry but the cold; he knew nothing else, and the shock of it was renewed with every pulse. As time passed, he came up with other possible reasons for his summons. Perhaps Antonio had caused some trouble. Perhaps someone had another job for them to do. He tried to empty himself of his fears – staring on to the dark, blank water – and keep himself open to these various explanations, but thrumming inside him like blood was *My son, my wife, my mother? A fall, a fever, a fire?*

Arriving at Whitehall, scrambling from the little boat, he slipped on the icy steps, scuffing his knees and one of his gloves. Picking himself up, he dashed to the Spanish office. There, though, the official looked baffled – and uninterested – before going off, leisurely, to consult elsewhere. Rafael stood recklessly close to the fire and failed to hear the door opening behind him. But when he turned around, there she was: the queen's lady, Mrs Dormer, the one from the garden, the one with the smile. She'd had good reason to smile when he'd failed to recognise he was in the presence of the queen. 'Come on,' she said. So, she'd happened upon him here and was thinking she'd have some more fun. 'No ...' his English deserted him and it was all he could do to indicate the desk, the official's vacated desk. He wouldn't have believed it possible for that smile of hers to widen, but it did. 'No, *me*,' she said. 'It was me: I sent for you. The queen wants to see you.'

His insides lurched, stopped dead, but resumed and he breathed a laugh of relief: *very funny*. Mrs Dormer's smile, though, faltered; she seemed to be serious. But no one had told him he'd be going to the queen, and he was a complete and utter mess. As she could well see. He'd come as he was, hadn't even had a shave and was mud-caked from his run to the quayside, scuffed from his fall. She could see that. Yet here she was, holding open the door for him. 'No, no, no –' he swept a hand down in front of him, showing her, making it clear: an utter mess. But she sighed as if this were a quibble and an endearing one, at that. 'You look lovely, Mr Prado,' she said, in her breezy way. 'Now, come on.'

He hurried behind her to continue his objections, trailing in the wake of her swishing, black wool cloak, his own footfalls on the flagstones mere echoes of those made by her thick, new soles. She was fur-coddled and kid-gloved, and she'd have washed, this morning, and properly, too, the water warmed for her. 'Please,' he called to her; insisted. '*Please.*'

'Mr *Prado*.' She stopped, turned, and he saw how she was enjoying objecting to his objections. 'You *look lovely.*' Again, that laugh, quick and low, and, 'You look *Spanish.*'

The first time, he bet, that had ever been offered in England as a compliment. And if only she knew: he didn't, not to true-blood Spaniards, he didn't. He tried anew, countering as best he could in his panicked English: 'But it's the queen.' Her response this time was no response at all, just a mock-glare, and he saw in those widened, resolutely staring eyes that he was losing. He was on his way to the queen of England, unwashed and in damp, mud-strafed clothes. At least could he be told why he was being summoned? That would be the very least she could do. 'Madam – please – why does the queen ask for me?'

For once, she seemed to give serious consideration to what he'd said, stopping and turning to him. 'Sometimes –' she specified. 'Today, the queen is unwell.'

Which brought him up sharp. 'She's ill?'

'Not ill. Just' – touching her forehead – 'headaches.' She'd pitched it high as if it were first on a list, but added no more. Her hand came down to touch her heart, though. Malaise, then. 'Tired. She works very hard, too hard, much too hard,' and a puff of despair as if to say, *I've told her, I've tried to tell her*, confiding not the fact of the queen's hard work but her own impatience with it. 'And today her head is bad. She needs cheering up.'

He was to be a diversion? No wonder she didn't care what he looked like: she must have tried everyone else and now she was scraping the bottom of the barrel. Because Rafael was no conversationalist – not even in his own language, let alone in English. He knew nothing. A sundial maker stuck on a cloud-clogged island: that was all he was. No good, here, to anyone. Oh, why couldn't he *go home*? Why wouldn't they *let him be*? The queen could do with some true-blood, church-going Spaniard to converse with – that's what she needed – and he failed spectacularly on both counts.

It was ridiculous. He'd refuse. Because what would Mrs Dormer do? Manhandle him into the room? Well, that would certainly be a diversion. He'd say he was ill. At the very worst, he could bargain: beg for more time, time to go back to the Kitsons' and tidy himself up. Two hours. Surely he'd be just as good a diversion, if not better, in two hours' time. Better prepared. But he was still following her and they seemed to be nearing their destination, turning into a guard-lined gallery. He could try making a run for it, but he was seriously outnumbered. How he must look to these men: a laughing stock, at best; a disgrace, more like. *This is not me*; he wished they knew: not Rafael de Prado, sundial maker to the king of Spain. This, instead, was the bedraggled, despondent man he'd become during four long months in England.

But who were they to judge? A couple of years ago these men would have had her die, the woman who was now their queen. Back then, in the reign of her little brother, she'd been a traitor for her beliefs. Here they were, now, though, lined up to defend her. They'd defended her a year ago when thousands of rebels arrived on the opposite bank, led by a charismatic commoner, and the new reign had looked already to be over. They would have been standing here while, behind the far door, the queen's ladies cowered and the queen paced at the windows: the ladies crying – this was what Rafael had heard – but the queen at the window, wishing aloud that she could go down there and join her men. Something else he was told was that she'd ordered no one risk endangering innocent people by firing across the river. Instead, she would wait for the rebels to come across to her. Her guards wouldn't have known that the rebellion would soon come to nothing, doors shut against it when it arrived in London's streets. Up here, they'd have heard every-where around and below them barricades being shoved at the doors. The clattering of makeshift weapons as grooms and gardeners and laundresses gathered up broom-handles and rakes and paddles.

The room was just ahead of them, he could tell from Mrs Dormer's slowing pace; she was collecting herself. She stopped short, to turn to him. No smile, now. 'She's fright-ened,' she confided. 'But your wife was the same age when she had your son. She wants to hear about your wife. Talk to her about your wife.' Ahead, the door was opening for them and, before he knew it, they were in the doorway, on the thresh-old. His first impression was of heat, and although just minutes ago he'd have been ready to give anything to feel heat like this, he recoiled: it was stifling. He didn't look ahead into the room, didn't dare; just followed his guide forward, his eyes on her fur-draped shoulders. She'd know what to do, for now: his tormentor and now his saviour. What she did, though, was drop away: gone behind him in a single graceful step. She was presenting him, he realised. And leaving him to it. *Talk to her.* He stared down at the intricately woven carpet and, on it, his pitiful, encrusted boots. His heart was punching into his throat. *Dismiss me*, was all he wanted to say to the queen, *dismiss me from your offended presence*, and in his mind he retraced his way to the office where it had all begun; and, there, he'd say, *Send me home*, and, furious with him, that's exactly what they would do.

He hadn't raised his eyes, but he'd glimpsed the centrepiece of the room, couldn't have missed it, an immense, gold-canopied chair. A throne. Occupied: that, too, he'd glimpsed. So, he did his bowing, scruffy and flushed.

'Mr Prado': that deep voice.

She didn't *sound* frightened. Should he look up, or not? What was the rule? He looked up, but cautiously, head still low, hedging his bets. She was tiny in the chair under the tasselled canopy, her face a scratch amid all the finery. How odd, he felt, to be sitting in your own room up on a dais. A companion occupied a floor cushion beside the dais, but the distance and difference in height didn't suggest ease of conversation.

The queen made as if to rise, but didn't, not quite. So, now what? *Talk to her.* But from here? He managed a glance up and around: horse-faced ladies in clusters on floor cushions, somehow observing him whilst avoiding looking at him. Clever, that. Years of practice, probably. Clearly he'd get no help from them. The queen solved the problem, suddenly free of the throne-chair and approaching, all gown and jewels swinging and swaying so that he marvelled at her posture. The gown was front-laced although her pregnancy – five months at most – had yet to show. How, in all that clothing, did she bear the heat? It had him by the throat. He bowed again – and there, again, the fabulous carpet and his awful boots – as she passed him with a rasping of fabrics. 'Come.'

She'd gone to a window and was looking back expectantly, her expression incongruous in a room of guarded faces. Rafael imagined her in just such a room – perhaps this very room – during her brother's reign, insisting bulge-eyed on the right to practise her religion; imagined, too, the looks of impatience and disgust that she would have encountered. With one strikingly bejewelled hand, she prompted him to join her. He obliged, but hung back respectfully. *Talk to her about your wife.* He was waiting for her to initiate the conversation, after which he'd do his very best.

'My doctor says I have to rest, today,' she began, matter-of-fact. 'No reading, today, for me, because of my headaches.' Scathingly, she repeated, '*Rest.*'

*All I ever do, here*, he reflected, ashamed. Except that, he realised, he didn't. He never felt rested, here in England. He did nothing, but nor did he seem to rest. As for the queen, she seemed incapable of rest. Even now, her hands clutched at each other. Scrawny hands, cruelly reddened: not the hands of a queen.

He offered condolences on her indisposition – that was how he put it – and followed with congratulations on the news of the impending royal birth. His English was inelegant, but he felt he'd managed and at least it was a start.

'Thank you,' she said, dutifully. She was looking out over her garden, despite there being little to see and not much light to see it by. Dusk, already. On this January day, it had hardly ever been anything but. Barely mid-afternoon, but dusk. All Rafael could see was grim yew and brittle, half-dead lavender. To his surprise, she called over her shoulder for her cloak.

Shaking off any attendants, she led him through a door and down a stone staircase into an open porch. And there they stood, looking over the gardens just as they had from the window. 'I needed some air,' she said. The air in the porch was ragged in gusts, and so cold that the taste was metallic. He was about to make himself speak up, but she was ahead of him, asking, 'How's Francisco?'

She'd remembered his name: Rafael was stunned. Very well, he told her, despite not actually having a clue, and thanked her profusely for asking. He'd have liked to have repaid her interest with some news, but he had none, the fact of which – coming afresh – giddied him.

Francisco had once asked him, with genuine interest, 'How will I die, d'you think, Daddy?' adding, 'I think I'll fall under the wheels of a cart,' and when Rafael had said he'd ensure it didn't happen, Francisco's response was, 'You won't be there.'

The queen's bulbous little eyes were turned to him and he became aware that he was biting his lip, hard, as if to hold on to something. Self-conscious, he released it.

She asked, 'Why are you still in England?'

He didn't really know and, even if he did, he probably couldn't have told her, because there was a lump in his throat. He was supposed to be reassuring her, he reminded himself, not unburdening his own fears. But she'd asked. He took his chances with an expansive shrug. Was it permissible to shrug at a queen? Well, he did, at this one. She didn't flinch. 'He should've sent you home.' Her irritation was audible. She was voicing disappointment in her husband more than she was sympathising with Rafael, but it was better than nothing. 'Yes,' Rafael said, and, again, 'Yes,' in the hope that she would not let it drop. His wild hope was that she'd say, *I'll tell him to send you home.*

She turned back to the desolate vista. '*He* wants to go.' A gust slammed into the garden; branches flailed. 'Not to Spain but to France. To war.' She sighed hugely. 'There's no need for war with France. There really is no need. Talk is what's needed. Not war.' She said again, 'He wants to go,' then let it drop with a weary, 'but you know all that.'

Rafael cringed because he did know, he couldn't help but know. Everyone knew, and she knew they knew. He pitied her the lack of a private life. It was bad enough even for him, in the small household of his own family. Here, though, he had nothing but a private life. Here in England, no one knew or cared anything about him, and he didn't like that any better.

Then she broached it: 'Was your wife well, during her pregnancy?' She peered at him: keen for the truth, he felt, rather than empty reassurances. The truth was, he didn't really know. As far as he'd been aware, she'd sometimes felt well and sometimes hadn't. On the whole, though, he supposed, she'd kept well. Yes, he told the queen. She'd made complaints – aches and pains, plenty of them – but there'd been nothing drastically wrong, he tried to explain, or nothing of which he'd been told and nothing which had had any consequence. He didn't say that she'd kept herself to herself during her pregnancy and he'd assumed that was how it was with women. He'd never known what she was thinking and there'd been times when he'd been grateful for that.

The queen said, 'I'm finding it very hard.'

Mrs Dormer was wrong: this wasn't for him to hear. This was for women to hear, those women up there in her room. He said he was sorry to hear it.

'The tiredness.' She was aghast. 'I am so tired. More tired than I've ever been, and I can't do anything, I can't think, but there's so much to do, so much to have to think about.'

He said, truthfully, 'My wife was very tired.'

She sighed. 'The winter doesn't help.'

Well, no. They stood looking at the dead garden with dismay. In that, united.

Then she looked around at him. 'I'm happy,' she insisted, staring at him as if to stare him down; 'I am happy,' her words so at odds with her expression that, despite everything, he could have laughed. 'I'm scared, though. And I shouldn't be. I should have faith in God.' She corrected herself: 'I do, but' – incredulous – 'I'm still scared.'

Nodding, he shuffled; his feet were freezing. He didn't find it extraordinary in the least that she or anyone should have faith in God but still be scared. Leonor had never voiced her fears to him, but he was quite sure she'd have had them. He certainly had, on her behalf, and he was about to say something of this to the queen but she hadn't let up.

'I've been frightened before, Mr Prado – I've lived much of my life afraid – but I've had faith in God and' – anguished, she unclasped her hands, splayed them, re-clasped them – 'it's been enough. But now ...' She shivered, shuddered. 'You know, Mr Prado,' her gaze scouring his, 'I'd worried that I'd lose God a little if I loved a man. I'd have less love to give Him, I'd be distracted. But it's not so, is it? It's the opposite. I

141

have more love for God.' She relinquished him, looked away. 'I don't know that I did love God, before. Not love. Worship, yes, of course. But *love*? Well, now I do, and so now, for the first time, I'm terrified of losing him.'

He felt for her. It was all he could do, standing there.

She said, 'I'm finding it hard to be a wife as well as a queen.'

He didn't doubt it.

'He wants me to make him king.'

Him: the prince. Rafael knew, of course. Everyone knew. A perfectly reasonable expectation, was the Spanish view.

'But I can't do it.' She glanced at him. 'I mean, I really can't. Council –' She flapped a hand, perhaps to demonstrate Council's dismissive attitude, perhaps to convey her despair. 'And the English people …' She shrugged, accepting, resigned: 'And they're my people; I serve them. But my husband doesn't understand, and he refuses to listen to me,' she said, plaintively. 'For so long I wanted to be queen, to be able to step up and do the job, but now sometimes I'd just like to be a wife.' She turned to him with the softening that was, for her, close to a smile. 'Having a baby is a lot to do, isn't it, Mr Prado.' She laid both hands on her stomach. 'Keeping the two of us alive, getting him grown, getting him born. A lot for me to do at thirty-eight, when I've never been strong. But he trusts me absolutely, doesn't he?' Gravely, she added, 'This is the only time I'll have him all to myself. He doesn't know how important he is, dozing in here. Important to everyone else, I mean. Of course he's important to *me* – he knows that. But to everyone else: little prince.' She took a breath, decisively. 'You're very good to me, Mr Prado.' And turned to the stairs, talking over her shoulder: 'I have confessors, and ladies, officials, doctors,' and reminded herself, 'I have a husband.' At that – at having to remind herself – she almost smiled. 'And of course I have him –' a hand again to her stomach. 'But ...' She didn't finish; just stepped ahead of him, leading him up the steps.

He wondered what it was that she felt he'd done for her. He'd done nothing. He was supposed to have reassured her, but he'd failed.

At the door, she paused and turned to him. 'You know, Mr Prado,' she said, fixing him with her watery stare, 'if there's ever anything I can do for you in return, you must come to me. Promise me you'll come to me.'

She'd arranged for him to be given refreshments before his journey back into the city. As he was escorted from the room, and then from the guarded hallway, he'd intended to say that he'd prefer to be going. He was desperate to get away with what he recalled of his time with the queen, hold it intact and cherish it. Hanging around at the palace would be to risk it settling, sinking and draining from him. But somehow it hadn't happened, this polite refusal, and then there he was, sitting at the end of a long table at the back of the Hall. A platter of thinly sliced meats came, served with a spoonful of a jelly made from some hedgerow fruit, and linen-wrapped bread – white bread – and even a glass of sack, Spanish sack. He had to remind himself to savour it, though, thinking instead of the queen, of her standing there beside him, small but steadfast in that freezing cave of a porch. Beleaguered by frailties, fears, and enemies. He wished he could have done more for her than just listen. He finished what he'd been given and took the platter, linen and glass to the buttery hatch.

Making his way back to the riverside steps, he tried to see himself through the eyes of the various Englishmen who glanced at him. They didn't know where he'd been, and they'd never be able to guess. He, himself, even, didn't quite believe it. Had he really stood there, a man from Spain – from a *converso* family, at that – with the queen of England, with her confiding in him? He loved her for it – for having taken him there to her side, and for having been so open with him. She'd shown him, when he'd ceased to believe it, that anything was possible.

For once, and despite the sleet, he didn't cower resentfully on the wherry but was keen to take it all in: London, crowding down to the river as if to get in on something it might otherwise miss. The red, regular brickwork and the unflinching gaze of so many big, unshuttered windows. And over the jostling rooftops, an endless exhalation of spires: London throwing its head back, devil-may-care. How strange to think of that anxious, humourless, dowdy woman trying to rule this brash, cynical city. For the first time, he saw what there was to admire about London. Gliding through snowflakes, he found himself listening as hard as he was looking. He was opening himself absolutely to the city, trying to love it, to be moved by it – but he knew it would never quite happen. This was a city that kept him at arm's length.

Going back into the house, lit up by the chill and rattling from the crowds, he almost bumped into Cecily. Drowsy with household warmth, she was wrapped in her cloak with her basket on one arm and, at her side, the child. There they stood, one coming in and the other going out: at sixes and sevens. He took two steps back, involuntarily. He hadn't been expecting to come across her, not so soon, although he'd only just been thinking of her. And now here she was, facing him with that big-eyed, enquiring look. She wanted to know where he'd been; she was expecting to be told, and he wanted to tell her, but how could he? Where would he start? He would tell her, but such a tale wasn't for a mere threshold exchange. He'd been standing in a dripping porch, listening to the genuine fears of the troubled queen of England and there wasn't any way that he could tell it that would make it believable. She'd think him a liar, a fantasist, or she'd think he was making fun of her.

'Going out?' he asked her, which was stupid of him because it was so clearly the case.

'Buttons,' she said in explanation, with a quick, flat smile: no real smile at all. 'You were called to the palace?'

'Yes.' He busied himself removing his cloak. 'Nothing. Just work.'

'Work?' Polite, but nonetheless making him uneasy.

He turned the attention back to her: 'Urgent, these buttons?'

She shrugged it off.

'Because it's snowing.'

'So I see.' She indicated the dusting on his cloak.

He asked her, 'Can I ...' ... *go for you*? Seeing as he was wet already.

'Buttons?' she laughed, derisively: what would he know about buttons?

Helpless, he tried again, 'But it's snowing.'

'I know it's snowing, Rafael.' Impatience, now. 'I've been snowed on before.' Then she asked, 'Are you going home?' and his heart contracted. She – like him, earlier – had assumed the summons was something to do with his going home. But it was how she'd asked that got hold of his heart: the appeal in it.

'No,' he told her. Just like that, nothing more. She'd asked and he'd told her – that was all that had happened – but somehow in that one brief exchange they'd become co-conspirators. He'd known it was what she'd wanted to hear, and that he'd wanted to tell her what she'd wanted to hear. He was desperate to go home – but he'd also liked telling her that he was staying.

She couldn't say 'Good' but he saw her thinking it and hating herself for thinking it. She turned to her son – 'Come on' – and, to Rafael's relief and his despair, the door closed behind her.

Although in need of a fireside and a warm drink, he went to his room. Standing at the window, he gazed at the obliterating snow. His hands were shaking; he held them to stop it. What had happened down there in the hallway? Nothing: a silliness, a madness. A madness that comes from being cooped up, far from home, for too long. He'd just imagined it. They were close, he and Cecily: that was all. They'd miss each other when he was gone, and there was no harm in that.

That evening, lining up to go into Hall for supper, Antonio confided that some people were claiming the queen wasn't pregnant.

Rafael regarded him uncomprehendingly.

'Not really pregnant.'

'She *is*,' Rafael refuted.

Antonio looked amused. 'How would you know?'

And Rafael half-laughed because, yes, how ridiculous he must have sounded. 'In my opinion, she is.'

Understandably, Antonio looked unimpressed. 'There are people who are saying she isn't.'

'Well, they don't know, do they? Why would she be saying she is, if she isn't? It's not something she can get away with, in the end, is it?'

'Could be a mistake,' Antonio explained. 'Women make mistakes.'

'Anyway,' said Rafael, as they lingered at the back of the queue to prolong the conversation, 'what people? Who is it that's saying this?'

'People in London. The French Ambassador.'

'Well, the French Ambassador would say that. He'll say anything to discredit the queen.' England and France were all but at war. The French favoured the Protestant half-sister.

Antonio allowed it: 'I suppose he would.'

As he ate, Rafael thought how those people – whoever they were – hadn't stood next to the queen; they hadn't experienced the new-found weightiness to her presence. She was a woman who believed herself to be carrying a baby. And she was a woman of so much self-doubt that she wouldn't have announced it, he felt, unless she was absolutely sure.

After supper, Rafael went to the kitchen to sit in the warmth and write to Leonor. He wrote how much he missed her, and how much he needed word from her. *Don't protect me*, he wanted to say. Even if what she had to tell him was bad, he needed to know. But to say it would seem to invite it.

He wondered how it was for her, seeing the black marks on the page while Pedro deciphered them for her. Did they sit together in the main family room? Or did she go to his office, stand beside his desk?

Cecily knew what he was doing, she could see from where she was sitting. Their earlier exchange by the door had made him wary of her although there was no need to be because she seemed entirely normal with him, and so his wariness felt faintly shameful. She was playing cards with Antonio. Seeing Rafael writing, Antonio was making much of giving him a wide berth; Rafael detected Antonio's derision. As if he were thinking, *I don't know why you bother.*

In the morning, Cecily stopped him – 'Rafael?' – and her manner was the same as by the door on the previous evening: the hush, the directness, an appeal. In spite of himself, he thrilled to it, his heart high, hanging on her next words. But it was about the sick kitchen boy, Harry: he was being moved to the tiny, unoccupied room opposite Rafael's. And so she was warning him: there would be comings and goings, was what she said, but he knew that she meant there would be noises and odours. And he knew why the poor lad was being moved: he was dying. He was being taken to the peace and quiet at the top of the house to die. Until now, he'd been in the kitchen, in a makeshift corner of his own – propped up on cushions – to benefit from the warmth, distractions and company, and have an eye kept on him. He'd been visited a couple of times by the Kitsons' physician and, on those occasions, removed to another room to be bled, but he'd always later returned.

Rafael knew from Cecily that the illness had been going on for months, perhaps six months, perhaps longer. He'd been complaining of tiredness, dizziness, weakness, and the cooks had been going easy on him, gradually excusing him his duties. There was never any fever nor a cough, so no one was worried for themselves. In November, he'd been brought to London with the household; he couldn't have been left at the country house. Rafael had asked Cecily, at the time, why couldn't he have gone home, to his own people, and Cecily had explained that he'd be better cared for in the Kitson household. His own home would be desperate, she said; it's warm, here, she said. Although Rafael took care not to be caught looking, he'd seen when he re-emerged after his own illness that the boy's deterioration over Christmas had been drastic. He was cadaverous and if Rafael hadn't known who he was – there on those cushions – he'd not have recognised him. That wasted figure was of indeterminate age; there was nothing of boyhood about him any more.

For Rafael, the prospect of his own son's death, even in old age, seemed a travesty. Indeed, old age itself, for Francisco: absurd, outrageous. Ageing in the face of such vibrancy and perfection was ridiculous.

Rafael hated to see the remorselessness of the kitchen boy's decline. If God had to take him, why not just take him? Why did it have to be so hard, his going? And now he was no longer manageable in the kitchen; the illness was beginning to get messy. 'Who'll look after him?' Rafael asked Cecily. She would, she said.

And so Harry did his dying upstairs while downstairs the pace was unaltered, kitchens were serviced and people were catered for. Cecily was occupied for a couple of weeks. Rafael was constantly aware of her presence in the room across from his. He longed to see her. Sometimes he glimpsed her on the stairs with a bundle of bedding, and sometimes he braved calling through the door to ask her if there was anything she or Harry needed. Thanking him, mostly she said no. A couple of times, he left outside the door whatever she'd requested. Once, when the door was ajar, he glimpsed enough to know that she was stroking the boy's head, smoothing back what little hair he had left. His head was too far back, his chin in the air: he sounded as if he were snoring, but the sounds he made were nothing so robust and carefree as snores.

And once, Rafael saw the eldest Kitson girl was coming up the stairs to take over. Faced with him, she stopped in her tracks, clearly nervous at having been seen. No doubt this was something she shouldn't have been doing. Rafael smiled sadly to reassure her, retreating back into his own room to let her pass. Whenever free of her nursing duties, Cecily must have been going to her own room. Rafael was always hoping to come across her in the kitchen, but never did.

Nicholas, though, he saw plenty of. The boy was often sitting on the top step, outside the two rooms, playing with something – nothing much, the buttons again or a chalk and slate (on which, Rafael noted, he could write N-i-c) or pegs, which he lined up and to which – Rafael was sure – he muttered under his breath. After several days of having to step past him, feeling awkward, Rafael dared to squat down and ask, 'What do you have there?' Pegs, in a line. Nothing, though, from Nicholas, but that frown. 'Well, looks good, whatever it is,' Rafael said, in his own language, trying to stay sounding cheerful as he gave up and continued on his way.

The following day, Nicholas had the chalk and slate and Rafael said, 'You can write! Your name.' He pointed in turn to the N-i-c. 'That's very, very good, Nicholas.' But the boy wiped it away with his sleeve.

Two days later, Rafael felt compelled to crouch beside him again and, in an attempt to find a shared interest, said, 'You had a king in England – many, many years –' *back*, for which he waved a hand, 'a thousand years. A very, very good king: Arthur.' He had to say the name in his own language; he didn't know it in English. 'Did you know?'

The boy had paused in his playing.

'But before he was king, he was just a boy. Not a prince, just a boy. Like you. Lived with his daddy and his big brother, and what he wants, he dreams … to be a knight.' 'Knight' said in his own language, but the emphasis – he hoped – conveying the grandeur. Rafael couldn't remember exactly what the fascination with knights had been when he was this lad's age, but he remembered that he and his best friend Gil had had it. He cast around, hoping to make the word 'knight' make sense for Nicholas: 'Ride a horse … have adventures …' and he realised he knew the word in English, '*tournaments*'. And, 'Be very good. Fight bad. Fight for good. Help people.' A pause, so that the boy might indicate if he understood. Nothing. But he hadn't resumed his playing. He just might be listening, Rafael dared to hope.

So, he continued: 'But, oh, it is a bad time in England, a bad, bad time for a long, long time. No king. Lots of men …

fighting. War. Years and years. *This* man, *that* man' – despite the restricted space, Rafael managed to enact some sword-strokes – 'and England is tired, everyone is so, so, so tired. England is nothing, now. But there is someone who can help: Merlin.' Again, the name had to be in his own language. 'He is a ...' how to say 'sorcerer'? 'He makes magic. And he knows who is good for England; he knows who can be king. He knows he comes soon, the new king. Merlin puts a –' again, Rafael had to enact 'sword', swish an imaginary sword around, making the swishing sounds, 'in a stone, a big, big stone –'

'Sword,' said the boy, to the floor.

'*Sword*, yes, thank you, a sword in the stone,' Rafael was careful not to falter, 'and he says to all the men in England: "Next week there is a tournament, and who takes this sword from this stone, he is the true king."'

He paused for dramatic effect, and to give himself time to remember the story that he and Gil had so loved. 'Arthur's dad and his brother come to the tournament, and Arthur helps. Two days, they ride; sleep one night in an inn. Then the brother – he is silly, sometimes, this brother –' and Rafael slapped his palm to his forehead: '"Oh! No! my sword! at the inn!" But Arthur says, "I go and get it." And he rides. But the inn is shut: everyone goes to the tournament.' A heavy sigh to portray Arthur's disappointment. 'Arthur comes back, but he' – Rafael raised a hand and crooked it sideways to illustrate that Arthur took a wrong turning – 'and he sees a sword in a stone. "Oh," he says, "good: a sword." And he takes it from the stone.'

Nicholas looked up at him, searchingly.

'Easy,' Rafael pronounced, 'for Arthur. And Merlin comes, he says, "You are the true king of England," but Arthur says, "No, I am a boy, I want to be a —"' Rafael squeezed shut his eyes, a parody of concentration.

'Knight,' offered Nicholas.

'"— a knight." But Merlin says, "You are king. You are a good, good king."' Rafael stood up. 'Tomorrow,' he promised, 'more.' All the way down the stairs, he was half-expecting to be heckled but – thank God – heard nothing.

In the ninth year of his marriage to Leonor, Gil had died. He'd sickened and died in a matter of days. He'd had a stomach ache – Rafael could remember him mentioning it – and then he hadn't appeared for a few days. Rafael hadn't thought anything of it, but then the messenger had arrived with the news. 'Are you sure?' Rafael had asked the embarrassed man, in utter disbelief, abject with grief. 'I mean, are you sure?' Gil had worsened rapidly, doubled up and sweating, groaning his way through something like contractions; then sick, then pale, and no longer acknowledging any pain. How could it have happened? – he'd always been so full of life; and a doctor, too. And Rafael's best friend. The only person who'd ever understood him. Except that had stopped long ago, hadn't it, even if Gil – good, loyal, Gil – hadn't known it. Not sure if Leonor would receive him, Rafael went to see her. She was polite but distant.

Rafael continued with the Arthur stories – for two days on the top step, and thereafter in the relative comfort of his room where they took up position, cross-legged, at opposite ends of the bed. Nicholas hadn't spoken again, he just stared at Rafael as if defying him to look away, which Rafael never did, or not until he was saying, 'And that's enough, now, for today.' He described Lord Pellinore's challenge to the new king, and his eventual, glad capitulation; the handing over of Excalibur from the depths; the foundation of Camelot and the round table; and the marriage to Guinevere and arrival of Lancelot, that brave, loyal knight who was to become Arthur's best friend.

The kitchen boy died, and although Rafael didn't see Cecily at all for a week afterwards, Nicholas still turned up daily for his story, peering through the door which Rafael had left ajar, waiting to be invited inside. Even when Rafael had finally had the troublesome tooth pulled and pain reverberated high-pitched in his jawbone, he had to manage the storytelling: sitting there, composed, on the end of the bed when he longed to collapse on to it and shove his head under a pillow.

With similarly spectacular bad timing, the Spanish office had chosen the day of the tooth extraction to call him in to listen to apologies, explanations and assurances from someone senior they'd rustled up. Word had come from Rafael's contact in Spain and, clearly, whatever the officials had heard had persuaded them of their earlier mistake. While Rafael nursed his jaw, the contrite nobleman assured him that his continued presence was much appreciated and that the sundial project was dear to the prince's heart. Funding was now on its way, he claimed, and the sundial could celebrate the birth of the prince. That was all very well, Rafael countered, but the royal baby wasn't due for three months. He'd be willing to return in due course, but for now he needed to go home. More than four months, he'd been away. Apart from anything else, his family was having to rely on his brother to provide for them. He needed to get back to Spain to do some paid work. The situation was absurd.

There was no answer to that; the officials and their nobleman merely looked hurt. Rafael told them that if they couldn't arrange passage home for him within a fortnight, he'd do it himself. In truth, though, he had no idea how he'd afford it.

Trying to take his mind off the situation, and to pass the time, he'd begun to do his walks around London again. With the exception of when he was telling Arthur stories to Nicholas, walking around the city was better than sitting in the Kitsons' house. He'd done enough of that during the past four or five months, and now there was no Cecily for company. Not that his walks were in the least cheering. Leafless trees could have looked delicate with their tracery of bare branches but in reality were stark and grotesque. Holly – so admired, it seemed, by the English – looked reptilian to him. Several times on his walks he passed groups of friars – Franciscan, Dominican – and this was new: back in December, there'd been no friars. They were returning, he guessed, from wherever they'd been in exile on the Continent.

Back at the Kitsons', he began to see Cecily around, but she looked exhausted and kept herself to herself. He would have to give her time to recover. He and Nicholas moved on to the arrival at Camelot of Morgana, Arthur's beautiful half-sister – but evil, if only Arthur knew it.

'Why?' Nicholas surprised him with the challenge.

'Why she comes to Camelot? Oh, to –'

'No.' Nicholas's hard stare. 'Why *evil*?'

Yes, why? Rafael found himself stuttering through an explanation of how she'd been unloved and alone as a child. It cut no ice, though, he saw, with Nicholas.

Out walking, later that week, in the first week of February, he became aware of a swell of disturbance. There was always something up, in London – an eddy around every corner – but this was a commotion: doors slamming, people converging then breaking away and moving fast in one direction. Mindful of having been stuck at St Paul's, Rafael wasn't going to make the same mistake twice, and he didn't like the look on these people's faces. But of course he was curious, so he began making his way in their direction, but tentatively, hanging behind so that he could stop, turn around, find his way back again at any time. He kept his head down, caught no one's eye. Kept his ears open, but heard nothing that told him anything. He had a sense, from the terseness to this hush, that something was being held back.

He came across the cause sooner than he'd anticipated; he'd seen it before he realised what he was seeing. The crowd had gathered to witness a man being shoved along by a handful of uniformed, armed guards. Suddenly, the prisoner arched, stretched out to reach into the crowd: startlingly graceful for someone in manacles. A guard put a stop to it with a prod to his back. On the fringe of the crowd, a bristle of hands had been thrust up in response to the man's reach, and these people rose forward in a wave which broke against two guards who stepped into the breech. A woman, Rafael saw, with children: a woman holding a small child and half-holding another, and around her legs more children – three? – whom she was also trying to hold but of course she couldn't, and those children were scrabbling at her and scrabbling at the man. One of them was screaming: proper, adult-like scream-ing, not childish protest. Rafael had felt their lurch towards the man as if it were his own: his own blood crashing. The crowd lobbed words at the guards, giving voice to their outrage like no one would dare in Spain. Rafael saw now that there were in fact many more guards than the handful shep-herding the man: there were guards linked, braced, tottering with the pressure of the crowd at their backs.

That was when Rafael saw what looked like a pyre. But they didn't do that, in England: burn people. In Spain and countries under Spanish rule, yes, but that was one of the main objections of the English: that the Spanish were savages who burned people alive. The Spanish tied people up, made a fire at their feet and left them to it, to burn like rubbish. But the English didn't do it. They had different methods. That was a pyre, though: the stack of wood, the stool, and the stake in the middle; the clearing all around it. Was this, then, some kind of display? A threat, an elaborate enactment? But if it was, the people didn't know it because there was nothing fake in their outrage.

A man was officiating: Rafael watched him losing the battle, reasoning and imploring and berating and threatening all at once. He was utterly at a loss: just making a noise, or trying to, but making a lot less than the furious crowd. But still it was happening, it hadn't stopped: a manacled man was going to be burned away in front of these people.

*But the English didn't do this.* Their executions were done by hangings and cuttings: sharp, precise actions; the jerk of the rope, the slash of the knife. Not the chaos of flame. There was method to English executions: they were done in stages, for display. The body – usually dead – was acted upon, degraded in detail. Not burned away. Their savagery was of a different kind, a cold kind.

Rafael turned away. He could no longer see the manacled man and in any case he didn't want to see – or hear – any of this. Whatever that man had done – the man being shoved towards the pyre – he had a family who loved him: that had been clear. A family denied a last touch. That bawling child. And this whole crowd: so many, many people, but helpless. And now here he was, turning and leaving that man to his appalling fate. But what else could he do? What could he do that this crowd couldn't? Still, he despised himself for it.

He half-ran back the way he'd come but was too late to get out of earshot, because then it came: the cry, in unison, of disbelief. The fire was being lit, he knew: the touch of a torch to the kindling, the bestowing of flame and the instant of its taking hold. *There's nothing you can do*, he told himself with every breath, *nothing you can do, nothing you can do*, but what he intended as a vague comfort rang inside him as a taunt: *nothing you can do*. The crowd might still kick away the faggots, trample down the flames, cut the man free. They might. He could hope. He'd hope that the English rabble would do their best, their worst.

He recalled the nick of a flame to his hand and the reflex, the yanking back to safety. If there was no escape, would the burning – in time – cease to hurt? Wouldn't sensation be burned away into numbness? He was desperate to believe it, but it was not what he'd heard. And, anyway, there wasn't just the burning; there was the smoke, that scalding smoke and the smell of it: suffocating on the smoke of your own burning body. He made himself think of it because a person who didn't think of it was capable of lighting such a fire.

He didn't go back to the Kitsons'. He went instead to the river. It was flotsam-pocked, the swans slit-eyed and sour-beaked. News of the burning didn't seem to have reached there, yet: there was none of the confusion he'd encountered in the streets closer to the cathedral. The beggars were serene by comparison. Men loaded and unloaded boats, verbal exchanges limited to the necessary. Other boatmen lolled, conversing as they waited for custom. Rafael envied them their all-too-temporary ignorance of what was taking place within walking distance.

What had that man done, to be burned for it? Heresy. Couldn't bishops have argued with him, instead? Why burn him? He was being burned for having the wrong ideas, evil ideas, for denying God, for saying black's white and for keeping on saying it, because what if everyone said it? It would bring the whole world down. Rafael knew it all – heretics were evil, they aimed for chaos and darkness and there was no place in the world for them; but he couldn't stop seeing those hands reaching for that man, those little hands, and he couldn't reconcile it. Would that man really have wanted chaos and darkness for those children of his?

And that man himself was someone's son. Perhaps thirty years ago, he'd been someone's baby and that someone had got up at night, into the raw cold, night after night, month after month, to feed him. And then, later on, on other nights, that someone had sometimes swallowed down hunger so that the child could eat. That someone might have walked in stocking feet, boots sold, so that the apothecary could be paid. And prayed to God to be taken in the child's place. In better times, that someone would have daydreamed of the life awaiting the boy. Would have told him stories of his ancestry and his past, of London and England and of other places both far away and imaginary.

And that child had grown into a man who, only the other day, might have kissed his wife in passing for just a little too long, the kiss widening into a smile. A man who, just last week, might have looked at his child's shoulder turned away in sleep and marvelled again at the loveliness of it, small enough and smooth enough to roll in the palm of his hand. A man who, a mere couple of months ago, might've filched a sole blackberry, guiltily and gleefully, from the household's bowlful.

And all for this.

Where were the man's children, now? Why had the woman taken them there? But she'd had to, he realised. If she hadn't, they'd not have said goodbye.

Rafael remembered a night when he and Leonor were woken by Francisco crying. The little lad had wet the bed, which he only rarely did. Leonor was quicker out of bed and got to Francisco's bedside first, but he was deeply distressed and she struggled to change him. He was crying, 'No, no, no,' and wrenching himself away from her, obstructing her efforts. Despite her best intentions, her temper, Rafael saw, was fraying. Then Francisco was crying, 'I need to —' then something undecipherable. 'I need to — I need to —'

And Leonor was asking him, 'Need to what? Need to what, Francisco?' and continuing, 'Come on, now, please, darling: let me do this and then we can all go back to sleep, yes? Come on, now, let's get you dry. Let Mummy do this.'

Rafael was chipping in: 'Yes, come on, Francisco, let Mummy do this.'

Suddenly Francisco's last word was clear: *Mummy.*

Leonor said, 'Yes: Mummy.'

And then he managed it, got clear — even through the sobs — what he'd been trying to tell them: '*I need to find my mummy.*'

Leonor reeled, looked up at Rafael and back to her son. 'I am your mummy, Francisco.' And to Rafael: 'He doesn't know it's me!'

'He's asleep,' said Rafael, realising. 'He's not properly awake.'

Leonor said, 'Oh Jesus, Rafael, he doesn't know it's me,' and, frantic, 'I'm here, Francisco, it's me, I'm here.'

Just as stunned, Rafael could only say again: 'He's asleep, he's not quite awake.'

Leonor was incredulous: 'But —'

Yes: the candle was burning and they'd been talking to him for some minutes and he'd seemed to have been talking to them — well, crying at them — in reply ... How could he not be awake?

Leonor was continuing, 'It's me, darling, I'm here,' but Francisco suddenly got it and accepted it, stopped his sobbing; he was back in a peaceful sleep.

There'd been something horrifying about it: Francisco sitting there square on the bed, with busyness all around him, yet utterly bereft. He'd been so lost, and, for those few minutes, whatever his parents said or did for him, he was beyond being found. Rafael had never forgotten it, but he didn't understand at first why the memory had come to him on the day of the burning. And then he realised: it would be those children, some nights, crying desperately like that, in grief and terror, needing to find their daddy, except they'd be wide awake and there'd be no comfort for them. He'd be gone. No grave, even, to visit.

The atmosphere at the Kitsons', that evening, was radically altered, distinctly subdued, and Rafael guessed it was due to news of the burning. Cecily kept herself blank, looking through him if she ever looked his way so that although he was desperate to go to her, he didn't dare. Her son fared little better, her glances at him perfunctory as she performed various maternal duties such as cutting up his food.

Antonio had — as ever — been talkative on the way into supper: 'You heard? – they burned a priest today.'

'Priest?' A second burning?

'Near St Paul's. Burned him. Heretic. Married, with children.'

That was the man he'd seen, then. And Antonio would believe — and repeat — anything. 'If the man was married,' Rafael was scathing, 'then he was no priest, was he.'

'Married priest,' insisted Antonio. 'They could get married, here. Can't now. Have to renounce them, now, their wife and kids. Deny them, or something, and never see them again. Do a penance. I don't know, do I.' They were taking their places at the table, so he rushed to add, 'But whatever it was he was supposed to do, he didn't, so they burned him.' They were sitting, now, so it was too late for Rafael to respond, for which he was glad. Whatever he'd have said would have done no justice to the enormity of it.

That night, in his room, he pondered it: a married priest. A priest with responsibilities to a wife and children before his flock. In Spain, plenty of priests did have children, and everyone knew it. They were known as 'nephews' and 'nieces'. Priests were supposed to be above the distractions of family life, free from the complications, the mess. But the queen herself had told him that her love for God had grown because of her love for her husband.

Two days later, a bishop was burned. He was married, he had children. The burning took almost an hour, Antonio informed Rafael.

Rafael was aghast: 'You were *there?*'

Antonio rolled his eyes. 'You're joking, aren't you? I'd have been hauled up there by that crowd and thrown on there, too. This is all down to us – didn't you know? That's what they think. The prince can get his chaplain to preach against it, but it's still our fault. It's what we do, isn't it, burning heretics, and now their queen's married a Spaniard. So, she's one of us. That's what they think. There wasn't any burning before she married.' He paused. 'No wonder they never burned people, what with this weather. The wood's damp and the wind sends the flames one way then –' Antonio waved an arm, *away*. 'Half-burned, he was, that bishop – legs gone – but then the flames were off –'

'*Antonio.*' He didn't want to hear it.

Antonio shrugged. 'But he took it all,' he finished, admiringly, 'preaching forgiveness and giving his view of it all for close to an hour – God, do the English ever shut up? – until his throat was burnt out.'

The burning had been at Smithfield, just the other side of the city wall. Rafael feared that he could have unknowingly breathed in the smoke.

The bishop had been silenced, but London hadn't. Later that evening, there was a riot, and it even reached St Bartholomew's Lane. Rafael heard it before he saw it: heard a buzzing and, intrigued, opened his window. Crowd-noise, it was, trouble, all at once louder and nearer. He drew back as it splintered into the lane: two men running; then three, the two running and stopping, turning while the other one scooped something from the ground – a stone? – and chucked it. They were shouting at the closed doors, blaring their indignation. More people came as if thrown into the lane but landing – just – on their feet. Perhaps seven of them, nine or ten. Women, Rafael saw. Behind them came horses, instantly among and ahead of them, wheeling back around to scatter them, their riders thrashing at them. Someone was screaming. Rafael pressed his back against the wall. Somewhere close, glass smashed. The Kitsons' house? Were they now one window down? Were they under attack?

The trouble moved off as suddenly as it had come. When he was confident it wouldn't be returning, Rafael went down to the kitchen. A Kitson window had indeed been smashed: word was, one of the children's bedrooms. Various men had gone to board it up, he gathered. Even so, the kitchen was packed: everyone there, reeling and commiserating. Everyone except Cecily.

'Stupid fucking bitch,' Rafael heard a man remark, his companion adding, 'Wicked stupid fucking bitch.' When the first man said, 'With any luck, she'll die having the kid,' Rafael realised they were talking about their queen. How sickening to talk like that of any woman, let alone that they should be blaming their queen when she'd have had nothing to do with the bishop's burning. It was easy for the English people to blame her – they didn't really like her. Oh, they'd liked the idea of her – the rightful heir, the underdog; they made much of that – but they didn't like her, intensely Catholic and dowdy. The bishop's burning would have been the doing of the ecclesiastical courts: the Church's doing. The queen wouldn't burn people, Rafael knew, and certainly not the fathers of children.

The officials had called his bluff: the two weeks were up and they hadn't arranged transport for him, although they were talking of a ship due to leave in ten days' time. Reluctant though he'd been to do it, Rafael had written home to Pedro to explain the situation – an impossible task in itself – and to ask about the possibility of a loan. If he didn't hear back beforehand, he'd send two copies of the letter during the following three or four weeks, just in case, just to make sure.

Cecily continued to keep herself to herself. Once, when they passed each other in the kitchen, she said an expressionless, 'Hello, Rafael,' even-toned and low-pitched, but he was convinced he caught a trace of something in it: challenge or dismissal, or even contempt. She didn't pause, which put him in his place. Nicholas scampered after her and, albeit uninvited, took his place at her side. Which, after all, however bad his mother's mood, was still his place.

Rafael missed her. He missed those evenings, back at the beginning, when they'd sat in companionable silence. Watching her with a needle and thread, hands raised into the light, cuffs slipped a little down her wrists. He yearned for those evenings and sometimes he felt he was wishing for the whole world, and sometimes nothing much at all.

The Kitsons were still in London because the winter was so hard, the journey daunting. They'd stay, now, until the royal baby was born in May, and — all being well — then partake of London's celebrations. Rafael had still heard nothing from home. There'd been time enough, now, to hear back from her. Why the silence? He had no news of his own to tell. He didn't mention the burnings.

For a couple of weeks there were no more burnings and it was then, during that lull, that Cecily knocked on his door one evening and said, 'Come for a walk, Rafael.' He was so taken aback that he found himself unable to muster even the simplest response. His heart beat at him; his blood took flight; he placed a hand on the doorframe to steady himself. She, by contrast, was the very picture of calm. She'd spoken warmly enough, but it'd been no mere suggestion or request. It was so unlikely that he wondered briefly if it had been code. Was he in trouble? She mistook his lack of response for reticence in the face of the curfew — or that was how she decided to take it — because she added, 'It's quiet out there; there'll be no problem.' Then, 'And Nicholas is asleep. Alys is there, if he wakes.'

166

Rafael didn't know who Alys was, and didn't ask. Spinning his cloak on to his shoulders, he glimpsed Cecily eyeing the lining. She saw him, and smiled – *the lining I made for you* – and he smiled, too.

Not until they were outside and off down the lane at quite a pace did he ask her where they were going, hoping her reply would reveal the reason for the escapade.

'Nowhere,' was all she said.

In the absence of anything more enlightening, he liked the sound of that. Nowhere sounded good to him. Suddenly this lane, which he'd been going up and down for almost eight long months, was nowhere he knew. He might never have been here before and might never come again. There would be just this one time, with Cecily. Letting her lead the way, he took no note at all of where they were. Their breath scythed through the tangle of woodsmoke and river-air. Side by side, in step, their footfalls could have been one person's. She'd tell him in her own time what they were doing; he was in no rush, now, to know. He liked not having to know.

Rainwater showered from eaves, and for once he saw the drenched buildings as impressively unbowed. The rain – heavy all day – had just stopped, and everything was slick and gleaming, even the mud and muck. Somehow that sheen was on him, too: he felt it rushing up to him with each of his inward breaths and he tingled with it. He was part of this shining, after-dark world. In on its secrets.

More watchmen had been appointed, Rafael knew, since the previous week's riots, and indeed a pair stood at most corners, idling, only belatedly curious when he and Cecily passed. She strode on and Rafael did the same, and each time they got away with it. And why should they be challenged? They were doing nothing. They were up to nothing. His stomach felt high, braced as if he were on the lip of something and stepping off, unsure of a landing.

At last, Cecily spoke, surprising him with her question: 'Are there a lot of burnings in Spain?' He didn't know what he'd been expecting her to say, but not that. She hadn't let up on her pace and the question came on a rush of hard, fast breaths. She might've been asking him the time of day. Matter-of-fact. Fact-finding.

'Before I was born,' he said. Not quite the truth. '*Most,* before I was born.' Spain, she'd asked about. Nowhere else, no mention of elsewhere, of Spanish burnings nowadays in the empire, in the Low Countries. He couldn't quite believe that she didn't know about the persecution in those countries, but he wasn't going to bring it up.

'Did it work?'

The Inquisition? She'd got ahead of him by a step or two – he'd faltered – and turned to him, expectant. She was serious, he saw: did it work, yes or no? Put like that: 'Yes.' She gave him a terse nod: he'd confirmed her suspicion. Ostentatious obedience to the Church. He could have said, *Every second man's a priest. Take my brothers.*

She walked on. 'Cecily,' he called after her. 'It'll … stop.' Soon, he meant. But saying so, he felt he was playing it down and betraying those who'd already suffered.

'Oh, I don't know about that,' she threw back.

'Yes,' he reasoned, hurrying after her. 'This is England. In England …' *you don't do this, you don't burn people.*

'I don't know that this is England, really, any more, Rafael. It's half Spain now.' She stopped again, faced him. 'We have a Spanish king.'

'He is not king! He is not king.' Then, with something like an exasperated laugh, 'Believe me, Cecily, England is nothing like Spain.'

His turn, now, though: he wanted something explaining. 'Cecily, listen —' they'd resumed walking and he puffed to get his question voiced: 'Is it true? — priests here have wives?'

'Had.'

No more, though, from her. The air between them was crazed by their breath. He was considering what to ask and how to ask it when, 'Rafael?'

Now it was coming: the explanation for their being on this walk. 'I just needed you with me.' Matter-of-fact, again. 'Not in there —' she flapped a hand in their wake and he took her to mean the Kitsons' house. 'I needed you with me, just for a little while. Just ' she threw up both hands, glanced up into the black sky. *Here.*

'And I am,' he said, with feeling, 'I am with you,' and he marvelled at it: that here he was, in the dark, the desperate cold of this unforgiving city, his blood singing as he raced to keep up with this long-limbed Englishwoman.

She smiled at him, amused because he'd stated the obvious: here, indeed, he was. Her smile made it a mere statement of fact and he allowed it, smiling, too. But he decided to chance something: 'You're in trouble, aren't you?'

'No —'

'No' — fist to his chest — 'in here.' But that, of course, could be misinterpreted. 'In *here* —' fist to his forehead.

'Troubled,' she corrected. 'Don't try to make me talk about it.' Not a plea but a warning, and he heeded it. She'd not denied what he'd dared to put to her, she'd not thrown it back at him, and that was enough, at least for now. He knew something about her – she was troubled. She'd let him know it. That much had changed. He had to say something, though, so he said, 'I am your good friend.' It didn't sound right, though. There was something wrong with it, with having said it.

'Good,' though, she said, 'good,' but she said it absently – for the sake of form, he felt. 'Come on,' she said, 'let's go home,' so they walked back up the hill and nothing more was said.

The more he considered it, it seemed stupid: *I am your good friend*. It'd struck the wrong note. It wasn't what he'd meant to say, although what that was – what he *had* wanted to say – he didn't know. Not that it wasn't true. If anything, it was too true. Obvious. Not worth saying. Of course he was her good friend. Why had he had to say it? To him, she'd said, *I needed you here*. Direct and trusting. Why couldn't he have been like that, in return? Instead, he'd been awkward, and not just because of the language barrier. And in being awkward, he felt, he'd let her down.

And then there they were, already back indoors, behind the closed door, and there was nothing for it but to say goodnight. Bejewelled with chill – eyes and cheeks a-glow – she turned from him with a smile and was gone. He felt more awake than he'd felt in months, but this wakefulness wasn't welcome, not at this time of night. A beer, he decided.

The warmth in the kitchen was a whole day deep and many of the staff had already bedded down in it. Others lolled on sacks at the fireplace, and among them was Antonio.

Rafael recoiled from Antonio's amused look and resented his tracking of him – he could sense it – to the barrels.

Up in his room, in bed, he was unable to sleep. He felt Antonio's gaze on him still, he couldn't shake it off; it rattled him. There'd been times when Rafael could have – should have – looked at *him* like that.

Leonor had been Gil's wife and she would always be his widow. She would always be that, first, before she was Rafael's wife. But Rafael hadn't seen it.

He didn't ask her to marry him until after her year of mourning and then a few more months. An interval that was more than respectable. Not that being respectable had been his concern – he'd just had no idea how she was feeling. She gave no clues. She remained composed.

And anyway he didn't know how to ask her. For a year and more, he went over and over it: how to tell her what he felt for her and to ask her to become his wife. He imagined various approaches, from the seemingly accidental – somehow letting it slip – to making a formal, written request for an interview. Her possible responses, too: he worked hard to imagine every possible variation. He kidded himself he was prepared.

One day, Leonor was bemoaning being a widow, disparaging her status. Rafael didn't dare raise the question of marriage for fear of seeming to pity her, but he knew this was his moment. He just said, 'Leonor, I love you.' Amazed himself by saying it, as blunt as that. More than a year of pondering, of thinking through strategies, and that, in the end, was what happened: he just said it. And that was how he said it, too: a statement of fact. No great declaration. If anything, it had sounded weary. Resigned. Which was a fair reflection of how he felt, after all that time. 'Marry me,' he then dared to ask, 'please.'

She blushed, having been caught unawares, which wasn't what he'd intended. She was wrong-footed, and she didn't appreciate it. And he wasn't keen on being the subject of her displeasure. It'd had to be done, though: that, now, was his conviction. He'd been right to do it. Recovering herself, she acted dismissive: a brief, humourless laugh – not unkind – and she said his name in reproach. But he wasn't having that. Rafael *what*? He'd done nothing wrong in telling her how he felt. In putting it to her. It made him vulnerable, not her. Surely she could see that. 'I'm serious,' he told her, in the hope that this was helpful.

She raised her shoulders and turned away. There was something bleak in it: the stiffness, the turn, the distant gaze. She didn't give him an answer; she said, 'Give me time.' So relieved was he that she hadn't declined, he'd have given her anything she asked for. There would be no coming straight into his arms, but he'd known that would never happen. Only as they left the garden for the house did he wonder: *How much time?*

After several weeks, he was wondering: How much more time? Eventually – three, four weeks later – he was forced into having to ask her, 'Have you thought any more about my offer?' *Offer.* More like *plea*; he should've said *plea*.

She said, 'You miss your friend.'

It took him a moment, but then he understood her to mean that he was grieving for Gil and looking to her to be his consolation. 'No,' he urged, 'no,' impassioned, 'I've always –'

But he stopped in the face of her obvious alarm. He saw that it wasn't what she wanted to hear. This was what she definitely didn't want to hear. He spread his hands – *I've said it; I'm sorry, but I've said it* – and allowed, 'Of course I miss Gil.' And he did, dizzyingly so, and all at once it came again, the disorientation, because Gil's disappearance from their lives felt like an elaborate trick and for a heartbeat Leonor was part of it, she was privy to something that Rafael wasn't.

The hitch of her eyebrows was a kind of shrug, as if to say, *Well, he's not coming back.*

Yes, but where did that leave them?

And then, 'Rafael?' No more than a puff of impatience. 'Why not,' she said, and there was that tilt of her chin, the hardness of her mouth, her eyes alight with challenge. Of all the possible responses, this was the one he hadn't anticipated, but it was utterly characteristic of her. It made it impossible for him to go to her, to hold her as he'd imagined he might. He nodded, a sharp little nod, an acknowledgement.

A done deal.

And his heart bled.

Oh, it had got better, over time. It had been all right. She'd thawed. Opened up to him. The first time her hand felt for his, gripped it – well, he couldn't envisage a greater happiness. Only years later did he realise it had been nothing much to her, not anything like as much to her as it had been to him. For her, it was just a hand to grasp.

Two evenings after their walk, Rafael was delighted to find Cecily in the kitchen, at the fireside, her son resting back against her knees with his eyes closed and the dog lolling in turn closed-eyed against him. Gazing into the flames, Cecily was rolling something in the fingers of one hand. Seeing Rafael, she remembered herself, stopped, and revealed what it was: a pebble. 'Harry's.' The kitchen boy's.

'Oh.' Harry: the oddness, again, of him being gone. Rafael couldn't quite believe that he wouldn't be turning up again – *Hello, there!* – now that the drama of his death was done. 'What is it?'

She shrugged. Nothing. A pebble. 'It was in his pocket.' She'd had the job of going through his clothes, his belongings. It was nothing much. Nothing at all, in fact: just a pebble. But it had been Harry's. Rafael was glad she hadn't thrown it away. She closed her hand over it again. Rafael sat down beside her and they looked together for a while into the fire.

Then she asked him, 'What d'you think people do in Heaven?' She was being mischievous, he saw, but was also waiting for an answer – to that extent, it was a real question.

*Heaven.* He felt the familiar clench of terror: *it might've already happened.*

'Do?' He'd never thought of it like that. If he ever got there, would he have to do anything? Seeing loved ones again was what Heaven was for, wasn't it? Being back with those you loved. But quite what you then did, in their company, he didn't know. He didn't know, either, if he believed it. For her, though, he was happy to go along with it: 'Why?' He was curious, and amused: 'What do *you* think people do?'

'Music.' She'd shrugged, but she'd spoken emphatically – it was something she'd thought about, something about which she'd had an idea. 'Learn music,' she said. 'Practise.' And presumably get very good indeed. Eternity was a lot of practising. Just how good could you get? He liked the idea, was tickled by it.

'Do you play an instrument?' he asked her.

She shot him that mischievous look. 'Not yet,' she said.

Then, 'Some people say the king's still alive.' She'd spoken emptily, carefully noncommittal, staring again into the hearth. He sensed she was testing him.

But he was confused: 'King?' Still alive? Did she mean the Spanish prince? But he *was* alive, wasn't he? Or had something happened? Something he'd missed?

'The boy,' she said, seeing his confusion. 'The queen's brother.'

Oh, the dead king. He understood. But, 'Still alive?' How could that possibly be? He'd been dead for over a year. Why would he have disappeared?

She shrugged. 'It's what some people are saying.' *That's all I'm saying.* 'That he's going to come back.'

Wishful thinking, he realised: that was what it was. There were people who wanted the dead king back instead of their queen, and wanted him so badly that they'd believe any old nonsense. That was how bad these times were, in some people's eyes.

He checked: 'You …?' *You don't think so, do you?*

She gave him a long, flat look. *He's dead*, it said. Rafael saw that she'd resigned herself to it.

So, she too hankered for the old days, the days before the reign of the queen. The days before people were burned. And perhaps, even, if she was like other people, the days before England was linked with Spain. It was understandable, but he wanted to say, *You have a good queen; she's a good woman and a good queen; she thinks only of what's best for England; she's hard-working and mindful of others, appointing that huge Council and listening to each and every man, and she's merciful.* The English forgot how merciful she'd been. She hadn't even executed the girl who had been pretender to her throne, not until the second attempted coup, after which, of course she'd had no other option. He wanted to say, *She has great dignity – which has survived intact despite years of assaults on it – but no airs and graces, none.* And for England's sake, she'd weathered great changes in her life in a mere year, changing herself from spinster noble-woman living a life devoted to God, to monarch, wife and expectant mother. *She will see you through*: he was certain of that. She'd need to stop the burnings, though, yes. The burnings were a mistake, of course. And she would stop them, he was sure.

Or so he'd assumed. Later that week, coming into the kitchen, he was aware of a commotion in the back yard and ventured to the threshold. A lad whom Rafael didn't recog-nise as from the household – backed by a further dozen or so strangers – was proclaiming something. Gathered around was an agitated crowd of household staff. Rafael spotted a window open, above: the Kitson boy who walked with the sticks was watching, listening. The proclaiming lad ushered someone forward – a woman – and she threw her hand into the air. There was something in it, something small.

Cecily came to Rafael's side. 'Cecily?' he asked. 'What is this?'

At that moment, the steward came barging into the yard, forcing Rafael and Cecily to step aside, to opposite sides of the doorway. He began clearing everyone from the courtyard: for the strangers, an emphatic sweep of an arm towards the gate; for his own staff, a clap-clapping, *Back to work!* Cecily obeyed immediately; she'd have gone if Rafael hadn't stopped her. 'What was that?'

'Oh —' She looked worried, shook her head, *It doesn't matter, don't ask.*

But he was insistent. 'Cecily?'

She reconsidered and said that five people had been burned in Essex the day before, but had managed to make speeches and their words — their resistance — had been written down and had come to London. To be readily received, judging from what he'd just seen.

'But what was in the woman's hand?' he asked her.

She looked flat into his eyes and gave it to him: 'Bone.'

'Bone?' *Bone.* Fragment, relic. From the ashes. The ashes had been combed, and those five people had been made martyrs.

Francisco had once asked him, 'Daddy, what's inside people?'

'Bones,' Rafael said.

Francisco had reeled in horror: 'But dogs eat bones!'

'Not *your* bones,' Rafael had laughed, 'not people's bones. Animals' bones — dead animals' bones. Your bones, Poppet, are safe.'

That evening, Antonio appeared in the queue for supper and, having expressed his voluble dismay at the English failure to observe Lent, said, 'Guess what?'

Rafael couldn't even feign interest.

'The new Pope has decided he loathes the English queen. Loathes us, of course – war mongers that we Spaniards are – but loathes her, too, now, because of the marriage. Going to excommunicate us all, did you know that? England and Spain. Poor cow, she can't do right, can she. She hauls England kicking and screaming back to Rome, and Rome shuts the door in her face. She can burn as many people as she likes, but it'll make no difference.'

'She doesn't "like",' Rafael objected. 'She isn't burning anyone.'

'She signs the warrants,' Antonio countered, chattily. 'Fifteen-year-old blind girl, yesterday.'

Rafael tried to steady his revulsion. 'You shouldn't believe everything you hear.'

Antonio smirked at what he clearly regarded as Rafael's naïvety. 'You don't believe it? – fifteen-year-old blind girl? Which bit don't you believe? Fifteen? Blind? Girl?'

Appalling though it was: 'It's Church business.'

'She still signs.'

'She probably doesn't even look at what she's signing.' But even as he said it, he doubted that anything would get past her. In his mind's eye, he saw her peering at the warrant and raising a query.

'Oh, well, then,' breezed Antonio, 'that makes it all right, doesn't it – don't look, just sign.'

'Someone probably signs for her. She's not been well.' Again, though, to his considerable unease, he doubted she'd ever delegate.

Antonio half-laughed, relishing the sparring. 'And did that someone sign the letter she wrote to the sheriff – wrote at length – to tick him off for letting a heretic down from the pyre? A heretic who'd recanted in the fire. Heretic no longer? Doesn't matter. "Don't do it again," she said. "Don't ever let anyone go, even if they repent. Burn them anyway."'

'All these stories' – Rafael blustered – 'no one knows what's what, any more.'

'Oh, I don't know,' mused Antonio. 'What the English are good at – the only thing they're good at – is seeing straight to the point.'

No word back from Pedro, but the Spanish office had informed Rafael that the prince's long-promised loan had arrived and, in a matter of days, just as soon as they could balance their books, they'd be making him a payment. As to how much, they wouldn't say. Couldn't say, more like, until they'd seen what they'd been granted and had sifted through the hundreds of claims on it. Nor did they say whether the payment was intended to be compensatory or towards completion of the sundial. Rafael didn't ask. He was determined to use the money, if at all possible, to get home.

Then, though, the Spanish office moved away. On Good Friday, April the fourth, the queen and her husband and court moved upriver to Hampton Court Palace to prepare for the birth of her baby in just over a month's time. Everyone had gone, including all the Spaniards who'd been resident at Whitehall. Antonio had seen them go, or some of them, on boats. He'd been at Whitehall, watching them embark on their five-hour river-journey, and now here he was, in

Rafael's room, with that news and more. 'Not Windsor,' he announced.

'Windsor?'

'*Not* Windsor.' Antonio had made himself comfortable: he was lounging on the end of the bed. Rafael had sidled away to the head. Antonio had got some comfits from somewhere: sugar-coated seeds and spices, held in a cone of paper. Neither of them had money spare for comfits, nor did anyone whom Rafael knew. Antonio had, of course, offered them; Rafael had, of course, declined. 'Windsor's where she *was* going.' The crack of a seed between Antonio's teeth. 'But it's too far away. Better protected if she's closer, at Hampton Court.'

Rafael frowned his incomprehension.

'Well' – a delving into the cone – 'they can get troops there, quickly, can't they. Whereas getting them to Windsor …'

'But who's the threat?'

Antonio paused, to make his own show of incomprehension that Rafael should have to ask. Then a shrug, a dismissal: *anyone,* the shrug said; *everyone.*

But Rafael wasn't having it. 'You think they'd – what?' Attack their queen? He'd heard talk of wishing her dead, but that was just talk. Attack their own pregnant or nursing queen?

Antonio made a show of stifling a laugh: again, Rafael's naïvety. 'I tell you,' he said, 'they're already on their way. There's a lot more river-traffic than usual, all of it heading upriver.'

'But they'll be going there to wait for news of the birth.'

More amusement. 'With firearms?'

'This is London,' Rafael said; 'everyone has firearms.'

Another shrug: *If you say so.*

Rafael pushed it: 'And, anyway, aren't those firearms for us?' Spaniards. 'Aren't they going there for us?' Not to threaten her, but to threaten all the Spaniards surrounding her.

'No difference, now. She *is* one of us, as far as they're concerned.'

Rafael was about to take issue with that – was that really what the English believed? – but Antonio blew a sigh and said, 'If she dies, how do we get out of here fast enough?' *If she dies*: purely conversational. But she was nothing to Antonio. Nothing but the reason for him being stuck here. 'They'll forget us, probably. Leave us behind.'

*Our own people*: flee, forgetting their few fellow country-men back in the city. That hadn't occurred to Rafael, and panic prickled in his stomach.

Antonio was complaining, 'What d'you think they *do*, in that month?'

Rafael didn't follow.

'Women. In the month they're shut away.' He was merely registering his scepticism; he didn't require an answer.

They try to relax, Rafael presumed. They sew and sew and sew: make everything that should be needed, and make it beautiful. Bedcovers and pillow cases and nightdresses and cradle-canopies and swaddling. And in the particular case of the queen, he supposed, there'd be official business to be done in preparation: letters to be prepared, declarations, a blank left for *prince* or *princess* and the date. The letters' carriers to be selected and briefed, their safe passage planned – cleared, costed – and prepared for.

'Anyway,' Antonio got up, stretched, scrunched up the paper cone, 'this gives us a problem.' Whatever it was, he didn't seem bothered. 'Lunches – no longer available to us at Whitehall.' He said it as if quoting. He raised his eyebrows in mock triumph, because although the officials would assume this to be a problem for them, he and Rafael were already lunching at the Kitsons'. 'Lunches available for us, of course, at *Hampton Court …*' Five hours away.

The impracticality of their going to Whitehall every day for lunch had belatedly occurred to Cecily and she'd suggested that they stay at the Kitsons'. Just slip into Hall, she'd said, it's a full household and no one'll notice.

'So, anyway,' Antonio continued, 'I was told: make your own arrangements with your host household and we'll reimburse you soon. So, of course, I said, Yeah? How soon? Next week, he said, So I said, Heard that before, and he said, No, really; and I said, I bet, and he said, Listen, the prince's loan is through from Spain, it's here, we're just sorting it all out now.' Antonio raised his eyebrows: a flourish. 'So, we're going to have money.'

Rafael had so far avoided telling him about the promised payment and, now, didn't comment, asking instead, 'But how do we keep in touch with the Spanish office?'

Antonio shrugged. 'Dunno. Didn't ask.' Leaving the room, he added, 'Sorry,' his tone giving no indication that he was.

On Easter Sunday, the Kitson household went to Mass, and because he couldn't pretend that he was going to church at court in the company of his fellow countrymen, now miles upriver, Rafael joined them. It was something to do. It got him out of the house.

They'd been back a matter of minutes – Rafael halfway up the main staircase – when a cry went up: 'Mrs Tanner? Mrs

Tanner!' It was Mr Kitson's secretary, calling with considerable urgency. Rafael came back down to see what was going on, and there was the secretary — amid milling servants — ushering in a well-dressed but bloodied man. There was blood all over his jacket. The man was wide-eyed. Cecily was there, mid-gasp, her hand at her mouth, but the secretary was quick to say something to her that had her drop the hand and hurry forward, unalarmed and practical. From the downward sweep of the secretary's own hand in front of the man, Rafael understood that the problem was the blood on the clothes: there was no bleeding from this man; the blood had originated elsewhere.

Cecily encouraged the man to follow her into the kitchen. She knew him by name — or, at least, someone in the household did and she'd picked it up, because she was using his name, Mister Something. Something indecipherable to Rafael. Entering the kitchen, she turned, aware that her son was following her. 'Rafael —' she looked across the crowd at him, and indicated Nicholas: would he take him? Rafael stepped up to do so. Cecily had already moved on, was requesting water of someone else.

Rafael led the boy away with the gentlest of physical prompts, but suddenly he turned, ducked and ran back the way they'd come. Rafael's pursuit was hindered by servants gathering to gawp at the unfortunate visitor. He did his best, mortified by the prospect of Cecily witnessing such ineptitude. Nicholas was already at the kitchen door, had already opened it, but, a few steps in, came to a halt. Rafael saw Cecily glance up at the two of them — Nicholas free, Rafael following — but her face registered nothing. No surprise, no disapproval. She seemed to regard it as inevitable, Nicholas's absconding, his truculence; she was trusting to Rafael to put it right. Her priority was to wash the man's hands. He looked incapable of doing it himself, his hands were hers for washing and she held them in a bowl and stroked blood from them into the water. Rafael heard something of what the man was saying: 'I held his head … I held his head … on the ground, I held his head.' Cecily murmured back to him and Rafael couldn't catch her words but knew from her tone that she was reassuring him: *Quiet, now. Let's clean you up.* Rafael stepped into the kitchen – there was someone else there, too, a man behind him, beside the door so that Cecily and the visitor weren't left alone – and whispered to Nicholas, 'Come on,' adding as an inducement, 'Let's have an Arthur story.' And the boy, presumably having seen all he'd needed to see, complied.

When Cecily came to collect her son, she said to Rafael, 'Later,' meaning that when they were away from listening little ears, she'd tell him what had happened. And that evening, in a corner of the kitchen, she did. 'A priest was shot,' she whispered. 'Dead – I mean, shot *dead* – during Mass today.'

Rafael didn't understand. During Mass? Shot? Who would do such a thing? For a moment he was baffled enough to think she meant that the priest had been married and the Church had had him shot for it.

'Some man,' she said, 'a man, just – some man.'

A man who didn't like Catholics. The gravity of it hit Rafael. If a man could walk into a church and fire at an officiating priest, there was no sanctuary and no one could be considered above attack.

She said, 'The man who came here, he's one of Mr Kitson's colleagues, from –' Rafael missed it; somewhere other than London. 'He's in the city for a week to work. He'd gone to Mass …' She shrugged: *You know the rest.* He'd been a bystander.

*I held his head.*

'Stay in the house, Rafael,' she said, 'from now on. Until that baby's born. Until you go home. Stay in the house.'

And he did. For two and a half long weeks. Two and a half weeks of giving up on pressing the Spanish office for news or money, and waiting instead for a summons that didn't come. Two and a half weeks of sending no letters home nor being able to check for any that might have arrived. Two and a half weeks without a shave. Antonio was still taking his chances, being immeasurably better than Rafael at passing for an Englishman, and he could get away with it as long as he kept his mouth shut – which, somehow, he was managing, because he came and went unscathed. Where he went, Rafael didn't know, but seeing as he'd go for several days at a time, it was most likely to Hampton Court, where he was probably sleeping on someone's floor. Or in her bed.

Once, a couple of years back, Rafael had gone to find Antonio during the afternoon because his mare was foaling and in trouble, and when there'd been no answer to his knocking on the main door, nor to his calling, he'd gone inside to wake him. The bedroom door had been ajar, and before he'd realised that he'd looked, he'd glimpsed Antonio naked on the bed, face down, and, beneath him, also face down, a woman: a woman's bare legs alongside Antonio's. The two figures were so still and quiet that Rafael might've thought them to be sleeping – albeit in an odd position – if not for the rhythmic flexing of Antonio's buttocks. Rafael had drawn back, mortified, paralysed, unable to believe he'd been so stupid as to come unannounced into the house and to the bedroom door, and unable to believe that Antonio hadn't heard him. No change, though, in the quality of the silence; no one shifting inside that room to check around or reach for a bedcover. Rafael contemplated owning up – coughing – but already the instant of having seen them was receding and, with it, the opportunity to confess his presence. He'd backed to the main door, very careful to make no sound. Outside, he tried to compose himself. He hated having seen Antonio's nakedness. Couldn't bear to think of Antonio as even having the capacity to be naked. Couldn't bear for nakedness even to exist where Antonio was concerned. Let alone the rest, the actual activity, which he now tried to persuade himself was not what he'd seen. He'd headed for the stables, shaking, to deal with the mare himself as best he could. Passing his house, he'd glimpsed Leonor in the courtyard with Francisco and was overcome with relief that it hadn't been her in Antonio's room.

For two and a half long, Kitson-bound weeks, the only fresh air Rafael had was in the various little courtyards – where there was plenty of it, gusting and buffeting against the walls, as trapped as he was. He wandered around the stables, exchanging rueful smiles with the more approachable of the grooms. Talked to Flynn and the friendlier of the other dogs. Sometimes he was so tired of the courtyards that he'd stand just outside the gate – only just outside, and only in the early morning or dusk when he could be fairly sure of no one else being around. The weather was nothing much of anything, but always unpleasant. No breath of spring. Always wet, even if it wasn't actually raining. Steady seepage from the sky. And cold. Sometimes there was something that was almost snow and he learned a new word from Cecily: *flurry*.

He told Arthur stories to Nicholas. Morgana's wickedness was uncovered — Gawain was no fool — and she fled, realising that Arthur had the protection of Merlin's magic, cursing, *If I can't hurt you, I'll hurt the ones you love.*

'I'll hurt the ones you love,' Nicholas repeated, whispering, wondering, his eyes huge.

Then, in the early afternoon of the last day of April, dozing in his room, he heard a commotion below. Something being shifted, hefted, by the sound of it. Glad of any excuse for something to do, he slunk downstairs for a look. Two men were hauling a tabletop from the Hall towards the main door. That was all, then. Just as he was about to retreat, the men paused to re-align the tabletop and one of them glanced up at him there on the staircase, smiled and told him, 'A prince!'

Rarely was Rafael addressed by any man in the household, let alone with a smile, so he didn't immediately register the actual word or even its tone. Only as he was rustling up a smile in response did he realise: *prince*, and the relief with which it'd been said, the surprise, the delight.

'Now?' he managed. Already? More than a week before the due date? And, suddenly fearful, 'The queen?' The man had said nothing of the queen.

But he made the same gesture — eyebrows, shoulders — and said, 'Fine.'

*Really?* Could it really, in the end, have been so easy? Incredulous, they laughed together, Rafael and that man. And then he was gone, swept up in the passage of the tabletop through the doorway.

Celebrations, Rafael realised, watching the men go with the table: there would be food in the street. Somewhere upriver, far from all this kerfuffle, with her newborn son, was the queen. That small, tense, downcast lady. *See?* he said to her under his breath, willing it across the miles to her. *See? You did it. You did it fine.* It was over and done with, and early, too, but only by a week. Not too early. Perfect timing.

He wondered how Cecily was taking the news. She'd favoured the old days, as had most English people, but wasn't it different, now? Because there was a future, now, and even if it wasn't the one for which you'd wished, it was here and to be lived. No more waiting and wondering and worrying. Here was this future, against all the odds, and wasn't that – in a sense – to be respected? Rafael craned to watch the men with the tabletop: eager and intent, they were, getting on with it. They probably hadn't been in favour of the idea of a half-Spanish heir, but now the birth was to them a kind of miracle. And Cecily was a woman to get on with things. As long as the prince survived, the queen's reign would be secure, and a secure reign can relax. And a woman with a baby isn't going to burn people.

There was a future too, suddenly, for Rafael. The prince would be leaving, now, with all but the diplomatic staff. Even in the unlikely event that the sundial did still have to be built, Rafael was sooner or later – and not very much later – on his way home.

The Kitson kitchen rose to the challenge of getting food on to the tables at no notice at all; relished, even, this chance to show what they could do. Fleet-footed came the serving lads to replenish supplies, and their invisibility was itself a kind of display, accentuated rather than diminished by the occasional lapse, a momentary lark-about, a feigned lob of a bread roll. Out came platters of meat and trays of pies, and cheeses, some so fresh that they were still slick and milk-pale and had to be chopped into cubes rather than sliced. Family and servants from the Kitsons' and nearby houses stood reverently at the tables to make their selections, and their catching of crumbs in cupped hands looked like acts of tenderness. The Kitsons had dressed up for the occasion and looked self-conscious, the girls uncharacteristically demure in their finery. The Kitson boy with the unfocused gaze was unsettled and retreated almost immediately to the house with his elder sister.

Rafael and Antonio held back from the food, keen to partake but wary of being seen to muscle in. Rafael eavesdropped on speculation as to forthcoming festivities: pageants, processions, and wine to flow from the conduits. He spotted the two grooms he'd once overheard speaking so viciously of the queen — *bitch, witch* — and found it hard to believe, now. There they were, restrained and appreciative in helping themselves to the food, their faces benign, even comical: the long, red-tipped nose of one of them like a child's drawing.

*So, it's over,* Rafael dared to think: the people's suspicion of the queen, their loathing of her. No jubilation — nothing so extravagant — but people were conducting themselves with an absence of caution and dread where before they'd been cowed and belligerent. And what did they choose to do with their new-found freedom? Stand around chatting and sampling cheeses. Relief, Rafael realised: that was what it was, that was all it was. But it was everything. It was all they'd wanted, all they'd needed. Happiness was small and sweet, he realised, and each of them was rich today on a pocketful of it. Even he and Antonio were exchanging small talk which belied a profound gratitude. Because this was it, at last: this day of chatting and cheese-sampling was truly the beginning of their leaving England and going home.

A viol-bearing trio who'd appeared from a neighbouring house with an air of graciously fulfilling an obligation had no sooner bestowed bows to strings than the sky was cracked open by bell-ringing, and for a while everything was sky instead of street: the life of the street rolled up into each immense swing and enacted to each tuneful bang. Rafael and Antonio were able to cease attempts at conversation and give their attention as commanded to the great growling bells and those that were higher but faster and just as insistent. They were inescapable, those bells, and wherever Cecily was, she'd be pausing alongside everyone else and glancing skywards despite there being nothing to see.

Children, though, played regardless, tracked by dogs hopeful of dropped food. The Kitson girls and others in velvet tagged along with mere lockram-wearers, making their own alliances. Making and breaking them, as well as pacts and challenges, skirmishes and truces, all in the blink of an eye. Children busy being children. Even Nicholas.

*Nicholas?*

Yes, there he was – definitely him – across the street, with a boy of his own size, his eyes fixed on those of the boy but not with the usual challenge, *Leave me alone.* Quite the opposite: it was clear that he was holding the boy hard in his gaze and defying him to break away while he was talking to him. *Talking to him*: Nicholas, *talking.* Yes, definitely. Plain as day, even from where Rafael was standing. And the other boy was listening: that, too, was clear. Wide-eyed with scepticism, but listening.

*I'll hurt the ones you love*: Rafael remembered how Nicholas had repeated it, his imagination obviously captured.

Where was Cecily? But too late: her son was circling his companion and off, with a lolloping gait to portray himself horse riding. Rafael hadn't taken a breath, hadn't dared, but now he willed that other boy to follow, to join in. Nothing happened. Still lolloping, Nicholas disappeared from view behind a group of people, but the other boy remained where he stood and appeared to lose interest, glancing around but nowhere near the direction in which Nicholas had gone. Lost to Nicholas and whatever game he'd proposed. But then, suddenly, it did happen: the boy was in pursuit; he, too, galloped from view.

Francisco was always desperate for friends. From his first weeks, he'd seemed to recognise children as his own kind, craning towards them, enthralled and fascinated. The first time he'd ever laughed spontaneously was when a little girl skipped past him in the village square. He'd burst into giggles. Rafael longed to be able to give him friends, to make friendship happen for him. No one's happiness mattered to him as much as Francisco's, and the intensity of it was beyond anything he'd ever experienced or could imagine. Leonor's happiness was important to him, as was his mother's – as much as there could be happiness for his mother – but Francisco's was imperative, perhaps because it meant so much to Francisco himself, more than anything except the love and protection of his parents. As yet, the little boy understood nothing of mitigation, compromise, deferment. He was new to happiness and thrilled with it, but there was usually very little or nothing at all that he could do to bring it about for himself.

Once when he'd put Francisco to bed and all the good-nights had been said, Francisco added in his still-new, stilted, formal language, 'I will miss my friend.' Puzzled, Rafael asked, 'Who's your friend, darling?' and Francisco confided shyly but with obvious pleasure and pride, 'Daddy is my friend.'

The bell-ringing died down after an hour or so to become more doleful than celebratory, a distant tinkling instead of overhead clamour. Rafael and Antonio had braved the tables when some food remained to be had; now, the tables were crumb-littered, forlorn. Still no sign of Cecily. Rafael assumed she was helping in the kitchen, and, anyway, why would she want to stand around in the cold breeze? He was only doing so because he'd spent so long confined to the house, and because this would be one of his last evenings in London. He stayed watching, conscious of making a memory.

*I'll remember this.*

Here and there amid a mess of blue-black, gilt-edged cloud were patches of turquoise sky.

*This is what I'll take with me.*

A long, cold dusk wild with bells. The mustiness of beer and the spiciness of woodsmoke.

Firewood had been carried into the lane from the bigger houses and Rafael and Antonio headed for the bonfire with none of the reticence that'd been necessary for the food. Rafael was chilled to the bone and longed to be standing too close to the fire, barely enduring the heat. When they reached the newly lit pile, flames were already tearing into the wood, unleashed on it and racing to make nothing of it. Instantly, the spectacle – its grandeur – had him stupefied. The insubstantiality of fire, but its unsurpassed savagery: he stared into the flames to try to make sense of them, to track their wild work, but there was no sense to be made, the fire was hauling in the very air itself and turning it instantly into nothing. *And they put people in that.*

Later, back in his room, he wondered again where Cecily had been, all evening. His preoccupation the last few hours had been with memories, but now the future turned around and stared him down. Cecily would grow old here and he'd never see it. And surely he should be glad of that, but glad was the absolute opposite of how he felt. And even though he didn't understand it, he let himself feel that sadness and his utter desolation to be leaving her. He didn't understand it: he loved Leonor, didn't he? Yes, he did. He really did, often somehow in spite of himself. So, what was this, then? Well, it didn't matter what it was – he was going home, so it didn't matter how he felt. Already it belonged to the past. *This happened to me:* he nestled it away beneath his breastbone, this sadness of his, to take back with him to Spain. It was of no consequence. It would just have to be lived with.

That night, lying awake, he tried to remember if he'd been surprised when, after they'd married, Leonor hadn't got pregnant. Or had he expected nothing? Oddly, he really couldn't remember. He hadn't felt that much about it, he suspected. *So be it.* And perhaps, in a way, it'd been a relief. He hadn't been able to imagine being a father – that, he did remember. He'd paid lip service to the idea – *It'd be lovely if we were blessed* – but the truth was that life was good or certainly good enough. Better than he'd ever imagined it could be. No, that wasn't true – he had imagined it that good, of course he had. He just hadn't ever thought it'd happen. But it had. He'd got what he'd wanted: he'd married Leonor.

Except that he hadn't got what he'd wanted, had he. He'd wanted Leonor to be in love with him, and that hadn't happened. He knew it.

And sex: they did have sex, but not often, then even less often, then rarely. There'd been no problems in the early years of their marriage, no shyness from her, and she took pleasure in the act, liked to be on top. No, it wasn't her pleasure that was at issue, but his. There was nothing amiss physically, but he could never quite shake off the suspicion that his presence – the presence of him in particular, in person – was of no consequence to her. He felt he might've just as easily not been there: not him. He could have been any man. Certainly he never felt made love to, and that was what he wanted from her. She reached her climax with a muted sound, as if she'd been caught out and had to give in. It had the tenor of resentment, that small sound of hers, even though the climax was something she'd been striving for.

And then, one morning three years into their marriage, standing looking from their bedroom window, arms folded, she said, 'I'm going to have a baby.' Said levelly, businesslike, as if saying she were off to the shops.

'Baby?'

She didn't react; he'd got it right.

But she didn't have babies: that was a fact about her. Two husbands, twelve years of marriage and now thirty-six years old. And as yet, no babies.

She looked at him as he floundered – that faintly critical look of hers that she always had for him. In this, too, he was failing: she had big news for him and he couldn't take it in. 'Are you sure?' he asked, pathetically.

'Sure as I can be.'

They stared at each other.

'When?'

'October?' She shrugged: hard to know.

He said, 'Congratulations,' because wasn't that what was said, in these circumstances? He had a faint tingling in his stomach: everything was going to change and he didn't have the faintest clue how.

Arriving downstairs for breakfast, Rafael walked into an atmosphere that wasn't quite what he'd expected for a morning following celebrations. There was a blankness to people's faces and a carelessness in their demeanour – platters and cups slammed down and dragged across tables. He might've put the blankness down to hangovers if it hadn't been for that noisiness.

Antonio said, 'You heard?' and suddenly Rafael realised he was the only person who hadn't heard. Antonio enlightened him: 'No prince.'

Rafael's heart clenched before Antonio elaborated, 'No, I mean, there never was. Not yet. False alarm. Not born yet.'

But that was ridiculous. How could that have happened?

'Palace never confirmed.'

So, a rumour had gathered momentum as it rolled through London, and galloped away.

Antonio smirked, 'They'll have to do it all again.' But Rafael knew that'd be impossible. The innocence would be gone, the enthusiasm wouldn't be garnered.

After breakfast, he retreated to his room, not even having looked around for Cecily. He'd resolved that he was going to avoid her – he was going to *have* to avoid her – as best he could until he left.

For the next two days he was successful in avoiding her altogether, but she had a hand in his dreams. The first night, he dreamt they were at the market and she was with Nicholas at a stall, conducting her business, the very picture of competence, while he stood with one of the household dogs on a leash. The dog's neck was all muscle and he was rearing on his hind legs, desperate to be off. Rafael pleaded with the dog, appealing to him to behave, while passers-by gave him derisive looks because this was no place to bring a dog. And then the dog was loose, gone, the leash bouncing behind him. Barging through the crowd with spectacular disregard for obstacles. Boxes crashed to the cobbles and oranges rolled gaudily in the mud. Rafael was frantic; not for the dog – he'd be back – but as to how he could apologise enough to Cecily for shaming her. He woke and lay stunned, uneasy.

The second dream – what he remembered of it – was that he was travelling somewhere to see her. *Hang on for me, I'll get to you, I'll get there,* but the distance was daunting and time was folding down hard on him. He was on horseback but the terrain was sand and eventually he had to dismount and lead the horse. Each step – for both of them – was protracted. Then suddenly the terrain was rocky, every step jolting his spine up into the back of his head, and some of the rocks crumbled or rolled away underfoot, snatching his footing or that of the horse. His back was slick with sweat and he was shaking all over. Then came rain, drowning rain. The air itself was water and still they plodded on, Rafael and his horse, even though he felt as far away as he'd ever been and – worse – he couldn't go back because to turn around now would be as hopeless as pushing onwards. And then he woke, baffled and wretched.

How had this happened? He hadn't felt like this for years and he'd assumed he never would again. And to feel it for a colourless, frank-faced, almost eerily composed English-woman, of whom he knew next to nothing. Love was done with: that was how he'd felt, before Cecily. It had been a journey – the journey of his young life, long and exhausting – which had reached its destination in Leonor. What was happening made no sense. He loved Leonor. Didn't he? He'd just about always loved her; he'd spent his adult life yearning for her. He cringed to think how she'd look at him if she knew what he'd brought on himself with Cecily: amused, a little scornful, sceptical. Which was just how she always looked at him. He yearned for her, but she was forever retreating. There was no home for his heart in Leonor. He'd married her and had been stupid enough to think that was the end of it. In their married life, he was like a dog turning and turning, ready to make his bed, ever hopeful and trusting, but kept there turning, turning, turning.

It happened again, four days later. The news – if that was what it was – came shouted down the lane and Rafael, up in his room, heard it: 'A prince!' The proclamation delivered in a laughing yell, the clear implication of which was, *Really, truly, this time.* The first time in four days that Rafael had heard any reference from anyone to the previous mistake.

People were in doorways and on thresholds in a flash, but self-conscious, peering up and down the lane. Rafael hurried downstairs. The steward was already at the door and literally in an awkward position, his back to the open doorway as he tried to humour the restless Kitson crowd. Apologetic, he'd raised a hand, a palm, to hold them back. 'This evening, yes? This evening.' Asking them to bide their time, this time. If warranted, he implied, there'd be celebrations in the evening. By which time, presumably, there'd be confirmation or otherwise.

Someone had been sent to get confirmation, which did end up taking all day. Rafael kept himself to himself in his room until shortly before supper when he detected the return of the messenger. Downstairs in the kitchen, household servants had gathered by the door, obviously still curious but also clearly having lost heart during the day-long wait. Cecily was there ahead of Rafael and didn't see him. The bearer of the news was soaked, scarcely recognisable as one of Mr Kitson's secretary's assistants. Self-important but exhausted, he slung them the news – 'No' – as he pushed through on his way to whomever he was required to report to. Everyone dispersed without a word.

On his way back upstairs, Rafael reasoned that this was still before the due date, and first babies tend to be late, and it's easy, anyway, to get dates wrong. Impossible to get them right. And, anyway, the longer a baby stays inside, the better. The bigger, the stronger. *Stay safe. Rest up.* The queen would keep stitching. All those ladies around her, stitching, pacing themselves through the days, taking the tiniest steps – miles of them – around expanses of linen.

Rafael had been thinking, earlier, of the fastening on Cecily's cloak – how, one day long before he'd ever arrived, she'd have chosen that button and braid. He'd been thinking of her pleasure when she spotted them on the market stall – *Ooh, these* – and her anticipation on bringing them home. He'd been thinking tenderly, too, of her boots: just the fact of their existence, forever hidden away and unremarked upon. The *miracle* of their existence, was what he felt although he didn't understand why he felt that. And the little mole on her temple: she was so pale, but there was that tiny, rogue darkness, that small resistance to her pallor. The presence of the mole, the absence of eyelashes These had been some of his peculiar preoccupations – like dreams – during that long, empty day. He'd been thinking, too, of their walk together, revisiting it: her striding ahead of him, her freedom coming not from leaving the Kitson house but from walking into the darkness. How he'd admired her for that. How he'd envied her courage.

Every day, Rafael expected news but when the royal baby was two weeks overdue, the only news was that a woman was claiming she'd been asked to give up her own newborn boy. The story was everywhere in no time. An unmarried twenty-year-old daughter of a London apothecary: she was saying that two men and a lady had come to see her. Three times, they'd come, she said. She didn't know how or why they'd found her; they'd come from nowhere. They were kind, reassuring: the lady had said the loveliest things about the baby, *Oh, he's as bright as a button, isn't he! Look at that! — see how he looks into your eyes; he's keen to know what's going on, isn't he?* She spoke to the little mite himself: *You're keen to know what's going on, aren't you?*

You could still nurse him, they'd told the young woman. *Should* still nurse him. You should definitely do that. Keep him big and strong. They'd unswaddled him: *Look at those legs! You're a strong 'un, aren't you?* He'll be well looked after, they'd told her. He'll have a life better than you could ever imagine. A life of unimaginable splendour. You couldn't wish for more, for him, could you? Could you really turn that down?

But she did.

She's overwrought, was her own mother's word on it. Overtired. Confused. It'd never happened, the mother said. No one had visited.

She was in trouble for having made the claim. She'd been taken away for questioning.

A kitchenful of Kitson staff were listening to the story for the umpteenth time. Rafael was only there because he'd reached the limit of his endurance of the chill in his room. 'Arthur was a changeling, wasn't he?' Cecily piped up, addressing him over numerous heads. For two weeks, they hadn't exchanged more than greetings in passing. Startled, he didn't grasp what she'd just said. 'Your Arthur. You and Nicholas: your King Arthur.'

Still he didn't grasp it.

'Changeling,' she persisted. 'Changed. With another baby.'

'Was he?' Rafael managed. He had no memory of it. But there was so much to the story and he knew so little.

'Yes. You remember – Merlin took him and hid him. Took him from the old king and put him with someone else for safety. The man he knew as his father wasn't his father.'

He shrugged her off, but his heart was thumping him giddy and sick.

That night, he pondered again the circumstances of her widowing, something upon which he frequently dwelled. He pictured her first night alone with her fatherless child, putting him to bed and taking leave of the bedside, stepping back to be utterly alone.

He considered, too, the circumstances of her appointment to the Kitson household. Was it before or after her widowing? Did she enquire after a vacancy, or was one made for her? He recalled her change of duties when the Kitsons departed: the nonchalance with which she carried around her waist all those household keys. How she was called upon by senior staff, the varied and important duties with which she was entrusted. How she was deferred to in recognition of her capabilities. Her ease with everyone else in the house.

He wondered what she said last thing at night to her son, and with what kind of touch. A fingertip to the nose, perhaps. Or the palm of her hand over his heart.

He thought of how she pronounced 'Rafael'. Comically inadequate. A mere sideways swipe at it. And how, in turn, humour flashed into her eyes whenever he tried to say her name, although he couldn't for the life of him hear how he'd got it wrong.

That look of hers had often come for him as direct and secret as a dig in the ribs.

A few days later, someone came to London with a tale even less likely than that of the apothecary's daughter. An eighteen-year-old lad claimed to be the previous king and the answer to a lot of people's prayers. What else he'd been saying, if anything, Rafael didn't know, like how he was accounting for his supposed earlier death. Was he mad, or being manipulated, or was this a simple prank that'd got out of hand? By the time Rafael heard of it, it was over: the lad already apprehended and punished. Whipped, and his ears cropped, and paraded around the city with a placard proclaiming his crime. Antonio laughed, 'Well, he won't be doing that again in a hurry, will he?'

*But that depends, doesn't it.* 'Was he mad, or simple, or what?' Rafael asked.

'I don't know, do I.' Antonio sounded as if he resented the implication that there were distinctions to which he should have paid mind.

Rafael wondered if the queen had heard. Would she be told, or would she – in her condition – be protected? Or would she have demanded in advance, going into her confinement, to be told everything that was happening in the outside world? He suspected that her officials misinformed her or failed to inform her at their peril.

If it had been his own brother – someone claiming to be his own dead brother – how would he feel? It was different, of course – incomparable, in that nothing was at stake, let alone the ruling of a country – but still he dwelt on it. His brother would be thirty-seven. Even if – thirty-five years ago – the accident hadn't happened, he might never have reached thirty-seven. Something could have happened at any time. Any calamity.

Four years old at the time, Rafael had no memories of his little brother, but his absence had been alongside him for almost all his life. How would he feel if a man attempted to stride into that absence?

He imagined various scenarios: a man coming to town and telling tall stories; his brothers debating what to do and going to investigate. But it couldn't ever happen, because so many members of his family had been there, had seen Mateo die, had seen him dead. It could happen to a family of someone who'd gone missing or had been said to have died far away, but not to the Prado family, not in Mateo's case.

Rafael had had to be told that Mateo had died. He'd been outside, exploring, and when he came back inside, he'd had to be told. He had a clear memory of being told: standing there in the hall with his aunty bending down to him and speaking kindly, her eyes red. He was mortified that she was crying. He'd never seen an adult cry. He probably hadn't even known that adults could cry. He didn't remember if he'd listened to what she was saying. *Something has happened to Mateo.*

What it was that had happened, he didn't know. Whether he hadn't been told – *Something has happened to Mateo and he's gone to be with Jesus* – or hadn't listened, he didn't know. And he wouldn't have asked. In the face of his aunty's crying, he wouldn't have been ready with questions. Only later did it occur to him: What happened? How?

His mother was lying on cushions in the main room and looked to be staying there. At his own bedtime, he bedded down beside her, with no word from her nor any recognition from her of what he was doing. It was nothing so sophisticated as a decision. He just did it, probably because he didn't know what else to do. Someone put a blanket over him and there he slept. And there he slept, alongside her, every night for years. He only re-occupied his own room when he became sick, once, with a fever, and was moved.

All he'd ever heard his mother say of Mateo's death was, *It was God's will*, and, *He's with God now*. Rafael sensed she didn't believe it, that she said it because it was what she was supposed to say. What did she believe? That Mateo was somehow lost, was Rafael's guess, back when he was little. She stayed vigilant in the middle of the house in case he returned. And there she was, even now. She'd never gone back to her bedroom.

As for Rafael, how does one ask such a question? *How did my brother die?* So blunt a question itself was cruel. And to ask it would've revealed that he hadn't asked earlier. He had tried, when he was nine or ten. He'd chosen to ask his aunt, seeing as she was the only person who'd ever spoken to him about it. 'My little brother,' he asked her, 'did he suffer when he died?' But it didn't work: 'No, darling,' she said, smiling her appreciation that he should be mindful of his brother's pain. 'Thanks be to God, it was instant.'

In the end, he did it when he was nineteen, the day after his father died. He remarked to Pedro, 'You know, no one ever told me how Mateo died.' Pedro looked surprised, 'Didn't they? He was kicked by a horse. Kicked in the head. One kick.'

And Rafael nodded a kind of thanks.

A split-second, then. Only the tiniest adjustment to time would have been needed to stop it happening. He really did feel that. He really did feel that it ought to be possible.

For Francisco's life, he would bargain anything. The problem was, there was no bargaining to be had. If it was going to happen, it would happen. And then how would he continue to live his life? That was his terror: *How would I live with what might be asked of me?*

Antonio had come to Rafael's room. Not to say much. He'd complained about the rain and told of a minor accident that had happened in the kitchen. Then, 'Why hasn't the queen had her baby, yet?'

'I don't know,' said Rafael. Could the baby be dead, inside her? The doctors and midwives would know, wouldn't they? Francisco had kicked long and strong in his final weeks in the womb: he'd been alive for anyone to feel. Well, anyone whom Leonor invited to feel. Rafael had felt him and flinched, alarmed.

He had a headache. When would Antonio leave him alone? Before Antonio had invited himself in, Rafael had been pondering Cecily as a girl. Gawky, he imagined she'd been, and quick to learn, keen to please. He'd been wondering what hopes and expectations she'd had. Did she remember them now? He'd wondered what slights and injustices she might've endured in her girlhood. If he could have somehow got there first, before her, he'd have picked up her future and billowed it in the air to lose its creases: that's how he imagined it; that was what he would've liked to have been able to do for her.

He wondered if her husband had been her first lover. What man had first held her hand – did she remember?

He'd been recalling the way she once reached down absently for a passing cat and the cat's back had arched to meet her hand and prolong the touch.

He'd been thinking of how she was when she moved around the city, the few times he'd been lucky enough to be able to watch her in the streets. Her casual confidence. She wasn't a native Londoner; she'd had to learn that confidence. Her little braveries were lost to her, now, but he wanted to retrieve them and honour them. They mattered to him.

Had he ever loved Leonor like this? No, but it would have been impossible to love Leonor like this. She wasn't open to it, she wouldn't have welcomed it. She would have considered it an intrusion. Somehow she always managed to make him feel he was fawning over her. For his part, he had never felt loved by her. With Leonor, he'd had to love from a distance.

A week later, the queen had contractions. Another whole week had passed by, but now, at last, *contractions*: the word was everywhere and even if Rafael hadn't understood it, he'd have guessed from the sound, the hardness in the middle of it. There seemed to be no enthusiasm, but nor was there scepticism, because surely the time had come. This had to be it. If not today, then tomorrow. Certainly by the end of the week. There was a quickening of pace in the household, a gathering of wits, a meeting of cooks. The minimum was done in the kitchen to ensure that — be it in a day's time or three or five — they'd be ready. But then there was nothing: no more news, for five, six, seven days. Nothing.

Rafael kept to his room, waiting for word that he was to go. Whenever he saw Cecily, he did no more than greet her, despite, every time, deeply regretting the distance between them. But it had to be done. He'd retreat to his room, stung. He kept his door closed, not even answering Nicholas's knocks if he could get away with it. They'd reached Guinevere and Lancelot's bewitchment and he'd seen from Nicholas's frown that he hadn't been able to explain their falling in love nor why it was a betrayal of Arthur. *They wanted to be together, just the two of them,* he'd tried, *and poor Arthur felt very, very left out.*

The weather worsened. The sky was nothing but slabs of near-black cloud-cover sliding along in succession, no chinks of blue. Mostly, it rained hard all day. Sometimes there'd be an afternoon of no rain, but then the air was like wet cloth. A whole week of it, two weeks, now almost three. Surface water no longer drained away, there was nowhere left for it to go. The lane was under a couple of inches of floodwater. Inside, everything smelled damp: stone, wood, fabrics.

Antonio had told Rafael that an ambassador had arrived from Poland with congratulations because, it seemed, the first rumour had rolled as far as Poland but the retraction behind it had got lost along the way. He'd had to be received, of course. He'd been travelling for weeks in anticipation of a jubilant London. It was said that the prince and his men even laughed, if hopelessly, desperately: *I mean, you've got to laugh …* He had to stay, that ambassador. So he, too, now, was waiting.

Rafael was spending these last, desperate days trying not to think of Cecily. He'd have loved to switch one of her earlobes back and forth across his lips. And then he'd have lain his lips behind that lovely ear and stroked them along the channel beneath her jaw, down the flank of her throat into the dip at the base that deepened with each inward breath. He couldn't help but think of how poised she was and how, he felt, he might undo all that poise with a lick.

Antonio came to his door again, opening it uninvited and asking, 'D'you think the queen *is* pregnant?'

Rafael sighed. How could she not be? – this far down the line, this late into a pregnancy. He could understand there having been a mistake early on, but not now, and not with so many doctors and midwives involved.

He remembered when Leonor's pregnancy had continued into November. She was huge; he couldn't believe she'd grow bigger, but she'd said, 'The doctor says it'll be a while yet.' He must've looked impatient or irritated or something, because she warned, 'He's just taking his time, Rafael,' and that was him told.

'Is he all right, though? Is he moving?'

'*Yes.*' She sounded exasperated.

'Well, how much longer, does the doctor think?'

She'd shrugged. 'Weeks?' Then, 'It doesn't matter, as long as he's safe.' And duly, once again, Rafael was put in his place. *Of course, of course*, he rushed to agree.

His mother was unbothered: 'She's got her dates wrong, is all.'

Yes, that was all. And that'd be why she was so snappy with him, with his questions: she'd never want to have to admit to having made a mistake.

A new due date was issued: the fourth or fifth of June, which would be a full moon. But the fourth and fifth passed and nothing happened. Nor was there any change in the weather. The cloud-stuffed sky was featureless; obscenely so, it seemed to Rafael. An affront to anyone glancing skywards. No change in the weather and none in policy. Eight burnings, in the first two weeks of June, despite riots, one of which had London Bridge closed for a whole day.

Into the chilly air came the smoke from burning bodies, and it didn't blow away but was trapped under the lid of cloud. Rafael kept his window closed; he hated that he might be smelling it, breathing it, tasting it. Not only priests or bishops, now – but one day, two women who'd 'said things'. That was what Antonio had told him: 'They said things.' But to whom? Because someone must have turned them in.

One of the women had said that Jesus wasn't in the sacrament. *Is he here or is he not?* That was what she'd been asked at her trial. *It's a simple question.* She knew full well it was a simple question, one to which she had a simple answer: 'He isn't,' she'd said, with a half-laugh of disbelief, dismay. Clear enough, wasn't it? What was wrong with everybody? 'He's not there, is he,' and she shrugged an appeal to everyone in the room.

The English spoke their minds, that's how it seemed to Rafael. Not that the woman had been saying very much, really. Certainly, she hadn't considered herself to be saying very much – that had been clear from the shrug. The English were a practical people, with no love of magic and mystery. Their one legend was of a good king who did good deeds: just a boy, just a man from a homely background with the barest help from a magician at the beginning of his story and the very end. A magic sword: a piece of hardware, its handing over at the beginning and handing back at the end being magical, but in between it was just a sword. No wide-open spaces, in England, no far-off gazes, no dreaminess. Instead, an eye for detail – their gardens, their gold- and silverwork, their embroidery. No big ideas, no great statements. And there was no Jesus that the woman could see inside that sacrament, and she'd felt it needed saying.

But she was sentenced to burn for saying so, this twenty-seven-year-old mother of three. The date was discussed and fixed. Guards were requisitioned, a decision having been made as to the appropriate number. Men were appointed and funded to buy the wood and build the pyre. A stake had been found and fixed, a stool made, bindings bought and gunpowder funnelled into a little bag to tie around her waist in the hope of hastening an end to her suffering if the flames dwindled.

Mid-afternoon on the tenth of June, a messenger arrived at the Kitsons' to take Rafael back with him to the palace at Hampton Court. Rafael was having his afternoon sleep when a Kitson servant-lad knocked on his door to relay the message, and he woke in a panic. Surely this was his call home. All this time, almost a year, but now that the moment had come, he didn't feel in the least ready for it. He clattered downstairs only to discover the messenger relaxing over a substantial snack. Not yet having endured the river-journey between the city and the palace, Rafael didn't realise until later how welcome and how necessary that break would have been. Resenting the messenger's meandering chit-chat with the steward, he interrupted to ask if arrangements had been made, or needed to be made, for the transportation of his trunk. The messenger claimed to know nothing of any trunk, but advised Rafael to bring whatever he needed for an overnight stay because he wouldn't be able to make it back before nightfall. Rafael checked: nothing had been said about his trunk?

'No trunk. Just you.'

The journey took more than four hours. At least the craft had a canopy to protect Rafael and the messenger from the showers and the breeze which rattled and rustled it. No such provision for their four rowers, whose only respite consisted of frequent breaks to gnaw on hunks of bread and drain ale from flasks. Rafael had come unprepared, but the messenger was kind enough to offer a share of his own supplies, and sometimes Rafael took him up on it, feeling sheepish at his earlier impatience. The atmosphere between them was congenial but they rarely spoke, staring instead through the canopy's opening – politely avoiding the rowers' straining faces – as if there were something of more interest than mere, endless river life. Rafael looked at trees and the mess of clouds that was the sky. Birds. And the palace: he watched for the palace even when, he knew, they were miles away. From time to time, he closed his eyes and just listened to the oar strokes. What he didn't do was think. Just felt himself to be suspended there on the river between London and the palace. And that was something, at least, that did feel good: to be so far from London.

Eventually, they were travelling alongside high walls, which they did for a long time – the river arcing around the palace site – before arriving at the riverside gatehouse which was, itself, a little palace, pink-bricked and turreted, jade-windowed in the river-lit dusk. Their walk through yew-hedged, extravagantly shadowed grounds was welcome, despite his impatience, as a long-overdue stretch for his legs. He was taken with what he could see of the palace: so smart as to seem somehow stitched from brick.

They entered through a substantial double door, which was guarded, and on to a staircase which led up to a richly furnished gallery from where they were admitted, under the scrutiny of half a dozen more guards, into a room. An ante-room with two doors, the one through which they'd come and a second one. Someone high-ranking, then, he'd be seeing. It was a candlelit jewellery box of a room with no window or fireplace, nothing but floor-to-ceiling panelling, intricate and gilded. And a bench – similarly ornate – which the messenger helpfully indicated. Having just sat for almost four hours in a small boat, Rafael declined, ostentatiously pacing and rising on his toes to stretch his calf muscles. He gestured, *You?* The messenger smiled knowingly: he couldn't sit if Rafael didn't. Rafael's sitting down wouldn't solve the problem, because the bench was too small for both of them. So they stood, looking at the glorious panelling. Rafael turned to the wall and ran a fingertip around a tiny Tudor rose.

The mystery door opened, sending Rafael's heart into his throat, and a lady requested his presence. He'd been anticipating a man, a Spanish man, but here was an English lady. The messenger nodded cheerfully at him and was off, job done. Rafael followed the lady back into the room from whence she'd come.

It was dimly lit, in there — the window-hangings prematurely drawn — and the heat was an entity in itself. His skin swelled instantly, sticking to his shirt. Clusters of lighted wicks seemed not only illuminating but interrogative; he was dazzled. The room was scented, too, with the floral distillations worn by ladies. There they were, those ladies: there in the shadows, winks of jewels on headdresses as they turned to him. A year in London had made him wary of shadows, and even here he was prey to that unease. Even in a roomful of seated ladies. Perhaps because they were seated: their shapes collapsed, not quite discernible.

He followed the lady across a carpet so thick and soft that the sensation was of treading in warm mud. They were heading for a girl of twelve or thirteen who sat separately, alone on the floor, her back against the panelling, knees drawn up and arms around them. Puddled around her was lavish fabric, plum-dark, veined with gold. She was an intermediary, perhaps, to be sent scampering ahead somewhere in the next stage of this strange mission.

Then he realised that he was looking at *her*. That was *her* down there, looking back up at him. Not pregnant, he saw in the same instant, and his heart slammed to a stop before it rushed at her to find her like this, enduring what was befalling her. He knelt in front of her, not because she was queen – indeed, he'd forgotten the necessary preliminaries, offered none of the requisite verbal flourishes, said nothing – and not as one should kneel to a queen, but lower still, sitting back on his heels as if to tend to a child. Her gaze was on his; stark. 'How much longer?' came from her, as a kind of growl.

She couldn't be sitting here like this, knees up, if she were in the last stage of pregnancy. Or perhaps she could; perhaps she was just small. He didn't dare take another look. Some women would be smaller than others in their pregnancies. She was asking him, *How much longer?* The question to which no one, it seemed, had an answer. But there was, he realised, something he could tell her: 'My son was very, very late.' He was shocked to hear himself say it, but also thrilled.

The tiniest spark of interest from her, with an understandable wariness. Carefully expressionless, she asked, 'How late?'

'Two months.' For the first time ever, he was glad of it; he believed it or believed in its persuasiveness and loved it, and was grateful for it. He watched her wanting to believe him, and he understood. After all, he'd believed it once himself.

All the same, she checked, her tone properly incredulous: 'Two months?'

'Two months.' Leonor's pregnancy had lasted eleven months: that was the story. That was what he had been told.

He was repeating what everyone had been told and had seemed to believe. Repeated here, it had a purpose: to help her endure what she had to endure.

She entered into it, her tone hopeful: 'And he was fine?' But she knew he was.

Rafael confirmed what she knew: 'My son was fine,' and his insides tingled at the saying of it. *Fine*: the glorious inadequacy of the word. That was what had mattered, in the end: that Francisco had been fine. End of story. Happy ending.

Her eyes slid to one side, but unseeing: just to relinquish him and pursue her own thoughts. Then back to him. 'Were you worried?'

He hoped she didn't see him flinch. The question was genuine, he sensed, as always with her. She didn't require him to say yes, to join her in her anxieties. Solidarity was of no interest to her. What mattered to her was the truth, and he could answer truthfully. 'No.' What he didn't tell her was that he hadn't been worried because he'd trusted in Leonor, and he'd been stupid to do that. Leonor hadn't seemed worried, and he'd taken his cue from her. He'd trusted her. He'd had to. And, anyway, it was the story he was being told: late, late, late, later, a bit later, and later still. And so it had crept up on him: always late, which he'd never questioned. Not if late, but how late. He tried to remember how he'd explained it to himself, how he'd lived with it, and said to her, now: 'God moves ...' *in mysterious ways*. And, with a shrug, 'Women ...' mysteries aplenty. 'And dates ...' difficult. In Leonor's case, though, there'd been the unmistakable physical manifestation of a pregnancy. And that wasn't the case here.

But she took it, his story, with the faintest nod of acknowledgement. It was a good thing to have done, he told himself.

It was to help her. It was the only thing to be done. And that might have been how Leonor had felt, he supposed. *Leonor*, his heart called across more than a thousand miles and back four years. Four years ago, he should've been kneeling in front of her, looking her in the eye. *Leonor*, he could have begun. He should have taken the lead from where he was, outside the calamity into which she was locked. He should've done it then, when it was a lie laid over their lives and not yet stitched tight into it.

Because no pregnancy lasts eleven months.

Something was wrong, here, he knew. What he didn't know was what, or how wrong. And there were so many other people who were better placed to know: attendants and midwives and physicians. People who undressed her, people who examined her. The people who'd know: it was their business to tell her, when they knew. And when that time came, whatever it was that they had to tell her, she'd be ready for them, he was certain of it. She'd hear them. This was a queen who relished the truth, for whom nothing mattered but the truth – who lived her life to pursue it – and had always shown mercy to those who admitted it. They wouldn't be cheating her of the truth, surely, when she was in such dire need of it. They'd achieve nothing by it.

There was a relenting of her stare, an appeal – he felt – to him: *How bizarrely similar our lives*, it said, her look. He thought so, too, and – despite the circumstances – was glad of it.

'My husband –' she whispered, but there was no reticence; indeed, the hiss of the whisper gave it a fierceness '– he despairs.'

Rafael didn't doubt it. Her husband and everyone else.

'He's been so patient.' She needed that understood, and Rafael nodded. Understood, too, though, was an unspoken *but*. She hadn't moved a muscle. Could there possibly be a live, full-term baby inside her? Would she be able to sit here like this, if there was? Surely the baby would be testing its strength, revelling in it, dragging her around in its wake.

'He's ready to leave,' she whispered, 'my husband. Whatever happens, now, he'll go.' The same level delivery. She said it in order to face it, he sensed, to hear it said aloud. The studied absence of inflection made him uneasy: the effort it must've taken her. And it gave no clue as to whether or how he should respond. And he, too, was ready to go. She could have been speaking about him: *traitor, deserter*. He sat frozen as she was, buttocks on his heels, hands on his thighs.

'Ten weeks,' she said, 'ten weeks since I've seen him.' And her eyes moved, just a little, as if seeing beyond him. She was seeing nothing, really, though, he felt.

Ten months: ten months since I've seen Francisco and Leonor.

'I miss him.' Again, no complaint; just the fact of the matter. 'I write to him, every day. All day, I keep a letter going.' Like a fire, he thought. 'I know what people think' she frowned – 'there can't be anything for me to say, being stuck in here. But there's always something to say, isn't there?'

He didn't doubt that she always had something to say. He felt that he knew what she was going to say next. His lower lip was skewered beneath an incisor, he realised; he made himself let it go.

She had at last dropped her gaze, and spoke to her knees. 'He doesn't write to me.' Carefully free of recrimination. 'Not unless there's business to be dealt with. But men don't, do they? Write. Find things to say.' She corrected herself. 'Most men.'

Then, looking up again: 'He does ask me if I'm well. Whenever he writes, he asks if I'm well. And I am,' she said, as if it had just occurred to her and surprised her but somehow didn't particularly please her. 'I am well.'

And she looked it, or didn't look unwell. Rafael found himself taking a breath, as if he were about to speak; it seemed time for him to speak, although he had no idea what he'd say. But she was already saying, 'I'm glad I never escaped to Spain. My brother's men were plotting to have me killed, but I could've escaped to Spain. It was all planned. I dressed as a maid and went one night with Mrs Dormer to the boat. But I turned around. I had God's work to do here.' She sighed hugely, and closed her eyes. 'Still do. It's still all to do.' More – much more – than she'd bargained for, he realised. Suddenly, her eyes opened, shining. 'And I do it.' Said like a pledge.

But she didn't know what was being done on her behalf, in her name, while she was closeted in here. Rafael did know, and knew he should say so. The English people were shut away from their queen's mercy. The Church was taking advantage of her incapacity, and losing her the respect and trust of her people. *Speak*, he willed himself.

But she was the one who was speaking, daring with round-eyed wonder: 'Has God abandoned me?'

There was terror and dread in the question, but also sheer wonder at the notion of a Godless existence. All the rejections of her life, they'd been dealt with, lived through, endured, but this … The question had seemed to come unbidden. But it was what was inside her, this dread, he saw. It was this with which she was living. It was her life.

He had no answer for her. There was nothing he could say to her, nothing anyone could say, and she knew it. And so they stared at each other – neither of them, he felt, daring even to breathe.

Then, 'I do his work,' she said again.

He did speak, he dared. 'How hard, for you to know what to do.'

But she simply said, 'I do what's right, Mr Prado,' and sounded calm, her previously widened eyes softened. She didn't seem to have heard the doubt in his voice. He was confounded, said, 'The burnings?' Said it gently, and said no more. Did she even know there were burnings? Let alone of women who had babies at home.

'Mr Prado.' She said his name with feeling, as if she felt for him, for his ignorance. 'My subjects have hard lives. They work hard – so hard – and for what?' Her voice was so low that he could hardly hear, but the words were clearly enunci-ated. 'There's never enough food. And they're cold, summers as well as winters. Sick, a lot of the time. In pain. And their children, Mr Prado: their children die. They have to watch their children die.' He flinched but she held his gaze in hers. *Understand this.* 'And there's nothing I can do about it. I'm their queen, and there's nothing I can do. I can hand over some coins – I do, Mr Prado, of course I do – and they'll buy food and firewood, but I can't feed everyone in England, I can't keep everyone warm, and I can't cure anyone's sickness. All the coins in my kingdom won't stop a baby from dying, if that baby is going to die.'

She waited for him to look back up at her. 'What my people do have, in their lives, Mr Prado – if they're lucky, and I dearly hope they are – is love. The love of their parents, spouse, friends, and – God willing – children. But they die, those parents, the spouse, the friends, a child. They go,' she reminded him, gently. 'But there's someone else in every life, above and beyond all this, who doesn't ever go, and that's God. God's love, Mr Prado,' she urged, in her harsh whisper, 'His infinite love. And when a life is over, that's what's there: the love of God. My people trust to that. They can go to God. God is the light in all this darkness, and at the end they'll be reunited with their loved ones for all eternity in His presence.' She paused; then, as if – regrettably – having to break something to him: 'That's what heretics take from people, Mr Prado: God. They take advantage of people's innocence. Most of my subjects haven't had the luxury of schooling, and heretics take advantage of that. They tell them they can ask questions and know the answers, which appeals to people with no learning. It's a cynical play to their one weakness. Faith is not for questioning, Mr Prado,' she appealed, barely audible. 'That's not what faith is. You question, and your faith is broken. Broken before you know it, and never, ever able to be mended. You break a person's faith and you break them, you make them nothing. Heretics make nothing of people, Mr Prado – their lives, their loves, their hopes, what very little they ever had or could hope for – and they do it *just because they can.*'

He felt sick – hot, dizzy, unable to crouch for much longer.

'The cruelty of it, Mr Prado,' she hissed, aghast. 'The callousness. The ...' she frowned, searching for a word '... disregard.' Said as if it was the very worst that could ever be said and, hearing her saying it like that, he knew it, too: there could be nothing worse than a person's utter disregard for a fellow human being.

'They must … *be gone*. Every last trace.'

He shifted, swallowed, and returned – a little – to himself. And it occurred to him: why, though, was it wrong to question Christ's presence in the sacrament? How exactly did that turn other people from love? He tried: 'Some of these people, though, they just –'

'No,' she was emphatic. 'No. Not "just". Never "just".' As if he were naïve.

It was she, though, who didn't understand. She was so far removed, now, from her people. He had to try again: 'But –'

'There is no "but".' She spoke solemnly, as if reminding him. 'We are all in danger. If faith unravels, then there is no faith and we're all lost. We have to keep God with us, keep close to God. Faith is not for questioning,' she repeated, and he knew these were her final words on it: 'You question faith, and it's broken, and it lets the darkness in.'

He'd passed the night in a room in a gatehouse which was comfortable and peaceful enough, but he'd slept poorly, his restlessness having less to do with the unfamiliar surroundings than his fear for the queen. He'd seen that she was in the grip of her confinement and, until the hold it had on her was broken, nothing would change. It had to end soon.

In the morning he found the Spanish office and was handed a payment that was insufficient for the building of his sundial. The officials had clearly lost all interest in it. He was going home, was all that he could get them to tell him, and they'd send for him. The office was mostly packed up. There were no letters for him but, he was told, a ship from Spain had been lost a week or two ago in the Bay of Biscay. On his way back to the river, he found the big astronomical wall clock that had been built by the old king's clockmaker. Blue and gold, busy with roman numerals and zodiac signs, it displayed the hour, the day, the month, the number of days since the beginning of the year, and the phases of the moon. He read the time as being between nine and ten on the eleventh of June, and the moon was on the wane.

He was back at the Kitsons' by early afternoon. He'd only been in his room for a few minutes when he glimpsed from his window a group of the Kitson servants hurrying away down the lane, Cecily and her son among them. Intrigued, he watched for almost an hour for their return; then, seeing them coming back, nipped downstairs. They filed in, grim-faced – a cold was doing the rounds – with only Cecily sparing him a glance. He responded with a quick smile, but a hello was more than he could have safely said. A hello would have spoken loud and clear of a week in which they hadn't spoken at all. A week in which he'd altogether avoided her. If he said sorry, he was pretty sure she'd come back with, *What for?* She wouldn't make it easy for him, and why should she? His nerve failed him, yet he didn't feel able to move away.

She was busy with Nicholas's cloak. But then came a pointed, 'Look, Nicholas: it's Rafael,' which Nicholas obeyed, if warily. Even a four-year-old could detect the atmosphere. She told her son to run along, said she'd be following soon.

To Rafael she said, 'They had news, these men we've just seen.' She spoke as if he were somehow making her do so. She said, 'I wanted to hear it for myself. To make up my own mind.'

As to its likely truth, he understood her to mean. She'd said it as if he were the one telling her lies. 'I'm sick of rumour.' Again, as if rumour were somehow his fault.

Everyone else had drifted away; they were stranded alone together.

'And they were good men,' she insisted, as if to counter some contradiction from him. 'Serious, thoughtful men.' As if those qualities were rare; and perhaps they were, but why say it as if he were disputing it?

He had to ask, 'Who?'

'These two men,' she said. 'They have a job to do.'

*Unlike me?*

'They've come to London with the ashes of a man who was burned. William Pigot: that was the man. Burned for saying that we should be able to read the Bible in English. Those two men think we should know. And you know what? *I* think we should know, too.' She folded her arms, hard, staring at him. 'All of us.'

Even a four-year-old? Nicholas had been there, wherever she'd gone to hear those men speak. How much had he understood?

'Those men, they can read and they say the queen wrote a letter last week to the bishops, telling them to work harder at burning Protestants.' She'd lowered her voice, but it hadn't softened; if anything, it sounded even more furious as a whisper. 'Get more of them arrested, convicted, burned.' Her eyes glittered with defiance. 'You think I'm a Protestant, don't you, Rafael, to speak like this?'

He knew he should deny it.

She threw a hand in the direction of the kitchen. 'All of us here: Protestants – that's what you think, isn't it? But no one here's a Protestant,' she warned him. 'No one here's a Catholic. In England, Rafael,' she spelt it out, 'no one cares. God is God, and, beyond that, no one cares.' As if she were threatening him, she said, 'People, is what we are. Human beings.'

Still, before he knew what to say, she'd added, 'The queen thinks her baby won't be born until she's burned all the "heretics".' She quoted the word, sceptical, derisive.

She was throwing all this at him as if everything were his fault. Certainly he hadn't been acting well towards her, but he wasn't responsible for any of this. She was angry at him for everything. How easy for her. She spoke as if he were contradicting her, when he'd had no wish to do so, but now, cornered, he was coming close. He could question the veracity of that so-called letter to the bishops, but that would be quibbling. Instead, he simply said, 'You think I like this because I'm Spanish?'

It took her aback. Plainly put, it was clearly ridiculous.

'Spaniards are Catholics,' she blustered.

He couldn't believe it of her, especially not after what she'd just said. 'Catholics!' He dismissed it, his anger a match for hers. 'It's the same in Spain,' he insisted. If he was Catholic, it was because there wasn't anything else to be in Spain. But she wouldn't understand that, would she? She knew nothing of how he had to live: head down, watching his step. His turn, now, to spell something out: 'I am from a country where the Church is Catholic.' He added, 'I don't care what *England* is. Why would I care?'

And that was his mistake: he saw at once that he'd said something very wrong.

'Yes,' she countered, 'why would you care? You'll be gone in a week or so, and you'll never be back. It's nothing to you, is it.' And then she was off, leaving him standing there, watching her go. Her laced-up back, the tied-up back of her cap.

He returned to his room. He'd been getting more and more tired since he'd arrived here. Never had he imagined it possible to be so tired. He lay down on the bed. Somewhere below him were footfalls scattered in someone's wake on a stretch of stairs; voices here and there, sounding like idlings on a keyboard.

Darkness must have coincided with his own brief oblivion, because he woke in the early hours, the too-early English hours, and lay looking into the light that wasn't yet light and listening to the silence which – solid – seemed to be listening back. Inside him, pain held its one blaring note. Because Cecily had turned and walked away from him.

*Cecily* – he willed it to her   *Don't hate me.*

But she did. She did. He knew it.

*Please, Cecily. There's nothing I can do. You know there's nothing I can do. If there was anything else I could do …*

But he sensed her there, across the house, locked hard away from him, even in her sleep.

And that was why, a little later, he came to be standing outside her door. Not to wake her, but just to be near her. That was all he knew. *Cecily, if there was anything I could do.* He could be here, even if she never knew it. Because she'd never know it, his soundless trip across the house tucked away into these smallest of hours.

It was easy. The house had been abandoned, surrendered to night-time, and, lacking an audience, it lacked its usual glamour and failed to intimidate him. It hadn't cared to stand in his way, had turned a blind eye and let him get away with it, floorboards mute.

And here he was, on the stairs outside Cecily's room. He had no idea what he was doing; just that he couldn't have stayed in his room. Here he was, keeping a vigil at a door on which he'd never knock.

Looking at it, that unyielding English oak door, he recalled something from boyhood that his father had taught him: how to touch a door if there's danger of fire on the other side. Not as you'd touch anything else, with fingertips, palm; not open-handed, but with the back of your hand, the briefest touch of your bones to the wood. And then, if your hand burns, instinct bounces it back to you. Open-handed, the instinct is to touch, reach, hold on if only for the most fleeting of moments, but by then the damage would be done. He sighed. *Look at you, just look at you*: not even able to touch her door, not even to touch it. *Just touch it*. He put his fingertips to the cold wood. Then his palm, then his forehead. And there he stayed, for a while. And then he turned and laid himself back against it, and some time later he slid the length of it, squatted at the foot of it and hugged his knees. There in the darkness, where he didn't have to explain himself, he was hers.

*I can at least have this: nothing though it is, I can have this*. He'd come to her door in the hope of quelling his pain, quietening its clamour, but the feeling he had was of something being worked beneath his skin, shocking and to be endured. He was lodged here on this tiny landing and she was behind that door, in her room, in her life with her child, in the room that was her home. He'd had a life, before all this, a life that had been his and, yes, it'd had its problems and imperfections, but he'd lived in it; it'd gone on, day by day, year by year, a life of his own with a life of its own. But now, for the past nine months, it hadn't; it'd stopped, and he had no idea if it was still waiting for him.

He pictured Francisco asleep, how during his first year he used to sleep on his back with his arms thrown above his head, as if in protest. At about a year old, he was able to turn himself over, and he'd fold his knees up beneath him. He'd be kneeling, prostrate, in his sleep, and although he was folded up, this new position of his shared something with the earlier, open one: a fierceness of intent. Latterly, he'd slept as anyone else would: on his side, at the ready for waking.

'When you're dead,' he'd asked Rafael, 'can you move your arms?' He simply couldn't grasp the notion of lifelessness.

'When we're dead,' he'd said, 'can we be buried next to each other? Because then we can cuddle.'

Rafael knew he wouldn't need to shift for quite a while — the household was at least an hour away from its very first stirrings. He gave himself up to the silence which rose around him and hissed in his ears. Only a little later, though, came the chirping of shoe-leather on flagstones below him, and then the scuff of it on wood, on a stair. He scrambled up a few steps, around the corner, and stopped. The person was heading up the stairs. The person was *Cecily*: that was the pitch and rhythm of her footfalls. His own breathing seemed noisier than her tread; his heart, panicked, was throwing punches at him and thwacking blood into his ears. He was shaking so much that standing was hard, but a crouch would risk a crack from his knees. Half-standing, hands on knees, his noisy breathing was amplified, thundering back up at him.

Her door opened, then closed, and the silence down there washed in as if never displaced. He, too, stayed exactly where he was, didn't dare move a muscle, didn't dare even straighten. And there he remained, waiting for her to settle, to sleep. And beginning to make sense of what he'd heard.

He'd been outside her room for some time – and she'd been wearing her boots. Night-chill drifted up the stairwell like smoke. She'd been outdoors. She'd come back from somewhere in the small hours, the very smallest hours. So: an assignation. It had to be. *Got you*: a victory of a kind. He should try to savour it. *You thought I'd never know, didn't you,* but he'd laid her secret bare. Perhaps not quite so much a fool.

Someone else.

But of course, he'd known, really. Hadn't he? Of course he had. He'd known, all along, but hadn't wanted to face it. And now there it was, facing him, staring him down. Behind him lay the year he'd spent in Cecily's company, now shadowed. If he so much as turned around, he knew, he'd be going back through it, conversation by conversation, even smile by smile, to trace that shifting shadow.

He was still breathing hard, the air turning to nothing inside him as if he were ruining it by the act of breathing. Eventually, he relented and sat down, breathed a little easier, at an utter loss. *Now what?* Bed, he supposed. There was nothing else for it.

Back in bed, he gave himself a talking-to. So, Cecily had someone, and so what? He had no claim on her. Nothing could ever have happened between them. What business was it of his how she spent her nights? Couldn't he be adult about this? She was a free woman, free to do as she wished. And he should be happy for her.

He'd imagined a misunderstanding between them, but in fact she'd had no expectations of him. He could simply walk away from her and go home.

He wondered about the man whose bed, somewhere across the city, was warmed and scented by Cecily. He wondered if she loved him and how long it'd been going on.

Dawn deepened into day. He got up and got through it. At mealtimes, he didn't so much as glance at Cecily, although her presence persisted like a thumbprint. Night dawdled but finally began sighing into the house around nine and he took it up on its desultory offer, headed for bed. He was desperate for sleep but it played with him and at first light he realised he was lying there listening for Cecily and her surreptitious return. If he was right about what she was up to, she'd be doing it again. Her return to her room had sounded well practised.

He lay there hearing nothing. He'd have to be closer to her room. He got up and dressed, not keen to risk discovery at large in the early hours in his nightgown. He'd be better prepared for discovery, fully clothed. He listened hard for her ahead or behind him, taking up position in a stairwell opposite hers.

Once there, though, he woke to the futility of what he was doing and its shamefulness. What on earth did he hope to learn? He couldn't bear to imagine her expression of horror and loathing if she came across him. But he'd come here and he was trapped now, for fear of bumping into her on his return. So he stayed in the stairwell, cold and cramped and frightened, until what he judged to be close to five: beyond the time she'd risk a return, but just before anyone else in the household was around. Back in his room, he threw himself into sleep, only surfacing after midday.

The following night, he slept through, relieved to find himself delivered straight from sleep into a fully fledged morning. The night after that, he was unable to stop himself resuming his watch and felt cheated when he discovered nothing. The next night, sleep kept him in its grip until morning and then only reluctantly relinquished him, dogging him all day. The next two, he was awake before four and going about the grim business of surveillance, and it was on the second of these that he witnessed her return again.

Later that day, Nicholas tried his luck at Rafael's door. It was just as it had been, almost a year ago: the boy peering into his room. But Cecily's reprimand – '*Nicholas!*' – from the foot of the stairwell was very different, this time, in tone. She sounded aggrieved. Her son was placing her in an awkward position. Nicholas withdrew from the doorway, and Rafael could've left it at that, but he didn't; he went and looked down the stairs, and there they were, Cecily shepherding him away, just as she'd done that first time. No smile, though, from her, this time, and its absence hurled itself at him. He stood his ground; the two of them staring at each other, at a loss not just for words but even how to look at each other. Then she sighed – genuine, he felt, the sigh was, the sadness and exasperation of it – and offered an explanation for her son's intrusion: 'You were his good friend.' Carefully expressionless except for the faint emphasis on 'good friend': a quotation, a reminder: *I am your good friend.*

She was right, of course. He and Nicholas had built an odd little relationship of sorts, but lately Rafael hadn't been around for him. *I'll hurt the ones you love.* And regardless of what Nicholas felt about that, his mother would be furious. Certainly Rafael would be, if he were in her position. But for now she was withholding that anger, withholding everything, in fact; just staring at him.

She was right, but also it wasn't the whole truth. Neither of them was saying what needed to be said and – again – she was going to walk away. Someone had to say something, and it didn't look as if it'd be her. So, he made the move: opened his mouth and began to speak even though he didn't know how to say it. What came out was, 'There is someone you love,' and it sounded odd even to him.

Unsurprisingly, she didn't understand; she frowned, perplexed.

'At night.' He had to push on, to try to make himself understood. 'There is someone you go to at night.'

The child looked up at her, and Rafael experienced a twinge of guilt.

Realisation came like focus into Cecily's eyes. She didn't deny it but whispered, amazed, 'You're a spy.'

He had to translate before it hit him. *How could she think that of him?* 'No –'

'You're a spy!'

'No!' He'd had to shout her down, despite the risk of scaring the child. 'I was awake,' he insisted, 'and you come back …' He stopped, repeated it even though he knew it was a peculiar phrase: 'There is someone you love.'

'No.' So, here came the denials, tight-lipped. 'No, that's not it.'

But he could see the truth of it on her face. 'It is it.' Why deny it? 'Cecily,' he appealed, 'don't lie to me.'

She opened her mouth to deny it again – he could see the denial in the making – so he said again, much louder, 'Don't lie to me!'

And at that very moment, to Rafael's utter horror, Antonio sauntered past Cecily. *What the fuck was he doing there?* A deliberate saunter, it was. Even allowing for any self-consciousness, any awkwardness he might be feeling, it was outrageous, accompanied by a champion smirk. Rafael suspected he'd been on his way to badger him about something and had stumbled upon the situation – *but he could've retreated, couldn't he?* Why *saunter past*?

Both Rafael and Cecily bit back on any more words as they watched him go; he took his time going and every footstep put the two of them firmly in their place. When she judged him to be sufficiently far away to be unable to overhear, Cecily looked up the stairs again and Rafael saw that she had something to say. He saw it coming but he could never have anticipated what it was. She delivered it as if it were a reminder: 'There is someone you love, Rafael: your wife.'

And with that, and before he could find an answer, she was gone.

Perhaps only five minutes later, Rafael heard Antonio's footsteps on the stairs. He couldn't believe he had the audacity, and he didn't respond to the knock on the door. He wouldn't have answered to anyone; he was in no fit state, his heart floundering. Antonio, though, let himself in and came in saying, appreciatively, 'That was some row you were having with Cecily.'

Rafael got up and crossed the room to show him the door. 'You know nothing of what was going on between Mrs Tanner and me.' Antonio laughed at that, disputing it with a look and saying, 'Oh, but I think I do.'

And before either of them knew it, Rafael had hit him, and Antonio was reeling, bowing, cupping his face. *Oh, Jesus.* What had he done? *Jesus, Jesus,* had he injured him? Antonio straightened up and Rafael was swamped by panic and disbelief that he'd got himself into this position, because now there was going to be a fight and he had no idea how to fight. For want of knowing what else to do, he stood there to take it, whatever it was that was coming. But to his surprise, nothing came. Nothing from Antonio but a look of utter contempt: that was all he was doing, and – Rafael understood – all he was going to do. *Hit me*, Rafael found himself pleading silently. *Don't look at me like that.* But he did, he kept on looking at him like that until he turned and left.

Francisco had finally been born eleven days before Rafael's own birthday, and it was this proximity of his son's birthday to his own that had eventually tipped him off. Not, though, until his own birthday had come around. For eleven days, the first eleven days of Francisco's life, Rafael was oblivious. When his own birthday came around, the fact of it was acknowledged – *Your birthday!* – but otherwise it made little mark in a household reeling from a birth. Quite properly so, Rafael felt. He was glad to let it go. Birthdays in his household, from now on, were going to be for someone else. That afternoon, though, in his son's nursery, he reflected briefly on how different his life had been a year ago, and that was when he realised: his last birthday had been the last time he and Leonor had had sex. He'd known it'd been a long time ago – of course he had – but only now, sitting there beside his sleeping son, did he realise exactly how long. Until that moment, it'd been so long that he'd lost track; it'd been as long, he'd assumed, as a pregnancy. But it was in fact a year ago. Over eleven and a half months before Francisco was born.

Francisco's nursemaid was across the room and Rafael was terrified she'd see his realisation. So physical was it, to him, the jolt, that it seemed entirely possible she would've heard it falling into place. Perhaps she already knew. Perhaps everyone knew. Did everyone know? He couldn't believe that he hadn't known.

He could have cried, to feel so exposed. A cry for someone to make it go away. His mother, even. That was how desperate and helpless he was.

He understood nothing: that, too, was how he felt. How had it happened? When, why, *with whom*? Had Leonor been waiting for him to put it all together? Had he been slow? Would he ever have realised, had it not been for his birthday? A long time, was all it would ever have been. And even though she knew the truth of the situation, perhaps she herself didn't remember this exact date. It'd been his birthday, after all. Perhaps, then, she hadn't expected him to realise.

But even if it were possible, that it was never to be spoken of, would she one day throw it at him? One day, she would. And then it could never be unsaid and their world would be different and, with a mere handful of words, he would no longer be Francisco's father. Francisco would no longer be his son.

Her lie had already gone on for so long. It was made of so many moments in which she'd actively upheld it: all those moments, and each one of them a betrayal, and so many more to come. He was in awe at the depth and breadth of her betrayal; he couldn't begin to fathom it. He felt surprised, too; he'd never considered her duplicitous, nor interested enough in sex to take a risk. Well, he knew nothing, did he. That was clear.

He knew that she'd lied and was continuing to lie, but, really, that was all he knew and that was nothing. Because he didn't know who.

But he did know. Because there'd recently been another anniversary: that of Antonio's arrival in the household as his stonemason. Antonio had seemed like a good idea, at the time. He'd come highly recommended for his masonry, and it was clear in no time that those recommendations were more than justified. But it wasn't just with his work that he'd made an impression. He'd burst upon the household of women: a strong, good-looking man in his early twenties, young enough to be made a pet of, yet also all man. Rafael had been dismayed to see it: a man who adored to be adored; and they did, those women, as if to order, in the early days.

All except Leonor, of course, who could be trusted never to be in thrall to a man so full of himself. Antonio steered clear of her in those early days. She made him uneasy, Rafael knew. Antonio wouldn't be one for difficult women. Rafael suspected that he'd never had to win a woman over and hadn't learned how.

What was odd, though, was that they had gone on to form a kind of friendship, Leonor and Antonio, within a few weeks. Or an alliance, perhaps. Rafael had been aware of it, though he hadn't credited it with any importance. He'd come across them together, sometimes, and when she looked away from Antonio, her gaze would alight on Rafael but not take him in. So different from her habitual look of appraisal. Absorbed, she was. Elsewhere. She and Antonio were outsiders together in the household – she still saw herself as such, Rafael knew. Antonio, too, seemed different when he was with her. None of his usual ebullience. An impression was all it was: that was Rafael's suspicion. But, still, different, which implied she was singled out. And she'd have responded to that, Rafael knew. In her eyes, Antonio was true with her alone, and she'd have liked that. Of course she would have. Anyone would.

Rafael had scoured his memory but there'd been no one else around the household at that time. He'd never wavered, from those first moments in the nursery, in his suspicion of Antonio.

And from then onwards, he'd watched them intently on the few occasions they were in each other's company, but he detected nothing. Leonor was by now – he was sure – treating

Antonio with the faint contempt with which she treated her husband. Whatever it had been, it was over.

He wondered, even, if it'd been wholly consensual. He didn't like to consider it, but the fact was that he could imagine it of Antonio: a bit of pressure, keeping up the pressure, taking it a bit too far. Thinking this, he felt keenly for Leonor.

Perhaps Antonio himself didn't know. He might not have known that Leonor wasn't also sleeping with her husband; he'd only have known if she'd told him. And even if she had, she could well have retracted it later, lied to him: *Oh, well, yes, actually, there were a couple of times.* Casting enough doubt to free them both.

But if Antonio did know, he must think Rafael either stupid or spineless. Rafael didn't know which was worse. Did Antonio know? When he'd heard of Francisco's birth, he'd gone through the motions, offered congratulations, but he was no more effusive than anyone else. By that time, he was keeping his distance from the household. In all this time in England, he'd never once asked after Leonor and Francisco.

And as for Leonor: she was good at it. She really did appear to believe it: that there was nothing amiss and Rafael was the father of her son. Did she believe it? Had she somehow persuaded herself of it? Sometimes he doubted himself: perhaps there was a time, just the once, that he'd overlooked, or when he was half-asleep. But there hadn't: he knew it. He was certain.

In the nursery that day, as he faced the truth, he was staring at Francisco but not really watching him; he was thinking too hard. But then the baby had turned his head a little to search for him; the eyes intent, albeit barely able to see, the mouth pursed with the effort. This was a serious endeavour. That strangely humourless little face. The blind faith of the tiny boy: looking for the man he was learning was his father, expecting him to be there; expecting that if only he could turn his head, his father would be there for him to see. It was unthinkable not to honour that faith. Why should Francisco suffer for this? That was Rafael's decision, then and there: he must not suffer for it.

In company, Rafael had found himself making much of his adoration of the little boy: a challenge to Leonor and whoever else might know. *Ruin this, if you dare.* Alone with Francisco, he didn't need to make a show of it; it was genuine and, if anything, more intense.

*How dare there be any threat to our happiness.*

The two of them, together, were invincible. Even by Francisco's eleventh day, parenting had taken on a life of its own and was the only life there was.

That evening, Rafael skipped supper, retreated early to bed, in daylight. He woke later, in darkness, because someone was coming into his room. His heart flew at his ribs and he inched back the bed-hanging. There was a blaze of linen in the blackness of the gaping doorway.

'Shhh,' it said. *Cecily.* Her shape, long and lean. And the grace with which it was turning to close the door: definitely Cecily. His heart was beating so hard that she must have been able to hear it.

She said, 'It's –'

– *all right*: she hadn't been detected.

She'd come no further, though; she'd stopped by the door, her back to it. 'You hit Antonio,' she said. No reproach detectable, but his heart swallowed itself because he wasn't a man to hit anyone and he wished she knew it. 'Usually I don't,' he whispered back, his English failing him. He could have sworn he heard her smile: a change to the silence, although soundless itself; a lessening of its hold.

'Perhaps usually you should,' she said.

His turn to smile, if only he'd dared move a muscle. 'How did you know? Did he tell you?' That, he'd find hard to believe.

'His fat lip,' she said. 'I guessed.'

She came towards him – he didn't dare even breathe – and drew back the bed-hanging as far as it would go, then perched on his bed: the very end of it, the very edge. All he could see of her was the grainy illumination that was her nightgown. He kept himself still, didn't want to startle her, although there was nothing in her manner to suggest she'd be easily scared.

'Rafael?'

He waited. She was about to tell him something, he felt, that he should know even though he might not want to know it. He had a sense he should protect himself, but didn't know how.

'That man – at night? He's my husband.'

Husband? *You're a widow*, he wanted to protest. She'd certainly seemed like one.

But she'd never said so and he despised himself for having been stupid. Because what, really, did he know of her?

*Nothing.* It whipped his breath away, that he'd been so stupid.

Yet still it beat inside him like a pulse: *There is no husband.* Because what kind of a husband would she visit in the absolute dead of night? 'Husband' was definitely what she'd said, not 'lover'. Was this a trick? Some kind of English joke? But he knew it wasn't, from how she was sitting there, composed and grave, trusting utterly to him to believe her, and despite her seriousness she wore it lightly, he felt, this fact of her husband. She was accustomed to it. *My husband.* It hadn't sounded odd to her when she'd said it.

He tried, 'I thought –'

'I know what you thought.' *Because you wanted to. Because I let you.*

Complicity: it settled over them with equal weight. But Rafael understood nothing. And he didn't know where to start. 'Why – at night?' An explanation might just explain him away, this husband.

'He's a priest,' she said.

Priest? For a breath he forgot that England had ever allowed priests to marry, so what she said was ridiculous – priests weren't husbands, husbands weren't priests – but then he remembered that they had been. Some priests had married. So, Cecily had been married to a priest. *Priest's wife*: she'd had a life of which Rafael had known nothing. She'd told him nothing and let him believe a lie. And he'd been stupid enough to believe it. Stupid Spaniard: that was what he was. Stupid, stupid Spaniard.

'I – *see* him, Rafael,' she said, 'I mean, I just – meet up with him.' She spoke emphatically: this, too, was something she felt he should know, and he understood her to mean that she didn't sleep with him. The intimacy of the confession impressed itself upon him – she hadn't had to tell him, had she. 'I go to see him, sometimes.' And as if to justify herself – although of course he hadn't asked it of her – she added, 'He's Nicholas's father.' She said, 'We talk. There's a lot to talk about.' Of that, though, she sounded weary, even unconvinced.

'I'm sorry,' he heard himself whisper; and he was, very much so. He understood it, that weariness, that lack of faith. Separation, he understood. Distrust and hopelessness and disillusionment: those, he understood.

He made himself ask it: 'But he's your husband.' Not phrased as a question – nothing so intrusive – but that was what it was. He had to know. He had to get it straight.

'He chose the Church,' was how she answered. 'He says he's chosen us both: us – his family – and the Church. But there was no such choice, Rafael. It was us or the Church: that was the choice he was given. And he's still in the Church.' A pause. 'For him to stay in the Church, he had to abandon us, publicly. And publicly, he did' – Rafael winced – 'but privately, he didn't. That's his view on it. His setting aside of us was a sham: that's what he says. He'd already asked us to follow him to London and live near him. Which I've done,' but she emphasised, '*for Nicholas*, and Nicholas alone.'

'But your husband still thinks of you as married,' Rafael probed.

She considered before answering: 'He says he's biding his time. We did that once before, Rafael. Six years, because he was sure it'd come: a time when priests were allowed to marry. Only a matter of time, he said. And he was right, that time. It did come. And now he believes it'll come again, soon, very soon.'

She could only be referring to the imminent death of the queen, heirless, and the succession of her Protestant sister.

'What do *you* think?' he barely dared to ask. He didn't mean the queen, and she'd know it. He was asking her if she'd be there for her husband if and when the day came when priests could once more be married.

Again, she took her time. 'He chose the Church over us.' Not quite an answer, but also very much one. She added, 'I do think he had to,' and Rafael heard that she understood it; however she felt about it, she also kind of understood that he'd done what he had to do. Then, 'But I'd like Nicholas to have a family to grow up in.'

'Do you still love him?' Rafael was surprised to hear himself ask, but pleased with himself that he'd dared. It was what mattered, here.

'I don't know.' And it was no mere dismissal: she really did seem to mean that she didn't know. And that she wished she did know. And that, too, he understood.

'I did,' she mused, and he heard the wonder in it. 'Oh God, I did, Rafael,' hoarse with disbelief, not at the fact of her past love but its intensity, and Rafael's heart laid itself low.

'He's still Nicholas's father. They can make him my ex-husband, make me his ex-wife, they can say we were never properly married, but they can't ever say that Nicholas isn't our son.'

Rafael's heart folded in on itself. 'Does Nicholas see him?'

'Yes, sometimes. Whenever it can be done. That's the idea. It's why I see him,' she said: 'to make plans, keep it going.' She

sighed. 'He hasn't been able to turn his back on his little boy
– he'll never be able to do that, I know. Nor, though, has he
been able to turn his back on the Church: the faith, the fight'
– she shrugged – 'the people of England. He won't give in to
what's wrong, and I can understand that, of course I can, and
it's all very admirable, but how do I explain it to a distraught
four-year-old? He misses his dad,' she said.

'Yes,' said Rafael.

'He really, really misses him, Rafael. He hates this, and I
can't explain it to him.'

'No,' of course not. It made no sense to an adult, let alone
to a four-year-old.

'"Daddy's a couple of streets away but he's not supposed to
see you. No one can ever see him with you. He has to pretend
he never sees you. We have to pretend he never sees us."' She
sighed, a harsh, jagged sigh. 'I did try to make a game of it, for
a while, but it just didn't work.'

*I'll hurt the ones you love.*

Rafael said, 'Can't you pretend Nicholas is his nephew, or
something?'

'Too risky. They know he did have a wife and son.'

'Do they know you're in London?'

'I'm not in London.' And there was a wry smile in the
words. She explained: 'I'm not here under my own name.'

That was almost as big a shock as the rest of it. *You're not
Cecily?*

*Who, then?*

'No one here knows,' she warned him. 'No one, Rafael. I'm
a widow, to them.' She added, 'It was the first thing she did,
you know.'

He didn't follow.

'The first act she repealed: the one that allowed priests to marry.'

*She*: the queen.

The queen, who'd stood beside him spouting about families and marital love. These 'heretics' of hers were people, just people. If she could hear what he was hearing, she'd see what she was really doing. Perhaps she did have a point – Rafael had no idea, he was no theologian – in deciding that priests shouldn't have been allowed to marry. Perhaps they should be forbidden from doing so in the future. But those who already had – well, it was done, wasn't it? There were children. It was madness to pretend it hadn't happened and that the ties weren't there.

Cecily shivered.

'You're cold.' Rafael had drawn back the bedclothes before he'd realised he'd done it; and there she was, getting in beside him. The scent of her was instantly recognisable although he didn't think he'd ever noticed it before. Here it was, like a secret code or signal, a word in his ear. The fragrance itself was like that of the apples that'd overwintered on the rack near the kitchen. He was glad of the darkness, of the privacy it gave them. He understood her getting into bed for what it was – tentative and partial. This was no capitulation nor seduction. He was under no illusions, and he was on guard against them. This was the taking up of an unspoken offer of warmth and comfort, of intimacy but not of a sexual kind. That was all it was. And as such, there was nothing wrong in it: it seemed right, to him, to offer refuge to someone he loved.

She said, 'I don't want to talk any more about it. Not now. I'm so tired, Rafael.'

'Sleep,' he said.

They lay side by side, careful to avoid contact. To be in bed with her was more than he could ever have hoped for, more than he had ever dreamed possible: this, alone, was a privilege. Of course he'd have loved to be closer, but above all he wanted her to stay and he'd not do anything to jeopardise that. Any contact was accidental. In time, though, under cover of sleepiness, he did move a little closer and so did she, and then there they were: she turned from him, and he against her back, an arm draped over her. He was determined to honour her reticence.

He was aroused. No point in trying to hide it. He could either spend this time agonising over it, or accept it and try to ignore it, trusting that she'd understand he was ignoring it and would perhaps appreciate that. And he hoped she understood his arousal for what it was: a physical reaction, beyond his control.

He couldn't do more than doze, for fear of what – in this state – he might do. Anyway, sleep would've been impossible – a turning away, a turning inward when he was wide open to her presence, the shapes of her bones, the rhythm of her breathing, the abundance of her hair. Perhaps also he was awake because he was at the ready for any lead from her, even though he remained vigilant against any expectations.

Duly, some time later she turned over towards him, and he sensed intent. There followed a pause, and there was a questioning in it. He shifted purposelessly – just to let her know that he, too, was awake and responsive. He couldn't tell who made the first move but they kissed. Just the once: slow, measured, mindful. And light, too – a mere press of lips to lips, that was all. But there it was: a kiss. After all this time. A belated, mute declaration. Done. No going back. In recognition of that, and perhaps to make clear to each other that it was no mistake, no slip-up, they did it again: just the once, just the same, just a simple kiss; no more, no less. And then there really was no going back. So they did it again, but this time differently, very slightly exploratory, a stroke of lips over and around lips. Her breath was hot in his mouth – he was surprised by the heat of it – and flavoured with English cooking: salty and musty. His arousal was painful now – he felt helpless, and resentful that he had to risk offending her.

A peep of her tongue and then a slide of it against his own, and then they kissed and kissed as if kissing were everything and they could make a night of it. They were pressed closer together for all this kissing: one of his thighs between hers, one of hers between his. He was all too aware of her breasts and a womanly tang billowing up from inside her nightgown. He didn't dare move his hands, but eventually she moved hers, stroking down casually over one of his buttocks and letting her hand rest there, and then he was nothing but the skin under that hand, as if she were conjuring him. He had to make himself go on kissing because he'd stopped, his attention stuck under that hand of hers. He renewed his efforts at just-kissing.

But then she sat up. So, she was leaving, and of course she was. Of course. But no: she drew her nightgown up over her head. His eyes had adjusted and he could see something of her – shapes, shadows – and what he saw now were her nipples, big and dark, fruit-like, quite unexpected for a woman so pale. He followed her, shed his own nightgown – could hardly not, now – and was glad to be free of it. Her petal-soft skin was made to be touched and it took his hand around and around, over and over it. Down the length of her back, over the swell of her bottom, back up to the silkiness of a breast. With a fingertip she traced his nose, cheekbones, brows and lips – then re-traced them with the lightest of kisses, somehow all the more intimate for that. In turn, he took his lips along her hairline, her jawline, and into the tiny chamber of her ear. He moved them back and forth over her eyebrows, savouring their roughness. And her hair, the smell of it, and its freedom; he wanted it hot on his face, he wanted to drown in it.

'Cecily?' it sounded odd in the darkness; so close up, anything would have sounded odd.

'Yes?'

'You know I love you?' This was no declaration; he did mean exactly what he said: *Did she know?* He had to have her know; he couldn't have her think of this as being down to mere frustration, to having been too long away from home.

Her reply was a half-laugh, which failed to reassure him.

He pressed: 'Do you?' He didn't want to scare her off, but he had to have her know.

'Yes, I know,' and she sounded amused even as she was sad. He heard the sadness and of course he understood. It didn't do, to love someone who was married to someone else and was soon to be more than a thousand miles away.

They were stuck together; there was an unseemly sound as they moved to re-settle themselves, which brought to her lips

– on his – a smile, which teased one from his. He was on top of her, now, and he dipped to kiss her neck and down it, along to a shoulder. Raised on one elbow, he drew back to look at her breasts, laid his lips on and around one nipple and then the other.

She struggled a little to free an arm, a hand; she shifted their weight and reached down, took hold of him. And so she was moving them on; Rafael couldn't quite believe it. He felt light-headed, felt a release of tension that he could only have dreamt of at the same time as its predictable, almost unbearable intensification. Beneath him, her hips shuffled; she was positioning him. He intended to check – *You're sure?* – but his English wasn't there and instead he simply asked, 'Yes?'

'Oh yes,' she replied, humourfully.

In response – in recognition and thanks – he kissed her. But he was thinking: What about the risk of pregnancy? Wasn't she worried? She didn't seem to be.

She was closed against him.

If he just stayed there, she'd let him in; he'd melt into her. 'Don't worry,' he whispered, 'I won't hurt you.' He'd said it in his own language, but he sensed she'd understood and there was the slightest give. With her guidance, he began to find his way inside her; her hand still there as if to keep him hard, as if there were any danger of him not being so. And then he was inside her and they were both moving. It was like waking, for him: he wasn't quite there yet. Even though the sensation was exquisite, it remained slightly *over there* – he felt he was chasing it, not quite able to catch it, hold it. But then he did wake to it and was utterly in the moment: there was nothing else.

He took one of her hands, pressed it back and open beneath his, his fingers between hers. *I could die now, this would be enough; I ask no more than this.*

She said something – but more to herself than to him – and he didn't catch it. Even if he had, he wouldn't have understood. Or perhaps he would have, in a way. At that, he smiled mid-kiss and in response so did she, and somehow that was funny – two joined smiles – so his smile got bigger and then so did hers, which was funnier still. She wouldn't understand him, either: he could say whatever he wanted to say and she'd make of it what she would but wouldn't be far wrong. He longed to be deeper, higher, more fully inside her. More precisely – bizarrely, that was the word that came to him. It was impossible, though: there was no room to move; they were jammed up against each other. She was insistent, pushing for more, pushing against him, and her breathing was changing. He had to have her kissing him when she came, when he came. *Don't turn away, don't breathe, don't come up for air; be joined to me.*

Afterwards, they lay there, still joined, for a time; time, now, to relish it, to dissolve into the sensation of skin on skin. He told himself he should be ready for her regrets and recriminations, that he should ready himself for them, although he had no idea how.

*I should never have done that, Rafael. We should never have done that.*

The misgivings were there for him, too, hovering, and later he'd square up to them, he'd come to some understanding with them, but not now, not just now. For now, they had to leave him alone.

But no: he pulled away from her a little, so she'd know he was looking at her, posing a question, *You all right?* It was a risk: he was giving her the detachment she'd need to turn from him and explain it away, apologise for it – *Well, that was a mistake, wasn't it?* – and go. What she did, though, was sigh – a clear indication that she, too, didn't want to face any of that – and she rubbed his back and shoulder blades to reassure him that they were in this together, that she was with him on this. That was all he'd wanted and, avoiding the wet patch, they settled down to sleep.

But not quite. Because there was something bothering him. Did he dare ask her? 'Cecily?'

She tensed. She was ready for it, so he might as well ask. He said into the darkness, 'What's your real name?'

She remained just as tense and didn't answer. He regretted that he'd overstepped the mark, deeply regretted it. He'd come this far and then – just to satisfy his own curiosity – had asked too much of her. How reassuring, then, a minute later, was her touch of a fingertip to his back, and he let it soothe him. A long, sinuous stroke of her fingertip, then again – shorter, this time, more definite – and then a mere dab of it, but by then he understood: this was no reassurance, this was a message. She was writing her name.

S–i–c–

He lay there listening to her fingertip mute on his skin and then, when she'd finished, he said it: 'Sicilia.'

She left some time before dawn; he was too sleepy to manage more than the faintest acknowledgement of her going. In the morning, he woke alone but to the memory of her, the warmth and scent still there to be luxuriated in. *It had happened*: finally, it had happened. And she'd wrung every last pleasure from their encounter. Whatever else she might be feeling now, her enthusiasm had been unmistakable, was undeniable. How – why – before this, in his life, had he settled for so little? Had he not known there was such pleasure to be had? Not simply physical. No, he hadn't known. Well, now he did, and he could never unknow it. He was hooked. When she'd ground herself against him, it'd seemed to him that she knew him for who he was and that until then, he himself hadn't known. He felt he'd met his match, although he hadn't known he'd been missing one.

It wasn't as if Leonor would mind, would care, if she knew. Not really. Why would she care? She'd probably be pleased. Relieved to be free of him. He was sorry he'd burdened her; it must have been hard for her, he saw now. Him and Leonor: not meant to be, however much he'd wanted it. She'd known that, but he'd refused to see it. He felt sorry, too, that she didn't have in her life what he'd just experienced. She'd probably experienced it with Gil. As for Cecily's husband: well, he'd given up on her, hadn't he. Hadn't wanted to, but, in effect, that was what he'd done.

Rafael was at her mercy. He'd do his very best by her, but if she chose to turn away from him, he'd have to accept it. Perhaps even now, across the house, she was recoiling, blaming him for it having gone too far when he – not distressed, as she'd been – should've been the one to stop it. But worse, far worse than anything she could say or do to him, was the fact that, just as this had happened, he was going to have to go. Could be by the end of the week. There'd be more than a thousand miles between them. *How could this be happening?* It

couldn't be happening. It couldn't happen. He had no idea –
not an inkling – how he could endure it.

But he couldn't live here in London. He wouldn't want to.
Well, he could. People did. People survived it: married and
raised children, ran their businesses. He could ask the queen
for permission to stay. But he couldn't stay, because of Francisco.

What he wanted was to be left, somehow, to love Cecily.
The two of them in a room: that's all. Put like that, it didn't
seem much to ask.

He was standing at his window, looking over London roofs.
Down there somewhere was the man who'd been Cecily's
husband and still considered himself as such. That man knew
nothing of what had happened in Rafael's room. For him, this
morning was, presumably, the same as any other, which was to
say it was lonely. Perhaps he was thinking of Cecily. Of her
absence. Rafael presumed to know something of what he
might be thinking and feeling; but for that man, Rafael didn't
even exist. *She's gone from you*: sympathetic though Rafael was,
he felt the man should know. He willed the message across
the rooftops to find him. *She's been gone from you for a long time.*
Regretful though it was, he should face it. Rafael didn't envy
him those fraught, early-hours meetings with Cecily; the
thought of them made him almost grateful for how little
Leonor usually said.

There was a knock on his door, the door was opening and
in the doorway stood Antonio. Antonio and *the lip:* the lip
simultaneously demanding attention and demanding that he
avert his gaze. The split was still open, the blood in it barely
congealed, and for a single breath Rafael felt the tenderness

of it as if it were his own. If it was any consolation to Antonio, he'd have seen Rafael blanch. He showed no recognition of it. 'Listen, Rafael: there's been a …' – he blinked, a kind of rapid frown – 'a battle. Outside the palace. My friend Alonso has been injured and he isn't likely to survive.'

Rafael floundered: *battle*? Someone not survive?

'A messenger just came. Six dead, lots injured, it's being kept quiet, what with …' He didn't bother to finish. *What with everything.*

'Yes,' said Rafael, at a loss for words, his blood whirling inside him. No wonder Antonio wasn't bothered about the lip.

'He's a good friend,' Antonio said, 'He's been a good, good friend to me, and I have to' – a shrug – 'sit with him.'

'Yes,' said Rafael, his pulse noisy in his head. 'Yes, but –' *How will you get there?* The streets, the river, the palace steps and passageways: all harbouring potential danger.

'Well, I won't try to come back, I don't think.' Just the one journey. 'I mean, not until –'

*– until the baby is born dead or alive, until the situation is resolved one way or another and we're released and on our way.*

'No.'

'I'll just stay there.'

'I'll come with you,' Rafael offered, suddenly convinced of it. This called for solidarity. 'It'll be safer.'

Antonio's response was a pointed, amused look which Rafael took a moment to read: his company, recently, hadn't exactly done Antonio any favours, had it? He cringed. 'I'm sorry.' He'd said it before he realised, and was glad he'd said it.

Antonio looked as if he were going to say something but then settled for something else: 'I'll be fine on my own,' he said, 'but thank you, Rafael.' And then he'd turned and was gone.

Rafael hadn't seen Cecily, that first morning, when he'd gone for the water for his wash. He'd seen her that lunchtime, though: she was smiling at him as he came into Hall, and his heart shimmered. And with that smile, it began: her coming to his room, most nights, and sometimes in the days, sometimes once but on several occasions only to say hello and start back downstairs again as soon as she'd arrived, which didn't matter because all that mattered was that she'd come. He lived for her coming to his door, suspended himself between those knocks of hers at his door. That was what he did – all he did – now: listened for her footsteps. Oh, he sketched and designed, but then there she was and those sketches and designs were nothing, just scribbles and doodles, and all the time he'd spent alone had dissolved into nothing. And they'd be kissing before she was properly through his door and laughing at their own fervour and subterfuge, at their own sheer delight and the ridiculousness of it, two grown people.

The nights she didn't come, he drifted in the shallows of sleep and didn't give up on her, not until the household's day could be heard to be under way. He never knew, those nights, if she'd gone to the priest, her ex-husband. And later, when he could have asked, he didn't. He tried not to even think about it. Tried to accept that she had her own reasons for staying away. She couldn't — he knew — come every single night, leaving Nicholas and chancing her way through the house. For her part, she never explained her absences, never even referred to them. She let it be: and so, then, did he.

Not that they didn't talk. For two people with so much that couldn't be talked about, they did a lot of talking. They pondered their very different upbringings and their brief shared past.

*And when you said …*

*That time you …*

And together, they made a story of it: their story, the story of them. Nothing about their predicament, though: never that. Because what new or illuminating could be said about that?

Did others talk about them? Did people know what was going on between them? Rafael didn't care, because what could they do about it? And even if people did know, did they care? They had a more serious preoccupation, but about which, likewise, there was nothing new to say: the queen's predicament, the country's predicament. There was the possibility that there'd be trouble for anyone who even mentioned it, and who needed more trouble? There was more than enough of it about already, and no one could risk it hitting home.

The waiting for an announcement from the palace went on and on: for days after Cecily came first to his room, then a week and into a second week. It probably had no purpose, now: there was little likelihood of good news, this late on.

Rafael wondered often what had happened to Antonio's friend. Had he rallied? Or was he buried, now, in English soil?

He told Cecily that he loved her; he said it often.

'And I love you,' she'd reply, just as insistent, but her manner was different from his, was calm, as if she were correcting him.

Once – genuinely puzzled – he asked her: 'Why do you love me?'

She had to think. 'Because of how you look at me.' She revised, 'Because you look at me.'

He was ashamed, apologetic.

'No …' she tried to explain better. 'It's trusting,' she said, 'that look of yours. You're trusting.'

Which was exactly how she looked at him. That very first look – first smile – on the stairs, a year ago, had been exactly that.

And once she told him he was beautiful. She was holding his face in her cupped hands and she'd sounded grave, perhaps even puzzled. 'I've never seen anyone like you.' Dark, was what that meant. Differently shaped, possibly, too: his face was – he knew – quite unlike most English faces, which were long and flat. The faces of some Englishmen were bone-thin, the skin taut and translucent across the bridge of the nose; whereas on others, abundant flesh had the look of potted meat. Most English people were either fat or thin, but – Rafael was sure – the cause was the same: their abysmal food, which either washed through them or somehow stuck on them. No good to a body. But that was when there was food at all, and a winter of hunger was on its way.

Rafael saw from his window that there were more people on the streets despite the downpours, despite the official cancellation of festivities for the feast days of St Peter and St James, and despite the armed guards, the liveried men of one of the dukes, who patrolled on horseback in fours and sixes. The patrols had begun after the burning of a twenty-three-year-old pregnant woman, Perotine Massey, who'd gone into labour on the pyre. Her baby had been rescued by the crowd but thrown back into the flames by the sheriff. During the night that had followed, it'd sounded to Rafael as if every church window in the city was being smashed, and he'd willed the rioters on. On and on and on, through the night. And even though he knew it was impossible, he'd willed the clamour to reach Hampton Court Palace so that the queen might have to be told what monstrous act had been done in her name. She needed to wake up to what was happening; the people of England were in desperate need of her.

Despite the troubled atmosphere, more and more of them were coming to London. The failure of the harvest was the cause: the second year in succession, which was a year more than people could cope with. Rafael had heard talk in the household of widespread flooding in the countryside: of animals dead in the fields, and crops putrid. Many of the people walking down the lane beneath his window were, from the look of them, coming from the countryside in search of work and food. Whole families weighed down by bundles, and trailing children. They didn't stop to shelter from the rain beneath overhanging first floors, as Londoners did; they hurried on, but not purposefully, because the same people would often pass again in an hour or two. Walking in circles. They might be exhausted, but they hurried, expectant, heads up, taking it all in. They were conspicuous and they knew it; they were self-conscious, wary, obliging, stepping out of others' way.

That was when they were new to the city. They ended up sheltering, Rafael saw, but not as Londoners did, with a view to moving off during a pause in the rain. They didn't move on until they were made to, because they had nowhere else to go. They crouched: obstinate, hopeless, confounded; not knowing where to put themselves. He'd seen − although he wished he hadn't − such people relieving themselves in the lane. They did it surreptitiously and miserably, at first; but later, carelessly. One day, he witnessed a squatting child kicked over by a furious passer-by. He heard the child's wounded cry, his outrage, and saw the mess on his legs. He felt for the boy, but he felt at least as much for whoever was caring for him, faced with that mess and no change of clothes, no water except from the freezing conduit.

He feared for Cecily. Food would be imported, but at a price: a price that the Kitsons would probably be able to afford but, as housekeeper, Cecily would be getting up in the small hours, into the stinging cold, and half-running for miles with her bundle of baskets to the docks, chasing rumours of shiploads. And the frantic crowds at the quays, her chances of getting through them and then, if she were successful, getting away from them with her goods and then getting home safe: he didn't want to dwell on all that. And then, whatever she did manage to bring back: how much of it would be for herself and her son? How generous would the Kitsons be, in the face of their own children's needs? And even if she and her boy had food, she'd be living among people who were famished: locals and friends whom she'd pass in the street, flinching from their slow, swollen eyes.

In a few months' time, some of those people would be selling their boots and blankets for food. Wrapping rags around their feet to walk in mud and snow. And even then, some of them would have to tell their children, at the end of the day, that – again – there was nothing to eat. Absolutely nothing. How would Francisco take that? He'd rage, at first, Rafael imagined. For some time, he'd rage, desperate, and refuse to accept it, chucking blame at his father.

Why *isn't there any? I want some! Why can't you get some?*

And then? Weariness would take over and he'd suck his thumb. And then, later, to try to fill the hole, he'd angle his hand and suck the fleshier base of his thumb, wedging it in his mouth. What happens if a child keeps on doing that? – the skin gets raised, raw, and thinner. *Where is God?* That was what Rafael would think, to see those people down below in the lane. Was it really God's will that people should starve? Children, babies? Mysterious ways, sins of the fathers: he knew all that. He just didn't seem able to believe it, and if that was a failing of his then so be it.

The Kitsons' front courtyard was flooded, ankle-deep. At Hampton Court, he'd heard, courtiers were having to troop around daily in procession, whatever the weather, in a court-yard under the queen's rooms, and she'd appear in a window to wave. The courtiers' display was supposed to be wishing her luck, cheering her up, but her arriving at the window to wave back at them was giving her the opportunity to prove she was still alive. Which it didn't, to most people, from what Rafael heard around the household, because they were saying the waving figure was an effigy or someone in disguise. Mrs Dormer, the smiling companion of the queen, Rafael wondered: would she do that? But he did believe it was the queen at the window; he didn't believe she was dead. There'd looked to be nothing seriously wrong when he'd seen her. As to whether she'd ever been pregnant: well, who knew? He found it hard to believe that she was perpetrating a conscious act of deception; he suspected she simply didn't know how or when to stop. If you were waiting for something – someone – how did you know when to give up?

Around the house, he'd often see someone at a window or door staring confounded into the sun-deserted sky. No one remarked on the sun having given up and gone: it was so horribly obvious that it didn't need saying. At most there'd be a raising of an eyebrow, a silence that was telling. When Cecily was with him in his room, he quite liked the rain restive on the roof. They could be adrift on a sea. Inside his bed-hangings, he strove to do his utter best by her, to magic up pleasure for her and lay it on deep. Sometimes, though, he could do nothing but to drive into her and have her unyielding against him, just as hard, and marvel and marvel again at how strong she was, how definite.

One evening, when everyone was in place for supper, the steward stood up on the dais to make an announcement: the queen had come out of her confinement and would be going away with her husband for the weekend before resuming her duties. From that, he went straight into leading Grace, and then dining commenced in customary silence. On every face that Rafael could see – he couldn't see Cecily – was a contrived lack of expression, and eating was brisk: people were bursting to get out of Hall to discuss what they'd just been told.

If the announcement was true, the queen was alive and well enough to travel. And the marriage had survived – at least for now, at least as far as a public view of it. She still had a husband: she'd gone to him and he was taking her away for the weekend. He was supportive, he was publicly at her side. The glaring omission, of course, was any mention of a baby, as if there'd never even been a prospect of one.

To give up, childless, on that absurdly long confinement and offer no word of explanation: there was dignity in it, or at least an attempt to be dignified in the face of a humiliation that Rafael couldn't come close to being able to imagine. To have made such a mistake, such a fundamental miscalculation, not just under the gaze of your husband but everyone in the whole world, from monarchs to peasants who hadn't even known where England was. To know you'd be the subject of children's songs and games for years to come: the queen who dreamt up a baby, who pushed out her belly and walked around wincing and rubbing the small of her back. The ageing queen who'd deluded herself that she was young enough to be blessed with a baby. And even worse: to know there were so many people who considered that you deserved what had happened. The Kitson houseful did, Rafael knew. He could see it. Not a smidgeon of pity in any of those faces, just a desperation to get out of the room and gossip about it.

In his mind's eye, he could see the queen: the set of her face, and those bright, staring little eyes. He imagined her resolute busyness within a put-upon, pained air. The visible tension across her shoulders. Beyond that, he couldn't imagine – he couldn't imagine how she must be feeling. 'Dismay' was a weak word for it. A fierce dismay, then. A scorching dismay. To have believed herself to be cosseting a little one for those many, many months. To have *been* cosseting him: breathing his breaths for him, eating his food for him, and at the end of each day settling him down, inside her, to sleep, while she dreamed up futures for him. And then to realise that in fact there'd been no one, there'd never been anyone there. Just herself, alone as ever.

For Rafael, though, the news meant something quite different from what it meant to everyone else in Hall. The royal couple's weekend away was the beginning of the prince's leave-taking, he sensed. A show of husbandly concern before he deserted her. This was the beginning of the end. After the weekend, the prince would raise the subject of his going to France. Rafael imagined the prince's impatience to return to his life, his relief that it was finally over for him in England. He could get back to the proper work of a prince: ruling his lands. Ruling, not sitting around waiting to be invited to share rule here: an invitation that now would never come, now that the blessed marriage had been proved to be anything but. And England, anyway: why on earth would he want to rule this place? – a country that couldn't even burn a handful of heretics without descending into anarchy. That was probably how he saw it. And there'd be no talking him round, Rafael guessed. He'd done his duty, as far as he was concerned. He'd endured more than he should ever have had to, and now he was off.

After supper, Rafael went to his room. He waited up for Cecily until midnight, but she didn't come. He'd thought she might, but wasn't surprised that she didn't – and, in a sense, he was relieved. He didn't know quite what he'd have said to her. He didn't know what *she*'d have said to *him,* but he did know that whatever he'd have had to listen to, it wouldn't have been good. This wasn't good news for her. Nothing had changed, and that was the worst possible news for her. Even bad news – what *she*'d have regarded as bad news, the birth of a healthy prince – would have been better, because at least she could have tried to make decisions. At least she'd have known what she was likely to be in for, at least for the near-future. But this: this just meant more of the same, more waiting, more nothing. An ageing, heirless queen but still, despite everything, alive, and still married, and still, presumably, with a chance – however slim – of a future pregnancy. Despite all that England had been through, for a whole year, it was back exactly where it'd started.

Rafael had no idea of what he'd have said to Cecily, but he'd have liked to try to offer comfort. She probably wanted to be left alone, which he understood, but he doubted it was for the best.

And, anyway, there was a change coming, for her. Hadn't she realised? – he'd be gone, within days.

He barely slept, lying there in his bed while the hours turned slowly around him and drew back the night.

In the morning, Cecily, too, looked exhausted, and the child appeared clinging, fractious. Rafael only saw them from a distance – a distance which, he felt, she'd contrived. She half-met his gaze, to give him a brief, wan smile. It twisted his heart. *Talk to me.* She didn't come up to his room that day – a day during which there was a burning, news of it reaching the house by suppertime and spreading along the queue for Hall. The victim of the burning was a woman whose crime had been to advocate the Bible in English. How wonderful, she'd declared before the kindling was lit, to be able to hear the word of God. The burning had been bungled, was what people were saying: no one fanning the flames, the guards and officials battling instead with the crowd. Her legs had burned away to mid-thigh but then she had to wait until reinforcements arrived and the pyre was re-built, re-lit, and properly tended.

People were saying, too, that the woman's first grandchild had been born on the previous day. After Francisco was born, Rafael had been surprised by his excitement at the prospect, one day, of a grandchild. He'd never have foreseen that. Then had come the realisation that, because fatherhood had come so late for him, he'd be lucky to know any grandchildren.

He couldn't believe that the queen wouldn't be horrified when she discovered what'd happened, if she learned about that grandchild. She couldn't be unchanged by what she'd just endured. Surely she'd be humbled: it'd be hard, now, to believe that God was on her side. And she'd know, now, what it was to lose someone. Yes, she'd lost her mother and her little brother, *but this: a baby*. And she *had* lost a baby, that's what had happened to her: there should've been a baby in that now-abandoned nursery. That nursery, which she'd furnished by months and months of meticulous stitching.

Cecily warned him she wouldn't be coming, that night: she whispered it as she brushed past him: 'Tonight, I'm … going visiting.' He was pleased she'd told him; he was grateful for that. And of course, of course: she'd have to go and see

Nicholas's father. That, he understood; he'd been expecting it. They'd have to talk about what to do now that nothing had changed: now that what could have changed, hadn't. He lay awake for a long time, that night, wondering what exactly they were discussing. He knew nothing of the terms of their discussions, knew nothing of any understandings – or indeed misunderstandings – between them. He'd tell her anything and everything about his marriage, if she wanted to know: he'd tell her whatever she wanted to know. He *wanted* to tell her. True, he hadn't told her about Francisco – about Francisco's conception – but he *would*. He was sure he would. It just hadn't yet come up. But as far as he was concerned, it was no secret between them.

Knowing she was away from the house, he wasn't listening for her, that evening; but he did listen for Antonio's tread on the stairs. Possibly, though, he wouldn't ever return; perhaps he'd just go. Perhaps – as he'd once said – everyone would just go, every Spaniard, before all Hell broke loose. Perhaps he'd join them and go back to take over Rafael's life, or try to: his work, his wife, his son. Rafael was adrift from every other Spaniard in London. It was as if he wasn't Spanish, any more, living in this English household, speaking English, loving an Englishwoman. He could so easily slip through the net, sink down here and stay. But he couldn't let that happen. He'd give it a week and then, if he hadn't heard what was happening about a return home, he'd somehow get to Hampton Court Palace and make his presence known. Because of course he was going home. Of course he was. He was going to go home to his little boy. He remembered Francisco once telling him, 'When you're old, you'll still be my daddy.'

He would if he could.

The next day, Cecily didn't come to him. Nor the next. She was avoiding him, he realised, and she was good at it; he couldn't even catch her eye. He recognised what she was doing: after all, he'd done the same, back when he'd first realised he was in love with her and that there was nothing he could do; he was going to lose her. Not only was she focusing on squaring up to her future, but she was withdrawing from him in anticipation of the wounding that was coming her way. Better to get it done, was how he'd felt when he'd tried to distance himself from her, but he knew from his experience that it didn't work. *Don't do this*, he willed her. But he didn't go to her. He knew he shouldn't try to force this. He'd have to give her time. Wait for her to come round. She was reeling, that was obvious even from the mere glimpses he had of her. She wasn't alone in that – a sinking-in was visible in all the Kitsons' servants' widened eyes, distracted gazes. Rafael could see them thinking, *We're lumbered with a queen who's mad and, even though we're all excommunicated now anyway, she's going to keep on trying to turn us Spanish and she's going to go on and on burning people.*

Nights, he didn't sleep, not properly; he waited for her. On the third day, he did approach her, on the way into Hall, but she was flustered, exasperated and unwelcoming – 'Rafael – don't – please – not now' – and declined to meet his gaze. There was no give in her. This was worse than he'd anticipated: he suspected she was trying to put him away from her as if he'd never been close. Well, that really wouldn't do. *I can't help you, Cecily, unless you let me*. He didn't know how he could help, but he'd find a way. He'd be able to ease her misery somehow, if only for the briefest time. If she'd give him a chance. But she was shutting him out, hard.

Thereafter, he stopped going down to meals. He couldn't face a repetition of her rejection of him. Besides, he had no appetite. His stomach was busy enough, gnawing at itself. Occasionally, feigning malaise, he visited the kitchen when everyone else was in Hall and begged a little bread and cheese. That was how he kept himself alive. Otherwise, he mostly kept to his room. He had to be where she could find him, as soon as she was ready. Somewhere they could have privacy immediately, giving her no chance to back off, to try to postpone. This waiting for her was so unlike his usual dozy wishing away of time. He was alert, poised. He wasn't giving up on her while she was trying so hard to get him to do exactly that.

He didn't write to Leonor and Francisco. It'd always been his intention to write ahead in case he didn't survive the journey but, now that the time was near, he simply couldn't imagine a letter of his ever reaching them. They seemed utterly beyond his reach. Inhabitants of a different and long-ago world. It was as if he didn't quite believe in them, any more.

He couldn't have written, anyway: physically, he couldn't have done it, because he couldn't hold his quill properly. He was afflicted by a tremor. The sensation was of his blood being fundamentally altered: no longer liquid, perhaps; not smooth, warm and settled, but grit-like, chafing at him from the inside. And there was a pain above one eye, too, like thumb pressure. When it was at its worse, its most insistent, he had to sit for hours concentrating on his breathing to hold it at bay.

Sometimes he found himself blaming Nicholas for Cecily's non-appearance: if it weren't for that pathetic, needy child, she'd be here. Other times, he missed the little lad intensely and blamed her: if only she'd allow him over here, then Rafael would be telling stories to open up that sullen little face.

He was waiting for Cecily and for his call home, not knowing which would come first, but willing her to be ahead of any messenger. The gap was narrowing, though, was shutting down on her. He willed it to stay open; he felt his vigilance might just be able to keep it open.

On the fifth day, the realisation turned hard inside him: she wasn't coming. She didn't feel able to come, or didn't feel she should. Maybe something had been said when she'd been to see her husband. Whatever the reason, her failure to turn up at his door was a message which he could no longer pretend not to be hearing. She was going to stay away.

And she thought he'd just melt away as if he'd never been. Well, she was wrong about that.

His decision was instant and compelling: he knew what he should have been doing. He'd been trying to keep the peace, he'd spent his whole life trying to keep the peace and look where that'd got him. Up here in his room, he'd been lying low, keeping his head down, and it'd solved nothing. *I will not do nothing.* He could do better than that. He could do better by her.

The queen was the answer – if he could get to her, if she permitted him to see her. Hadn't she said to him, 'If there's

ever anything I can do for you …' Cecily and Nicholas aside,
no one in England had more than spared him a glance, the
sole exception being, bizarrely, England's queen herself. And
her small, bright, serious eyes had seen straight to his heart.
He felt now – was it fanciful? – that she'd known that one day
she might be in a position to give him the help he needed.
They'd shared an extraordinary intimacy during those few
brief times together. She'd understand. He still believed –
more than ever, in fact – that everyone in England had her
wrong. They had her more wrong than ever, regarding her as
a deluded, ruined, vengeful queen. He believed that she
hoped and tried, and if she was sometimes slow to see her
errors, she was then quick to admit to them. She had no pride
– none at all – and never offered any defence. She was his only
hope and he prayed that despite her recent trouble – perhaps
even because of it – she'd rise to what he was going to ask of
her. *If there's ever anything I can do for you …* It was a far from
good time, to say the least, to be asking anything of her –
asking even just to see her – but he had no choice, had no
time and had to trust that she'd forgive him the intrusion into
her grief.

He braved a quick trip for a shave, then went to the steward
to tell him that he needed to get a message to a contact in the
queen's household: could that be done? He acted confident,
and the steward didn't question it. He wouldn't have known
Rafael's role – or lack of it – in relations between the Spanish
royal household and the queen's, and he'd seen him called to
the palace before. It certainly could be done, he assured
Rafael: no problem. And he took the letter addressed to Mrs
Dormer, for passing on.

In the meantime, if Cecily did turn up, he wouldn't tell her what he was planning; he didn't want her to feel that she had to try to talk him out of it. That night, he surprised himself by sleeping, waking later than usual so that he was anxious that he might have missed a response from the palace. Not until late morning, though, did a liveried messenger arrive: a pallid, wall-eyed lad who was to accompany Rafael on that long river-journey to Hampton Court Palace. The lad said nothing for the whole journey but there didn't seem to be malice in the silence. Irritation, perhaps, but no malice. Rafael guessed he might've been drinking the previous evening – he had that look about him. As did most of the English, although it didn't usually keep them quiet.

The weather wasn't bad – there were spangles of sunlight, even, on the water – which was wonderful to Rafael, and fitting. He drew in the tingling river-air and rested his gaze, having been so long hemmed into his room, in the middle distance. He'd envisaged spending the journey thinking through what he intended to say, first to Mrs Dormer and then, if successful in his mission, to the queen. He didn't, though; didn't think of much, just let the journey take over. Slumped down in the boat, giving in to its rocking, he became aware of how wholeheartedly exhausted he was: the dead weight of his legs. He felt faintly sick, too, but the nausea had been niggling at him for days, had nothing to do with the boat's motion.

Not far on from Whitehall, he must have fallen asleep; he was woken by the cessation of the rowing. He shook some life back into his limbs, offered his thanks to the puffing, disdainful oarsmen and clambered behind the lad up some deserted riverside steps. Then they were off down a similarly unpeopled path – long, broad, gravelled – towards the buildings. There, the messenger headed for a small, plain, unguarded door, opening it on to a barely lit, elbow-cramping spiral staircase. Up they both struggled for two flights to a door which gave on to a gallery, the bare walls and floorboards of which seemed to extend for ever, even around corners, so that, after a while, Rafael wondered if perhaps they were back where they'd started or had even passed it again. They'd still seen no one nor heard a sound. Finally, through a guarded doorway and up a broader, wooden staircase was a gallery that couldn't have differed more from the previous one: many-windowed, thick-carpeted, and gilt-panelled. Not far along, under the impassive gaze of a quartet of guards, he was handed over to an occupant of a room behind an immense oak door: a young, expensively dressed woman who smiled distractedly at him.

Mrs Dormer was inside the tapestry-shimmering room; she rose from a chair. 'Mr Prado –' there was a faint note of enquiry in it. Her smile, though warm, didn't dazzle: those months of confinement alongside the queen appeared to have taken their toll. She came towards him and he hurried to greet her properly, already thanking her for having allowed so far, but she shook it off – the greeting, the explanation – by gently taking his arm. 'She's ready for you,' she said, guiding him towards a door.

The queen's room was east-facing and instead of sunshine was firelight. Ladies – six or seven – were at the fireside and the most richly dressed of them was the queen, her gown midnight-dark and starred with pearls. She was being helped

271

up, and a hefty, rubied cross swung and bounced at her bodice. Rafael bowed, and stayed bowed as she approached.

'Mr Prado,' her deep, level voice sounded no note of surprise. She indicated with the lightest of touches to his shoulder that he should straighten. Her face – fireside flush like a graze down each cheek – was expressionless, passionless where before it'd been lively with enquiry and concern. Her eyes looked smaller than ever in slack, puddled skin.

He said that he was very, very sorry. He didn't specify; he didn't need to.

She seemed to consider what he'd said, and he guessed she was unaccustomed to hearing it. Then, 'Thank you, Mr Prado.' Careful to reveal no emotion. Careful, too, though, to give it weight: 'Thank you.' She inclined her head towards the bay of a window.

There, looking down on to the now black river, she remarked, 'You'll be going home soon.'

In the entourage of her husband, yes. Uneasy, Rafael was dismissive: 'Oh, I don't know …'

She wouldn't have it. 'You will.' And, mustering an imitation of brightness, 'You'll see your son.'

He echoed her tone: 'Oh, I'm not sure he'll know who I am.'

That, too, though, she knocked back. 'He'll learn, again. Soon, it'll be as though you were never away.'

Blithely said, and he knew it could never be so, nor would he want it to be. He made himself say it: 'Your Majesty …'

Nothing from her; he had to assume she was listening. *If there's ever anything I can do for you …*

'In the house where I live in London, there's a four-year-old boy. Like my son,' he reminded her: four years old.

She did look around at him, and there was a chink of the old openness. 'He reminds you of Francisco?'

He shook his head, almost smiling because the notion was so unlikely as to be – despite everything – amusing. 'No, same age but nothing like Francisco.' Except that he didn't actually know, did he? He didn't know, nowadays, what Francisco was like. He forced down despair. 'This little boy,' he tried again, 'Nicholas: he's a very unhappy little boy. He doesn't talk –'

'Can't talk?' – the query so quick and the frown so hard that Rafael was taken aback.

'*Can*,' he blustered. 'Can. But ...' It was hard to explain, and anyway it was irrelevant; what mattered was, 'When he was three, he lost his father.'

She'd turned from him again and spoke distantly, towards the river: 'Are you worried that your son will be like this, when you get home?'

Again, he shook his head but what she'd raised allowed him to say, 'My son has been told that his daddy's away across the sea, working for a queen.'

She didn't respond but her silence had a softness to it as if she was faintly pleased to find herself in their story.

'And he's told that I'll be coming home' – he pressed on, the sensation one of sliding over an unexpected dip – 'and that everything'll be fine. And while I've been here, I've been able to write to him, draw for him –'

'Draw?'

Again, she'd thrown him off track. He shrugged: 'London Bridge ...'

Which seemed to be good enough, because she nodded.

'Pictures are better,' he felt he should continue, 'for –'

'−Yes.'

So, he looped back to where he'd left off. 'The other one, I tell stories − the boy here.'

She seemed lost to him, again; lifeless at the window, an absurdly extravagant rag doll. But then she surprised him with, 'Stories from Spain?'

'Stories from England.' He felt nervous: she probably favoured biblical stories; and King Arthur might be particularly poor ground to be on, what with his wicked half-sister and his doomed marriage.

'Oh?'

He felt she was merely following form, so wearily did she ask, but he'd have to answer. 'King Arthur.' He'd made sure to sound dismissive: *child's stuff*.

'England's last good king,' she said, airily, sceptically, as if quoting. Then, 'Did Francisco like those stories?'

'Oh, he was too small.'

'Maybe when you get home, then.'

'Maybe.' Home, again; he didn't want to think about home, not at this moment.

She surprised him again, this time by asking, 'Is it hard to leave the boy − the boy here in London?'

'Yes.' Grateful to her for raising it. 'Yes, it is.' Then, 'His mother, too: she's been a good friend to me.'

She'd already lost interest, managing only a dutiful, 'I'm sure they were glad of your company.' Then, though, something changed and she turned to him, looking at him with something like feeling. 'It's been a difficult time, for you; it's been a long time. I'm sorry.'

Unwittingly, he'd reminded her of her own awful time.

Not knowing what else to do, he pressed on with what he'd come to ask her: 'Your Majesty, is any father better than none?'

She replied emptily, 'God's gift, fatherhood.' Not to be questioned, was the implication. But she had questioned it and had taken some fathers from their children. His blood was stirring hot beneath his skin.

'The greatest of His gifts, perhaps,' she said, but without enthusiasm. 'the love between parent and child.'

He disliked talk of children as gifts from God, because what did that make of what he'd done? By being Francisco's father, had he misappropriated someone else's gift? Or perhaps God's gift was all the greater in his case, giving him what he otherwise wouldn't have had.

'It's a gift from God, and should be honoured.'

*But* you *haven't been honouring it*, he almost said. Instead, though, he made himself say what he'd come to say: 'I've come here to beg for your help, Your Majesty.'

She turned to look at him, that sharp little fold between her eyes.

'I can't just go back,' he implored her, 'knowing what I know. It'd be wrong of me just to go back as before. I can't pretend nothing has happened here.'

No change in her expression: she was waiting for him to deliver it, whatever it was that he had to say. Now that he'd come to it, though, he didn't know how. He'd been wrong to trust to knowing how when the time came.

But then suddenly he did know, or at least knew where – how – to begin. 'Your Majesty, I know a man who has to lie to be able to be a father to his son. A man who, if people

275

knew the truth, many of them would say he should give up his son.' His heart had taken flight inside his ribs, driving his air ahead of it and leaving him little to breathe. 'But is it wrong,' he rushed, 'can it ever be wrong to …' he faltered '… do the work of fatherhood, for a little boy?' It came convoluted in English, but struck him as being true: 'It is work,' he insisted, more to himself than to her. 'It's love, I know, but it's what God gives us to do, isn't it? It's what we have to do, and we can do it well or not well, and we can do it better –'

He'd forgotten what he was asking her. She looked blank, but had offered no contradiction. 'And the better we do it,' he felt blindly ahead, 'the stronger the child, and a strong child can be …'

*Be*: know and feel, and love and do, and … *wonder*. Yes, that was it, that was what he wished, above all, beyond all, he realised, for Francisco: that he'd look up at the stars or into someone's eyes with wonder.

He said, 'There's a man I know who lives his whole life as a lie just so that he can be a father to his son. Just to be able to ruffle his son's hair, kiss his head, ask him how his day has been.'

'But why?' Her question more than a question, an expression of frustration at an absurd situation.

Well, he could tell her that. 'Because he's a priest.'

He wouldn't have believed that so pallid a face could blanch.

'When priests were allowed to marry, he married and had a son.' He rephrased it: 'God gave him a son. But then he was told to give up the work God chose him to do, or give up being a father.' He shrugged. 'I think, neither of those can a man give up.'

Her eyes were glossed with tears. Never before – despite everything – had he seen tears in her eyes.

'His wife has come to London in secret; she lives a secret life close enough for him to see his son. They meet up for him to be a father, sometimes, to his son. It's a secret, the little boy is told, because to everyone else Daddy must say he doesn't want to be your daddy.'

She blinked, and the tears spilled. She didn't acknowledge them, nor wipe them away.

'And you asked why he doesn't speak.'

She nodded; she knew: 'The four-year-old in your house,' she whispered.

'Nicholas.' Nicholas's fate handed over to the queen of England herself for safekeeping. 'I had to tell you.' He was so glad that he had. He could see he'd done the right thing. What he'd come to do: it'd worked.

She looked down at her clasped hands. 'I understand.'

'I knew you'd see.' No one else would have dared, but no else knew her quite as he did.

Not looking up, she did at last wipe her eyes. 'I do see, yes, thank you, Mr Prado. I do see. Thank you. You were absolutely right to tell me.'

They'd said their final, formal goodbyes, wishing each other well. She'd said that perhaps he'd return to undertake the unfortunately stalled sundial project when relations between her people and Spanish visitors had improved, and he'd agreed. Surely she didn't believe it. He certainly didn't, and wondered anxiously how long her reign would last, and how it'd end.

He'd been taken to Hall just in time for the Spanish sitting and had slipped in, squeezing on to the table nearest the door, relieved to see no one he knew. He was happy in his own company. Glancing around, he considered how he might well have had to spend his entire time in England in this palace-bound, all-male Spanish household, and how utterly different – unimaginably different – the year would've been. He felt no connection to these dull-eyed men. His connection was to Cecily, and how strong and vibrant it was, somehow all the more so for the physical separation. Sitting there, his whole body sang with it. He was holding her close and carrying her forward: his memories of her and the certainty now of her future, her freedom.

He was famished and ate well before crossing the palace to present himself – as instructed – at the riverside gatehouse, where he was to spend the night. Settling down in the bed, he anticipated sleeping soundly. He felt that he'd handed Cecily back to herself: he'd arrived in her life and made it no easier, probably made it harder, but now, before leaving, he'd made good. He expected to feel something similar for himself but instead, all night, he felt shadowed, waking time and time again to the memory of what he'd done. The feeling was of being troubled, which made no sense.

At sunrise, he was down by the river to ask about the tide and was told that he'd have to while away the morning. Which was easy, in view of the length of the queue at the

Spanish office. Hours later, at the head of the queue, he was given the name of a ship and told to expect the call in two days' time. He paid a final visit to the astronomical clock before lunching in Hall.

Arriving at the Kitsons' as darkness was falling, he found that the house was being packed up. Just inside the door, two walls were bare, and the soles of his boots sounded on the uncovered floor. But of course: there was no longer a reason for the Kitsons to be in London. They'd been waiting for the royal birth but could now retreat to the countryside for what was left of the summer and for the autumn. Cecily, presumably, would be staying. For one anguished thump of his heart, he felt that, if only he were staying, too, then it'd be how it'd been a year ago, when for months the house had seemed to be their own.

The steward's sudden presence in an adjacent doorway made him jump. 'Ah! – message for you, Mr Prado: far side of London Bridge by ten tomorrow.'

Exhausted and distracted, Rafael grasped none of it, which the steward must've seen because he gave what looked to be a genuine smile and explained, 'You're going home.'

Rafael's heart hung in his chest like a stopped pendulum. 'Tomorrow?'

'By ten.' The steward sounded pleased to be able to tell him. 'Far side of London Bridge.' Where the ships docked. 'I'll have a couple of lads take your trunk.'

Disintegrating into shakes, Rafael could barely stand or breathe.

The steward was turning, resuming a dash elsewhere, and Rafael had to blurt it out to catch him: 'Mrs Tanner – is she around?' He hadn't been intending to ask for her, but the question had come and he was relieved. Because what on earth had he been thinking? Could he really have gone with no word of goodbye?

The steward halted – a definite, reluctant halting – but only half-turned back, and seemed to need to steady himself with an intake of breath. 'No.'

No?

What did *that* mean?

'No?'

'No.' Held in Rafael's stare, he said, 'Some men came for her, this afternoon.'

Rafael understood nothing by what he'd said. 'Some men?'

'The duke's men.'

The men who rode around the streets to keep order. 'The duke's men?' He hated parroting the steward but didn't know what else to do, what to ask.

'I don't know why,' the steward confessed.

Well, Rafael could guess. A guess was all it was, but surely coincidence didn't explain it: that he'd been to see the queen about her, and now this. The duke's men, though? The law-enforcers? Perhaps there'd been some misunderstanding, and the queen would have to intervene. And soon, he hoped, very soon, because where – now that it was dark – was Cecily? With a shock, he realised he hadn't asked: 'Nicholas?'

'Nicholas, too.'

Trying to gauge how it'd been when the men had arrived, he asked, 'Was Mrs Tanner – surprised?'

The steward answered simply, 'Yes,' and suddenly *surprised* was a euphemism. She'd been distressed: that was the implication of his abrupt, unequivocal *Yes*.

'And she's not back?' But he knew she wasn't back. The steward had said she wasn't back.

All he got now was a shake of the head.

His intention had been to make for the kitchen, but instead he retreated to his room to nurse his unease. Sitting on his floor, knees clasped, back against the bed, he reminded himself that the queen had taken Cecily and Nicholas's plight to her heart. He'd seen her sorrow with his own eyes. The duke's men had come for Cecily and Nicholas because there was no safer way, at this troubled time, to accompany a woman and child across the city. Cecily had been distressed because she hadn't yet known why they'd come for her. And if it'd happened sooner than he'd anticipated, wasn't that good? All this he told himself over and over again, but his disquiet persisted and he remained on the floor until the dogs were let out, their claws clicking over the cobblestones beneath his window. Hearing the steward's soft call for their return, he hauled himself up and got into bed.

He'd ended up leaving late, not that he'd been holding all that much hope of Cecily's return. He'd reckoned on a quarter of an hour for the walk to London Bridge, but the sundial on St Benet's showed that he'd taken that long just to get down Lombard Street. He was finding the walk hard going. He'd had a bad night. The day was unusually warm and he was burdened with his cloak. Turning into Gracechurch Street, heading south, he squinted against the sun and, above his left eye, the thumb pressure began again.

By the time Gracechurch Street became New Fish Street, the pain was flaring into the socket. He stopped – someone bumping into him – to press it with the heel of his palm. Somewhere nearby, a child was crying: a frantic crying that he recognised from the aftermath of battles with Francisco when protest had given way to helplessness and despair. The eye began to stream and he ducked into a lane for respite from the sun's glare. The bawling child was in the lane but at a distance and about to disappear around a corner. A boy, about Francisco's age. He was lagging behind an adult, or he was from one of the houses. In no time, someone would swoop back for him or bundle him indoors.

One side of the lane was so deep in shade as to be invisible. Rafael blinked hard, twice, and pressed the throbbing eye before trying again, scanning the row of dark buildings. He glimpsed the child being embraced by a little companion. The eye welled; wiping it, he saw that he'd been mistaken and the boy was still alone. Very alone, he realised suddenly; hence the crying. The boy was desperately alone, throwing himself on the mercy of the deserted lane. Rafael took a few steps up the lane, and the child became Nicholas. He slapped a hand over his bad eye, but the child remained Nicholas; the child *was Nicholas*. Definitely Nicholas. And no Cecily. Rafael's chest contracted with such violence that he clutched at it. Around the corner came a woman; she tentatively approached the boy, bending down to him. He blared his distress into her face. She straightened, a hand on his shoulder, and glanced around, called up the lane. A man appeared, similarly reticent at first but then he too was shouting. A single step backwards so dizzied Rafael that he vomited. When he'd steadied himself enough to be able to look up, he saw that doors had opened and more people had arrived. A crowd: a crowd had gathered around Nicholas, and it was outraged on his behalf. With hands on his head, his shoulders, between his little shoulder blades, people were shepherding him up the lane, proclaiming the news ahead.

In the end, Rafael wasn't up on deck with everyone else to witness England dwindling. He lay on his bunk, all around him the jockeying of timber and waves. And so he had no sense of leaving England, only of giving himself over to the sea.

# HISTORICAL NOTE

Rafael de Prado, Antonio Gomez, and the members of the Kitson household are my own invention. In all other respects, I have aimed for historical accuracy.

For further information about about the writing of this book, please visit www.suzannahdunn.co.uk.

# ACKNOWLEDGEMENTS

Many, many thanks to David and Vincent, for putting up with me – most of the time! – while this book was being written, which took some doing; Antony Topping of Greene and Heaton and Clare Smith of HarperCollins, for their very hard work on my behalf, their ideas and limitless good humour, patience and kindness; Jo Adams and Carol Painter, for so often letting me have the run of their lovely Bird-combe Cottage, where much of this book was written; Malcolm Knight, Secretary of the Thames Traditional Rowing Association (see www.traditionalrowing.com), for information on – you guessed it – rowing on the Thames during the Tudor era; and Matt Bates, who knows a thing or two about old queens.

The following books were very useful to me:
Erickson, Carolly, *Bloody Mary, The life of Mary Tudor* (Dent, 1987; Robson Books, 1995)
Loades, D. M., *Mary Tudor: A life* (Basil Blackwell, 1989)
Picard, Liza, *Elizabeth's London* (Weidenfeld and Nicolson, 2003; Phoenix, 2004)
Prockter, A., and Taylor, R., *The A to Z of Elizabethan London*

(Harry Margary, Lympne Castle, Kent, in association with Guildhall Library, London, 1979)

Ridley, Jasper, *The life and times of Mary Tudor* (Weidenfeld and Nicolson, 1973)

Weir, Alison, *Children of England: The Heirs of Henry VIII* (Jonathan Cape, 1996; Pimlico, 1997)

'The air of ideas is the only air worth breathing.'

EDITH WHARTON

LITERARY CORNER

## LOOK LIFE IN THE FACE
· · · · · · · · · · · · · · · · · · · · · · · · · · · · · · · · · ·

A Word From The Author

## SPREAD THE LIGHT
· · · · · · · · · · · · · · · · · · · · · · · · · · · · ·

Things To Think About

## IRREPRESSIBLE FRESHNESS
· · · · · · · · · · · · · · · · · · · · · · · · · · · · · · · · · · · · ·

What To Read Next

## THE CRITICS OVERLOOK
· · · · · · · · · · · · · · · · · · · · · · · · · · · · · · · · · · · · ·

Reviews for Suzannah Dunn

# LOOK LIFE IN THE FACE

......................................

'To be able to look life in the face: that's worth living in a garret for, isn't it?'

EDITH WHARTON

'True originality consists not in a new manner but in a new vision,' claimed Edith Wharton. Few would dispute the truth of this statement, yet the process by which such visions are vouchsafed is a mysterious one. What is it that inspires authors to put pen to paper: curiosity, sympathy, passion, obsession? In her own words, Suzannah Dunn reveals what fascinated her about the reign of Mary Tudor ...

We shy away from Mary Tudor. If she appears at all in fiction or films, she's dowdy and earnest if not also vengeful and deluded. Her problem is that she wasn't glamorous, to say the very least. Worse, for the English, she's embarrassing: that un-English religious fervour of hers, and the pitifully public nature of her lifetime of humiliations and rejections. And so she was – and still is, almost five hundred years later – eclipsed by the success story: her half-sister, Elizabeth. We all seem to forget Mary's own considerable claim to fame: she was England's first-ever ruling queen. And hard though it is to believe it now, she came to the throne amid such jubilation, it's said, as had never been seen before nor has been since. The English people were championing the underdog, displaying their much-vaunted sense of fair play. Mary – disinherited – had been denied her birthright, and the English people weren't prepared to tolerate it. Mary's tragedy was that, in her naivety, she mistook their jubilation for endorsement of her plan to return England to the Catholic faith. Within just five years, this once notably merciful queen was at war with her own people. And there she remains, to this day, as 'Bloody Mary'.

Into an already tense situation came the hapless Spaniards in Philip of Spain's entourage. The prince came to marry Mary (his maiden aunt) with his staff of hundreds of Spanish men. Someone had neglected to pass on the information that Mary had appointed a household in readiness for him, for which he was expected to foot the bill. So hundreds of Spanish men pitched up at a palace which had little room and no work for them. They were to discover that England was inhospitable not only in its weather (the summer of 1555 being one of the worst ever known). The English were dead set against their queen's marriage, which they considered compromised their independence (Spain was the empire) and their fledgling Protestantism. The Spaniards were faced not only with – as they saw it – the Godlessness of the English and the relentlessly bad weather, the lack of fresh food, the legendary drunkenness, but were also overcharged, swindled, attacked and robbed. The prince hadn't intended to stay long, but then, to everyone's surprise, the ailing, middle-aged queen announced that she was pregnant and made clear that she expected her new husband to remain by her side …

SUZANNAH DUNN

# SPREAD THE LIGHT

····································

'There are two ways of spreading light: to be the candle or the mirror that reflects it.'

EDITH WHARTON

From Socrates to the salons of pre-Revolutionary France, the great minds of every age have debated the merits of literary offerings alongside questions of politics, social order and morality. Whether you love a book or loathe it, one of the pleasures of reading is the discussion books regularly inspire. Below are a few suggestions for topics of discussion about *The Queen's Sorrow* ...

▶ Mary Tudor is portrayed in *The Queen's Sorrow* as a tragic figure as well as, increasingly, a tyrant. How sympathetic did you find her character? How much of her religious extremism can be explained or even excused by her personal unhappiness and difficult upbringing?

▶ What insight, if any, do you think the author's portrayal of Mary gives us into other historical figures and the ways in which personal motivations can underwrite the political? Is this a discussion that is relevant to today's leaders?

▶ The central characters in *The Queen's Sorrow* are unfaithful to their spouses. How harshly should they be judged for this? What factors drive the various characters to be unfaithful? Can their actions be excused as a side-effect of the nature of marriage in sixteenth-century England and Spain?

▶ Overall, is religion a destructive or constructive force throughout the novel? To what extent, if any, is the ideological debate in *The Queen's Sorrow* relevant to the modern day?

▶ Rafael spends much of the novel feeling uncomfortably 'foreign'. What does his experience tell us about the sixteenth-century world view, and the ways in which these attitudes have (or haven't) changed?

▶ Cecily's position throughout much of the novel is uncertain – she is neither married nor widowed, neither upper nor lower class. Rafael is similarly an outsider. What authority or insight do you think this marginal status gives these two characters? To what extent does this make it easier or more difficult for them to act in their own interests?

▶ What would you have done in Cecily's position? What would you have done in Rafael's? Could either of them have acted in a way that might have prevented tragedy?

▶ How responsible is Rafael for the events at the novel's end? Are his actions motivated by kindness, naivety or an unwillingness to accept the truth? To what extent does his motivation excuse the results of his attempt to intervene on Cecily's behalf?

# IRREPRESSIBLE FRESHNESS

'A classic is classic not because it conforms to certain structural rules, or fits certain definitions (of which its author had quite probably never heard). It is classic because of a certain eternal and irrepressible freshness.'

EDITH WHARTON

If you enjoyed *The Queen's Sorrow*, you might be interested in these other titles from HarperPress ...

## *Bone China* by ROMA TEARNE

Grace de Silva, wife of the shiftless but charming Aloysius, has five children and a crumbling marriage. Her eldest son, Jacob, wants desperately to go to England. Thornton, his mother's favourite, dreams of becoming a poet. Alicia wants to be a concert pianist, and Frieda just wants to remain close to her family. But civil unrest is stirring in Sri Lanka and Christopher, the youngest, is soon caught up in the tragedy that follows. As the decade unfolds, Grace watches helplessly as her family is torn apart and four of her children make the decision to leave. And yet in London, life is not as they expected. Only Thornton's daughter, Meeka, moves confidently into a world that is full of possibilities. But even she must overcome heartbreak, a terrible mistake and single parenthood before she is finally able to see the extraordinary effects of history on her family's migration.

*Published April 2008*

## *The Sisters Who Would be Queen: Katherine, Mary and Lady Jane Grey – A Tudor Tragedy* by LEANDA DE LISLE

Lady Jane Grey is an iconic figure in English history. Misremembered as the 'Nine Days Queen', she has been mythologized as a child-woman destroyed on the altar of political expediency. Behind the legend, however, was an opinionated adolescent who died a passionate leader, not merely a victim. Growing up in her shadow, Jane's sisters Katherine and Mary would have to tread carefully to survive. And yet both proved as headstrong as their sister. Beautiful Katherine changed her religion to retain royal favour, then risked everything in a secret marriage that threatened Queen Elizabeth's throne. Her younger sister Mary, too plain to be considered significant, also fell in love and incurred the queen's fury. Casting fresh light on Elizabeth's reign, acclaimed historian Leanda de Lisle brings the tumultuous world of the Grey sisters to life, at a time when a royal marriage could gain you a kingdom – or cost you your head.

*Published September 2008*

## *The Piano Teacher* by JANICE LEE

It's 1952 when 32-year-old Claire arrives in Hong Kong with her new (and dull) husband Martin. Using her marriage to escape a bitter mother and non-existent home life in England, Claire takes a position in Hong Kong as piano teacher to Locket, the daughter of wealthy socialite Chinese parents. She swiftly becomes intrigued by the family's unconventional English driver, the charismatic and mysterious Will Truesdale. As their love affair blossoms, the tensions and intrigues of 1950s Hong Kong are interwoven with events a decade earlier, during the island's wartime years – another, very passionate, and tragically doomed love affair, Japanese brutality and secrets betrayed.

*Published January 2009*

## *The Lace Reader* by BRUNONIA BARRY

Towner Whitney comes from a family of Salem women who can read the future in the patterns of lace, and who have guarded a history of secrets for generations. But there is one secret that Towner wants at all costs to avoid, and for seventeen years now she has been ignoring the truths concealed in the folds of the delicate fabric and living a life of careful exile. When she hears that her beloved Great Aunt Eva has gone missing, she must return to her hometown to unpick the mystery surrounding Eva's disappearance and to face the terrible events that drove her from home and split her family apart, in this taut, gripping, literary page-turner.

*Published April 09*

Visit www.harpercollins.co.uk for more information.

# THE CRITICS OVERLOOK

'After all, one knows one's weak points so well, that it's rather bewildering to have the critics overlook them and invent others.'

EDITH WHARTON

Here's what critics have said about previous books by
**SUZANNAH DUNN ...**

## Praise for *The Sixth Wife*

'My, what a story ... delightfully vulgar and utterly compelling.'

*The Times*

'Suzannah Dunn ... weaves ... a love story that is both moving and believable ... of second chances at love, and passion reawakened.'

*Telegraph*

'Mesmerising and beautifully written.'

*Scotsman*

## Praise for *The Queen of Subtleties*

'Suzannah Dunn is, as ever, a mistress at describing the material world through which her characters move.'

*Guardian*

'A boisterous historical recreation.'

*Independent*

'*The Queen of Subtleties* offers a stunningly refreshing way of retelling an old story ... I really could not put this one down.'

ALISON WEIR